Some Kind of Normal

a novel

Heidi Willis

This is a work of fiction. All characters and events in this book are fictional, and any resemblance to actual people or events is purely coincidental.

Copyright © 2009 by Heidi Willis

NorLightsPress.com
2721 Tulip Tree Rd.
Nashville, IN 47448

All rights reserved. No part of this book may be reproduced or transmitted in any form or by any means, electronic or mechanical, including photocopying, recording, or by any information storage and retrieval system, without written permission from the author, except for the inclusion of brief quotations in a review.

Printed in the United States of America
ISBN: 978-1-935254-18-8

Book and Cover Design by Nadene Carter

First printing, 2009

Some Kind of Normal

a novel

Heidi Willis

To Todd
I love you more today than yesterday…

Chapter One

I ain't one to bash being healthy, but it sure takes the fun out of living. My motivation to be the perfect mom starts about six a.m. when I swing my legs over the bed and ends fifteen minutes later when I stumble into the kitchen to make coffee and figure out what I can cook for breakfast that won't kill no one.

It wasn't always like this. I followed my own mama's footsteps for years, laying out a spread that included all four types of meat, and grits with cream and brown sugar if Travis was lucky. But during Travis's mid-life physical, his doctor told him my daily ham with sausage gravy on biscuits was driving him to an early grave. He slid the lab results across his desk at me, claiming Travis's LDL numbers were higher than a crackhead's. I said if a crackhead had my sausage gravy he'd give up the crack and rather die of plugged arteries. He didn't laugh. We switched to eggs and toast.

Then when Logan was young enough to run around bare-tushed, he developed hives and a tendency to up-chuck. His pediatrician pointed to the milk we poured on his Cocoa Crispies each morning. *Who the Sam Hill is allergic to milk*, I asked. We switched to Pop Tarts and apple juice anyway.

But now Travis's doctor don't want him having the fat in the pop tarts, and all Logan wants is Coke and Twizzlers, and Ashley can't make it downstairs in time to eat anything. So every morning I stare bleary eyed at the pantry wondering what to feed my family that won't kill them, and all I come up with is bagels and orange juice.

'Course, they're white bagels, not those whole wheat ones with all those grains in them, and I slather them in butter and honey 'cause they ain't got no taste otherwise. And the orange juice is really Sunny D, which I know is mostly water and corn syrup, but it's got all that vitamin c in it so it must be some kind of healthy.

"Ashley," I yell, walking down the hall tossing a Pop Tart package on Logan's bed as I pass. "Time to get up." I knock on her door. No answer. I know she's not in the bathroom because I can hear Logan drumming on the sink in there with his hairbrush and comb. I knock again, but there's no answer. I do the thing no mom of teenagers should do: I open the door without invitation.

She's dead asleep, a bottle of water and a stuffed armadillo she got at the state fair last year tucked under her covers. "Jiminy, Ash, the bus is going to come in less than half an hour." I pull the covers off her but she don't move. I got no time for laziness this morning. I shake her hard. "Get up."

She moans and rolls over. I'm not sure why God saw fit to give morning people like me and Travis a child who can't function like a human being until past ten. I grab her ankles and pull them over the side of the bed. "This is ridiculous. You were better when you were a baby."

"That's 'cause I slept twenty hours a day," she mutters, and I know she's awake.

"Get dressed. You can eat breakfast on the bus."

"I'm not hungry. I think I'm still sick."

"You're over the flu two days ago. The doctor said. Time to get back into the swing of things," I say over my shoulder as I leave.

When I check on Ashley twenty minutes later, she's dressed and sitting in front of her mirror brushing out her long hair very slowly. Her eyes are barely open. "I got you a bagel ready," I say. "And some Sunny D. You want it now?"

"Just water," she answers, holding out her empty bottle. I hesitate. "You need something more than that, Ash. You're shriveling up into almost nothing." She gives me a look that withers. I hold up my hands in surrender. "Okay. Water now. Bagel and juice for the bus." Who the Sam Hill drinks water for breakfast?

She turns back to the mirror and goes back to the brushing, her arm weighted like the brush is too heavy to hold easily. I try to see her for a minute like the little girl I knew so well, but she's not there anymore. This girl has sprouted up faster than a chain link cactus, the tallest twelve-year-old in her class, and I hate puberty for causing my baby to become this young woman I don't know. I go back to the kitchen and spread butter and honey on the bagel, sun starting to filter in through the front window.

Travis pops his head in the doorway. "I'll take Logan on to school," he says, clipping up his overalls over his flannel shirt. "I gotta get to the construction site early." I nod over my coffee and hear the back door slam shut. The truck growls loudly and I can see them pull out of the driveway, Logan happily munching on a Twizzler. I finish off the coffee and go back to check on Ashley.

She's trying to get her hair in a ponytail and acting like her arms weigh a hundred pounds. I take the brush and finish for her. She don't complain about me doing it, which strikes me as odd. "You that tired?" I ask.

She shrugs. It's her new favorite communication.

I sigh. That's mine. "Okay. Tonight it's earlier to bed. Let's go or you'll miss the bus."

She almost makes it out the door on time except she runs back to go pee. "You're gonna be late," I say through the door. "You wouldn't have to pee so much if you didn't drink thirty gallons of water every morning." She gives me a look as she opens the door and pushes past me. I don't think I've gotten ten words out of her this morning.

I hear the bus honking at the end of the drive as she's shoving her algebra book in her bag and flinging it over her shoulder. She tries to drain the rest of her water on the way out the door, but I grab it from her and hand her the bagel and Sunny D. "It's healthier," I say.

"I'm not hungry," she protests.

"I ain't sending no child of mine off to school without something in her belly." I press it into her hand and she takes it, but not happy.

She scowls at me and half-jogs down our long driveway where the bus is honking again. I yell at her to remember her flute lessons after school, but she's already too far to hear. I see her slow down before she gets to the bus, the jog becoming a walk, the walk becoming a stop as she leans over panting. And then she topples over. Just like that.

Chapter Two

By the time I huff and puff my way down the driveway, the bus driver has already called 911 and is alternately kneeling by Ashley like he might CPR her and trying to keep the other kids from getting off the bus. Some pull the windows down and lean out, their faces mostly pinched up and worried, although some look just curious.

I kneel down and pat her face. It's purplish and pale at the same time. "Ashley, darling. Wake up. It's Mama, now. If you're that tired you can stay home." I know this is stupid. It isn't as if she just decided to lie down and take a nap in the dirt.

"I don't know what happened, Mrs. Babcock. She was fine, then she fell over."

"I know. I saw."

"The ambulance is coming." He looks awkward, glancing back and forth between Ashley and all her friends, trying not to look at his watch; I know he's worried he'll be late to school. I want to tell him to go on, get the other kids out of here, but Travis is already at work and Logan left for school a half hour earlier, and I don't know what to do. I silently curse Travis for talking me out of that nice suburban house and into this ranch-in-a-hay-field.

I slip the straps of her backpack off her shoulders and push it aside. The Sunny D and the bagel are tucked under her body, and I roll her on her back away from them. "Can you get the water bottle I dropped by the porch?" He nods and scoots off to find it.

When Gus the driver gets back from the house, I'm sitting in the dirt with Ashley's head on my lap, stroking her long hair out of her face and wondering if maybe God is punishing me for the cigarettes I hide in my sock drawer. He hands me the water, and I wiggle her head a bit trying to get her to open her eyes.

"Ashley, now, wake up." I dribble the water over her lips a little and watch it run down her chin. I think I see her eyes flutter as a Buick pulls up behind the bus.

A lady I recognize from the beauty parlor gets out, looking like she's going off to a high-society social. A surly girl slithers out after her.

"Thank goodness. I thought we'd missed the bus this morning. I was afraid I'd have to take Chelsea in myself, and I just don't have time for that today. Are we having mechanical problems?" She comes around enough to see me sitting on the ground with my baby in my arms, and she stops suddenly, throwing out her arm and blocking her daughter from getting closer, too, as if we have some disease.

"What's wrong with her? Is she having a fit?"

"Of course not!" I have no idea what's wrong with Ashley, but I'm sure it isn't whatever this lady would like to think she has. I focus on Ashley and hold her tighter. "Come on Baby, take a little drink." I dribble more water, hoping I'm not drowning her. Her eyelids flutter and beneath them, I see her eyes rolled back.

"Go," I say to everyone. "The medics will be here. You ain't doing nothing anyway. Just get on to school so the kids don't miss nothing, and you tell them Ashley'll be on in later."

I don't see the expressions passed between them, but I know they're there. They're weighing moral obligation with the strong desire to leave. Their selfish side wins out. The surly kid climbs on the bus, and they all drive away. In the back window of the bus I see a couple kids with their noses pressed against the glass, unable to take their eyes off us.

I hear the ambulance, the siren wailing like my heart feels. I hear it far away and then getting closer until I see the lights red on the horizon. Ashley hears it too. Her eyes flutter open again, and this time she strains to focus on me, the pupils floating in and out, smaller and bigger, until she gives up and closes them again. She sighs a shallow breath, then again.

She begins to shake, small shivers turning into bigger ones, 'til I can barely hold her. Then, quick as they come, they leave, and she's still again. A tiny sigh again.

Three men are suddenly beside me, a stretcher on the ground and a heavy metal box I assume is the equivalent of the doctor's little black bag. I seen stuff like this in movies, where paramedics do all sorts of operations and life-saving stuff with the tools in the box. One man is kneeling, offering to take Ashley's head from me, but I hold on tighter.

"What happened, ma'am?" Ma'am is one of the most common words in the Texas language, a reflection of a good southern upbringing; but when he says it, it sounds condescending.

"She fell over on her way to catch the bus." I see them look around for the nonexistent bus. "It was here, but I told them to go on to school."

"Did she hit her head when she fell?" He has his fingers on her neck, feeling for the same pulse I first heard twelve years ago in the OB's office, all static-y and beautiful, beating loud through a microphone the doctor moved over my belly.

"No. I don't think so. She kinda fell on her knees first. I suppose she musta hit her head, though, 'cause I didn't see her break her fall with her hands. But it wasn't hard or anything. Almost like she was just lying down."

"Did she trip?"

"No. She just fell over." I see them checking for broken bones, but I know the problem isn't her falling down; it's why she fell down. "She's been tired lately. She had the flu a while back, and since then she's been hardly even eating. Drinking a lot, but not eating hardly a thing, so maybe she's needing nourishment." I see the two pass looks. "She seized too," I add, though I don't want to. "Just now."

"You know it was a seizure?"

I nod. "My cousin has epilepsy. I seen them before." My heart suddenly skips a beat. "You don't think she has that, do you?" *Oh God, I pray, don't let her have that.*

But he shakes his head. "She fainted first, right? How long before she had the seizure?"

"I don't know. A few minutes."

"I doubt it, but we'll run tests at the hospital." He don't look at me but clicks his pen on his clipboard and folds the top paper over to start a new one.

"How old is she?"

"Twelve."

"You say she's been drinking a lot?"

"Yes. Just water, mostly."

"Has she been urinating abnormally often?"

I give him my best peeved look. "She's drinking a gallon a day. Of course she's peeing a lot."

Two men lift her out of my arms and move her to the stretcher. I let them. One wipes the water dripping down her chin and looks at me as if expecting an answer. I hold up the bottle of water, and I kick the Sunny D behind me as I'm standing. "I tried to give her a little to wake her up."

"She can't drink if she's passed out." He rolls his eyes at the other medic the way Logan used to roll his eyes at me a few years ago before I took a switch and told him I'd beat those eyes right out of their sockets. I look this man up and down and decide he's not too old to need a beating. He's practically a kid himself, and I find myself wondering if he possibly is old enough to drive an ambulance, let alone dole out medical advice.

"How long she been breathing like this?"

I notice the heavy breathing I'd come to ignore over the last few days. "A while. Since the flu. It made her breathe real hard for awhile. Then it got better for a few days. Now I guess it's back."

A slightly older medic spreads a blanket over Ashley and buckles her onto the stretcher as if she might roll over on him and fall the two inches back into the dirt. He pries her eyelids and shines a light in them. She fights to close her eyes against the beam, and I can tell from his face this is a good sign. He opens his metal doctor bag and rummages through some packages until he pulls out a vacuum-sealed needle that he tears open and inserts in the back of her hand. They eye-roller is now writing something on a clipboard.

They seem too calm to my liking, as if girls like Ashley just keel over every day. Maybe they do. Logan never fainted on me, but maybe that's because he's a boy. Maybe girls Ashley's age do this now, some freakish pubescent result of living too near the power lines or eating vegetables with pesticides or having heavy periods. I expect the medic to tell me, "It's the most normal thing ever these days, Mrs. Babcock. In a minute she'll wake up fit as a fiddle. You just need to be sure to wash those carrots better next time."

Instead, he says, "We're going to take her to the emergency room, ma'am. Do you want to ride along?"

It's an inane question. As if I would let him take her and leave me here. I nod and follow them to the ambulance. They slide the stretcher through the back doors and hook up an IV, and I'm halfway there before I realize I might need my car. And I definitely need my cell phone to call Travis, and maybe Logan's school if it takes too long. And the women at church. I'm supposed to be there in an hour to help stuff flyers for the pro-life rally in a week or so.

"Actually, I'll drive myself. She'll be all right?"

"I don't know, ma'am." I'm sure I blanch at his bluntness. You'd a thought a mama who taught her son to say ma'am would have taught him how to use a little tact.

The driver is on a handset, talking to the hospital I assume. "We've got a twelve year old girl presenting with polyuria, polydipsia, Kussmaul's respirations and possible seizures."

Clipboard man climbs in and closes the doors, not even glancing back at me. The ambulance pulls away, the sirens screaming, leaving me still holding Ashley's water in its wake of dust.

Fire ants are already beginning to swarm over the honey slathered on the bagel. "Oh sugar," I say to no one.

It's the only swear word I can think of at the moment.

Chapter Three

"I don't know," I say for the third time to Travis, who is more than a little spun up on the other end of the line. "I told you all I know. She passed out. The ambulance came and took her. I'm on my way to the hospital." It's only twenty minutes cross town to Saint Joseph's, but I seem to be getting every one of the ten red lights.

"Is it serious, you think? Should I leave work and meet you there?"

"I don't know." My voice comes out shrill, and I realize I'm suddenly aware this isn't some normal girl thing. Somewhere between rationally gathering clean clothes for Ashley and some snacks in case we are stuck there half the day tied up in paper work and telling Travis "I don't know" for the fourth time, the panic settles in.

"Yes." My knuckles are white on the steering wheel as I tap my foot on the gas waiting for the light to change. "Meet me there."

I hang up and the light changes, but the car in front of me doesn't move. I honk. She moves, but slowly. I stick my head out the window. "It ain't going to get greener if you water it, lady!" The car speeds up a little and is finally far enough into the intersection that I can squeeze around her and take a side street. I gun the gas and blow through the next two lights without any traffic.

I'm in full-on panic attack now. I can hear my own heart. Not just feel it thumping in my chest, but loudly, like a stereo is playing it. Then I realize it *is* the stereo. Logan has turned down every tuner except the bass, and the drum of some rock song is playing through the speakers. I turn it off and realize my heart is fine. I ain't going to die of a heart attack. You'd think that would make me feel better, but it don't.

My phone rings, and I know the word is already spreading across the small town.

It's Gloria from church. "We heard about Ashley. Is she gonna be all right?"

I want to ask how she heard, and who we is, but I just say I'm sure she'll be fine, but the medics want to take her to the hospital to make sure. No use in giving her and the other gossip gals at First Baptist more to talk about.

"A few of us will get together to pray for her. How should we pray?"

I know the tactic because I done it enough myself. Cloak your own need for information in a prayer request. But as I know they will genuinely pray for her, and since I want God on my side and I'm not that good at praying myself, I ask her to pray that Ashley will get good treatment at the hospital, and that she'll get a good doctor, because I'm not too trusting of doctors myself.

"Oh, don't I know it! Eduardo went in for a cough and caught the strep from a doctor who didn't wash his hands. The doctor poked around in him, told him to sit in the bathroom with a hot shower running, and then sent him home sicker than he was to begin with. He had to go back for antibiotics later. He almost didn't go cause he was scared of getting something even worse. Hospitals are just teeming with germs, and doctors don't know more about medicine than a monkey. Almost everybody I know comes out worse than they went in." She paused, and then added, "But I'm sure Ashley will be fine."

"Yes," I say shortly, and hang up.

By the time I park by the emergency entrance of St. Joseph's I've lost the feeling in my fingertips, and a gripping headache is spreading from my clenched jaw to the back of my neck. I grab my phone and stuff it in my purse and leave the clothes and the food.

I've only been in St. Joseph's three times before. Once each for the births of Logan and Ashley, in which I walked through the front doors, and once when Logan fell out of the oak tree in the back yard and needed twelve stitches in the back of his head. We came through emergency on that one, bath towel pressed to his scalp, blood already seeping through it. They put Logan on an examining table, and when the doctor took the towel off I passed out, and when I woke up, Logan was in a chair and I was lying on the table.

I pass off the church sick visitations on the other women. I hate hospitals.

St. Joseph's isn't like the TV hospitals, where attractive young interns wander the halls making eyes at each other, interrupted by sudden chaos when fifty people are brought in after a train wreck or bridge collapses and all hands on deck have to rip open bloody shirts and slice the chest open to get a heart beating again. Although when Logan came, there was a man who got his arm chewed off by a combine, and that was rather bloody. But even then, there weren't no great commotion.

Today, the ER is empty. Elevator music is playing on the sound system, some synthesized version of a Reba song, and no one's even at the information desk. I look outside to see if the ambulance is in the bay, but it's empty too. I have this frantic feeling I've gone to the wrong hospital, as if there were more than one within fifty miles. I see a bell on the desk and I ring it.

"I'm looking for my daughter, Ashley Babcock," I say to the white-haired lady who appears from nowhere. "An ambulance should have brought her in."

She nods and opens a door next to the desk and beckons me back. I follow her through a maze of curtains to the single room with a door. Inside, Ashley is on the bed, her eyes open, watching the two distinctly not-TV-type doctors buzzing around her. One is poking at her veins, cussing under his breath.

"I need a smaller needle, Park. The veins are collapsed."

I see Ashley wince each time he pierces her, and already blood is gathering beneath her translucent skin. This is why I hate doctors.

"Can't you be more gentle?" When my jaw unclenches I realize I've been gritting my teeth. The doctors ignore me, and I see her thick, dark blood finally filling a test tube. Ashley's eyes wander to me, but they are glazed and unfocused. She don't smile at me, and though she smiles less at me since she turned twelve, I find this a bad sign.

"Can someone tell me what's going on with my daughter? What's wrong?"

I am still expecting someone to say maybe she's anemic and needs to eat more bacon for breakfast, but instead he says, "Your daughter has diabetes."

Just like that. He don't even turn to look at me. He finishes drawing the blood and marks the tube with a black pen. "Christ, it's thick as finger-paint." He shakes the tube but the blood barely sloshes. "Up the fluids and give her a shot of humalog," he says to the man named Park. "Start with four units and add a drip line as well. I don't want her seizing again."

"What's going on?" I think I sound angry and this is better than worried, which is what I am. I don't like that they are putting drugs into Ashley's veins.

"Your daughter's nearly DKA, ma'am. It's lucky the EMTs had it figured or we'd still be running tests. Her glucose doesn't even measure on our meters here in the ER, so there's not much doubt, but we're running the labs anyway."

"What's DKA?" I have no idea of half what he said.

"Diabetic Ketoacidosis. Coma," he says, and then I wish I hadn't asked.

He begins to walk out, his hands full of my daughter's finger-paint blood, then turns and says, "We called the helicopter in. We're going to medevac her out to Children's Hospital in Austin. She needs immediate attention, and they're more equipped to deal with this than us. You need to keep her awake. It's still possible for her to go into coma, and that would be bad."

I stand looking at the door that's swung shut behind him. Bad doesn't even begin to cover it.

"How can she have diabetes?" I say to the man at the IV. "It's not like she's fat or anything. She doesn't even eat sweets that much." I think of the Sunny D loaded with corn syrup and a sliver of guilt creeps in. The man at the IV shrugs and leaves. I make a mental note to write the director of the hospital and demand he provide a seminar on bedside manners.

I spot a swivel stool in the corner and pull it over to Ashley's side. I take her hand. It's hot and dry. I think of when I was a kid and my dog dragged around like he had worms and my brother told me to test his nose. "If it's cold and wet, he's okay. If it's hot and dry, he's sick." Despite the ridiculousness of it, I reach out and touch Ashley's nose. She opens her eyes.

"Hi sweetie." I move my hand to her forehead as if I'm testing for fever instead of hiding the fact that I'm treating her like my childhood pet. "The doctors say you need to stay awake. Can you do that?"

She looks like she might want to answer, but then changes her mind. She swallows hard, then whispers, "Water."

Now I feel like rolling *my* eyes. "Dang it, Ash, is that all you can think about?"

Suddenly she vomits. It's mostly just water, I suspect because that's about all that's in her. Still, the sight of it makes me queasy, and I jump up, letting go of her hand and sending the swivel chair crashing into the metal cabinets against the wall.

"I need a doctor," I yell.

One appears almost instantly, a different one, and I wonder how many doctors a small town like Collier Springs can hold. It's not as if people are lined up in the waiting room.

This one, though, I like instantly. He immediately lifts the back of Ashley's bed, grabbing a pink plastic tub at the same time and handing it to her with a smile. "That'll wake you up, won't it?" He strips the blankets off her as a nurse rushes in.

"I'll do that, Doctor Benton," she tells him, smiling in that way that actors in the TV shows smile at each other when they're in love. He doesn't notice. She takes the sheets away and returns with clean ones and a washcloth for Ashley's mouth. I notice Ashley trying to suck the water from it as the nurse passes it over her face, and I throw her a scowl she doesn't catch.

Dr. Benton rests his hand on Ashley's head the way I was doing before she threw up. "You're a pretty sick little girl, aren't you?" He doesn't say it in the kind of condescending way someone educated might talk to a twelve-year old, but in a grown-up, compassionate way. He recovers the stool and holds it out to me. He sits on the end of the bed and opens the clipboard Dr. Park had with him. I like that he don't seem scared she will hurl again.

"Ashley's got diabetes," he says to me. "Do you know what that is?"

I nod, but I really don't. I've heard the commercials for the blood test machines. It's on the news a lot lately too, what with America being so fat now they say. I don't know what it is for sure, but I know the people who get it are old, or have behinds wide as a bus, and end up blind and amputated. It has something to do with eating sugar, and I'm sure Ashley doesn't have it.

"There are two types of diabetes. We used to call them juvenile and adult-onset, but now we're seeing kids as young as six and seven getting the adult-onset, and adults can get the juvenile, so we differentiate now by calling them type 1 and type 2." He winks at me. "We in the medical profession pride ourselves on our creativity."

"What's the difference, then, if age don't matter?"

"Well, they're really two entirely different beasts. Type 2 is an insulin resistance, where a person's body might make enough insulin, even an excess, but not be able to use it. The body resists it. But type 1, which is most likely what Ashley has, is an autoimmune disease. Has she been sick recently with a cold?"

"She had the flu last week."

He nods, as though this explains it. "For most people, a virus, or the flu, is just an illness their body can fight off. In Ashley's case, though, the virus triggered her immune system to attack the pancreas and destroy the part that makes the insulin."

I don't know what insulin is, or what the pancreas does, but I nod because I don't want to open my mouth and look stupid. "So it's not because she's fat or eats bad?"

He laughs, and I like his laugh. It's honest and not patronizing. Patronizing is a big fancy word that means you think you know more than someone else. I learned it from one of Logan's school books.

"No. Type 1 has nothing to do with weight, or with what she eats. Even people with type 2 aren't always overweight, although being overweight does increase your likelihood of being insulin resistant. What Ashley has, the genetics have probably been dormant in her since she was born. It just took this particular virus, at this time, to set it off."

He looks past me at the door, and I turn to see Travis standing there, pale as a Pilsner. At the same time, Ashley begins to heave again, except nothing comes out. Dr. Benton jumps up and grabs the bowl and sticks it under her chin, but Ashley throws her arms out, knocking it to the floor. I scold her, but her eyes, which are wide open now, are wild and foreign. She pulls at the IVs, ripping the tape off her hand before Travis can get to her and wrap his arms around her, tying them to her sides. She struggles against it a moment before sinking back against his chest and sighing deeply. Her eyes close again.

"What the hell?" I've never heard Travis swear before.

"Is she in DAK?" I say to Dr. Benton, rushing to Ashley's side to take her hand and shake it.

"It's DKA," says Dr. Park, the rude note-taking doctor, who is now pushing me and Travis out of the way along with the two others who have come with him, steering a stretcher like the one from the ambulance. We are all crammed in this tiny room like clowns in a circus car, but I am not about to be the one to back out first.

"The Life Flight helicopter is here."

"Why the Sam Hill do we need a helicopter?" asks Travis.

Dr. Park doesn't even bother to explain. He flings a look my way that says it's my job to explain while it's his job to save. "Ashley needs to go to the Children's Hospital in Austin," Dr. Benton says, moving aside so the stretcher can line flush with the bed. "We just aren't equipped to help her the way she needs, and you as well. This affects your entire family. They'll make sure you get the best care, and that you are all ready to make the changes that need to be made before Ashley comes home."

"Changes?" I can tell Travis is not excited about that word. Lord a mercy, you'd have thought he'd had his arm cut off when I stopped making gravy every morning. He's been sitting in the same lazy chair since we've been married, driving the same dilapidated Ford truck, listening to the same Willie Nelson tape since I met him. Change is not his thing.

I stick my elbow hard into his ribs and glare at him. He shushes up. I glance at Dr. Benton, who is holding Ashley's head as they transfer her to the stretcher.

They are now pushing against us again, wheeling her out through the door and down the deserted hallway. "I'm going with her," I call over their shoulders.

"You get scared on a step ladder," Travis says, which I think is plain rude to say in front of everybody.

"I'll be fine. You need to pick up Logan and grab us some clothes and some sandwich stuff from the house in case there's no food places near the hospital. I'm not eating hospital food for supper. And call the church and let them know I can't come to the church today to help with the rally. And ask Janise if she will feed the goldfish until we get back. And call the flute teacher. I don't think we'll be home in time for lessons today."

I stop to think if there is anything else he needs to do when he says, "If there's that much on your list, why don't I go and you pick up Logan?"

"I'm sorry," Dr. Benton says, looking for all the world like he really is. "There's not enough room for you. Only Ashley and the emergency personnel are allowed. You can both drive and meet them there."

"We'll drive separate cars, then," I decide. "I'll go from here, you go get Logan."

"Why don't we all go together?"

"Because someone should be at the hospital when she gets there."

"You're not going to beat a helicopter, Babs."

I cannot believe we're standing in some hick hospital arguing over who's going to drive.

We're still following Ashley, though nobody now seems to notice us. Doors to a landing pad slide open, and we're greeted with a whoosh of air and the thwapping of the helicopter blades. "Make sure we got the paddles ready," one of them yells over the noise to the woman who is helping lift the stretcher and my baby in. "We may need them on this trip."

I am not educated. I do not know what DKA means and what a pancreas does, but I do watch ER and I know what paddles are. They are for people who die.

I whip back to Travis, whose slowly returning color has just drained again. "I'm driving myself – *right now* – because I drive faster than Jehu, and I'll get there before that dad-burned helicopter."

And that is the end of that.

Chapter Four

Ashley was born screaming. I think she came out with her mouth open, her eyes scrunched into tearless cries, which no amount of bundling could soften until the nurses put her on my chest and I said, "Hi there, baby girl." And just like that, she stopped crying. She looked up at me with wide blue eyes, not even blinking, like she knew my voice from all those months inside me. The moment they took her away, she cried again until they brought her back.

We've been tight like that ever since. People told me when she grew up we'd fight like rattlesnakes. This is the nature of preteen daughter/mother relationships, friends say. But this isn't so with Ashley. We are salt and pepper, sweet and sour, sun and moon. She is the blond to my brunette, the quiet to my loud. We are the opposites that attract. We need each other the way a bee needs the flower and the flower needs the bee.

I think about her first day of kindergarten, when we held each other's hand so tight it was hard to tell who was the most scared of letting go. I think about her birthday parties when I would invite her friends in and get the games started and be elbow-up with glue and paints and tissue paper crafts, and realize Ashley wasn't around. I'd find her in her room, reading a book, too shy to be the center of attention. I think of our fights in the grocery store over Doritos or Salt and Vinegar Chips. I think about her crying when she didn't make all-state choir and me baking her oatmeal cookies thinking that was all she needed to get over it.

I think about all this as I'm driving route 79 toward Austin. I wonder if she's crying now, needing me the way I need her. I want her to be. If she's crying, then she's alive, and God knows how I need her to be alive.

My cell keeps ringing, a dancing little Martina ditty, but I don't want to talk. They are all people from the church, and I know the news about Ashley is spreading like poison oak all over town. I don't know what to say because I don't know anything, so I finally turn it off and pray Travis won't need to call me.

Then I try to pray about Ashley, only I can't think what to pray except, "Lord keep her alive." I finally decide this is about all I have to say anyways, so I fish for one of Ashley's favorite CDs and pop it in.

I press the pedal hard until I'm riding the tail of a muddy foreign car. She drifts over on the shoulder so I can pass, and I wave friendly-like even though I'm thinking she shouldn't be on the road at all if she can't keep up with the speed limits.

I turn up the music to drown out the fear. It's the David Crowder Band, a group Ashley learned about from friends at church. Once, when I came to the church to put up Christmas decorations, I saw her with them in the basement. They were sitting on the floor in the midst of other junior high kids, singing these songs along with the youth minister, strumming on his guitar. Red and green twinkle lights bounced off her hair and lit up her face in a warm glow that seemed to go right through her. Her voice rose above the others, high and sweet. I'm not the crying type, but I teared a bit and knew her life was taking a turn I might not be invited to travel.

I linger in the music before I turn it off again, preferring the company of the silence.

It takes a little over half an hour to get to Austin and longer than that to cross the city to the Children's Hospital. There are long moments when I'm stopped in traffic on the feeder roads, and I scan the sky for helicopters that might be heading the same direction. The skies are quiet today, blue and clear as a song. I hope she's there already.

In my mind, I planned to arrive, park, and be in the hospital before the helicopter can land. In reality, I can't find the visitor parking lot or where I should enter. The building is huge, and the parking spreads out forever, and I start to panic. I think I see three or four doors, and I break into a sweat trying to figure out which one is the one I need. This is an emergency so I should go in there, except the sign says ambulance only, and the front says visitors but I'm not a visitor. I am the mom. I park. I move. I park again. Shoot.

I decide on the front doors 'cause I figure no helicopter is getting in those ER doors, and I don't see no landing pad in the parking lot. By the time I get in the lobby, I'm soaked with perspiration from the humidity and heat. Honestly, even though I'm here for my daughter and can barely think about anything but those helo folks zapping her with those charging paddles, the lobby takes my breath away. The AC is blasting, for one, which is a godsend, but nearly sends my system into shock. The entire inside is made of stone, and the ceiling is so high it might reach heaven. It's bright and light and filled with mosaics and art and glass displays. The waiting area's bigger than the entire maternity ward back home, and the chairs are the good kind, with the padded seats and backs and armrests, instead of those metal and plastic ones in ours. A few people are sitting in them, reading newspapers or writing on clipboards, and at first it seems so calm it's freaky.

Then a man comes blasting through the door behind me, fairly knocking me over, a gauze bandage wrapped around his head and fresh blood oozing through it. He brushes past me to the circle desk and begins making a scene that echoes against the rock walls. He's yelling about his kid and an ambulance and some people look up, but most ignore him. Soon the lady at the desk points him towards a hallway and he disappears down it.

He reminds me of the Mad Hatter in Alice in Wonderland, which fits because suddenly I feel I've been dropped down a rabbit hole.

"Can I help you?" The lady at the desk is calling across the room to me. Embarrassed, I dart across the hall before more eyes start looking up.

"I'm looking for my daughter. Her name is Ashley Babcock. They were going to fly her in by helicopter." The words rush out before I can collect myself. Now, I'm just a blabbering idiot.

She gives me a clipboard with a stack of papers and a pen. "We'll need you to fill these out," she says to me, her enormous bosom catching the sweat that is dripping down her neck, even though it's cold as the arctic in here. "You have insurance, right?"

I nod and bite my tongue because my tongue has a way of getting me in trouble in situations like this. I wonder if I didn't have insurance, if Ashley would be left in the hallway to die. I think about the fundraising table for Saint Jude's in the mall that I always cross sides to avoid. I vow to donate the next time I go.

I hunt through my purse to find the plastic card. I can't remember the last time I used it, so I hope it's here. She shoos me away from the desk saying, "Just bring it when you finish the forms, honey."

I start to take a seat and then go back and ask, "Is my daughter here yet? She came by Life Flight."

"What's her name again?"

"Ashley Babcock."

There's a lull while she clicks the mouse next to the computer a few times. "Hmm... looks like they took her to PICU." At my blank stare she adds, "Pediatric Intensive Care Unit." I must look stricken because she reaches out across the desk to pat my hands, which is a tremendous effort getting them past that bosom and equally large stomach and over the desk. "She'll be okay, honey. The doctors here are the best. Ashley is in great hands. It will probably be a while before you can see her, though. They need to get her settled in a room, maybe run tests. Why don't you finish the paperwork so we can get her completely checked in, and then I'll find someone to show you where she is."

I nod and take the clipboard to a chair by a window.

There must be ten pages front and back, all full of tiny lines and tiny boxes and tiny print, and my head hurts just looking at it. I fill out Ashley's name and birth date and a bit of medical history, which isn't much because she's always been a healthy child and comes from a pretty healthy family, breakfasts not withstanding. Some of the insurance questions I can fill out from my card but other information I don't know, so I leave it blank. I hurry through it mostly so I can find Ashley but even hurrying, it must take twenty minutes. If I'd thought getting here would mean sitting alone doing paperwork, I'd've sent Travis and picked up Logan myself.

When I get up to return the stack, a different girl is sitting behind the desk, a young, pretty thing, a mountain of file folders a mile high in front of her. "It takes a lot of paperwork to get someone healthy, don't it?" I say, handing over the clipboard and pen. I think she might be sympathetic. She smiles at me as she takes the papers and looks through them.

"I filled out everything I could. Do you think I could find my daughter now? They medevaced her in a while ago."

She asks her name, types it into the computer, and pulls out a map of the hospital from a file drawer under the desk.

"You are here," she says, circling the open space on the map that is shaded pink. "Ashley is here." She circles a purple section marked PICU on a different floor. I like how the people who work here call Ashley by her name, like she is a friend, or someone who matters. "You take these elevators here and walk this way. Here," she marks an X, "is the nurse's station. Ask there for the room she's in. They may not let you in right away. They're pretty strict up there about visitors and how many people go in and out of the rooms." She hands me the map but doesn't let go right away. "Are you alone? Is this your first visit here?"

Her eyes are sympathetic. I'd thought the sympathy would be for the paperwork. Turns out it's for me. "My husband's on his way."

She takes back the map and circles three more places. "Here is the cafeteria. The food is pretty good. And here's what's called the Family

Resource Center. They have great reference materials that can help you understand anything the doctor's don't tell you, or that you're afraid to ask. They also have books and CDs you can check out. Ashley, too, if she's up for reading or listening. Lots of parents pass through there, so it's a great place to meet people, too."

She hands it back to me, and I point at the third circle. "What's this one?"

"That's the Ronald McDonald house. I don't know how long you'll have to stay. There are pull out beds in most of the rooms, but they can be really picky about that in PICU. They like to keep people to a minimum. If you need to be here for a few nights, check with getting a room there. It's within walking distance, and I know they have availability. A family just left yesterday."

I get the impression it wasn't a happy leaving, but I'm afraid to ask.

I say thanks and turn to go. I turn back. "Is everyone here as friendly as you?"

She smiles. "You'll find this is the friendliest place in Texas," she says. "And the loneliest."

I take a couple wrong turns before I get to the PICU. Some decorator tried real hard to make this place not look like a hospital, but it still smells like one. Ammonia and disinfectant. That smell of being too clean.

For a Children's Hospital, it seems awfully quiet to me. Creepy quiet. In the PICU I see only one person not in scrubs, and I think it's someone delivering flowers 'cause it don't look like they're visiting. They set the flowers on the nurses's station; the nurse waves without looking up and he leaves.

There are several nurses walking around, mostly pushing carts with bulky machines or carrying medical supplies. No one is talking, or laughing.

I'd walk right on through if I knew where Ashley was, pretending I belonged just in case they tell me I can't be here, but the nice lady downstairs didn't tell me the room number. How convenient.

"I'm looking for my daughter. Ashley Babcock. I was told she'd be here." I feel like I've said this a million times today.

Gray beehive-hairdo lady looks up. "Yes. She was brought in about forty-five minutes ago. Let me check to see if she can have visitors yet." She gets up to leave, and I step in front of her.

"I'm not trying to be trouble here, but I'm not a visitor. I'm her mom. And I want to see her now. Can you tell me what room she's in?"

I thought this might rattle her, but I underestimated the amount of times she must hear that 'cause she don't even blink.

"If you're not a patient, you're a visitor. I need to check first, to make sure she's stable. I'm sure you wouldn't want your visit to be harmful."

"I'm her mother."

"Yes, well..." She trails off.

"Okay. Go check." I give in, since maybe this argument might last longer than just waiting would take. I look at my watch. I give her thirty seconds before I'll start poking my head in every door on the floor. I don't have to, though, because beehive nurse is back lickity-split and tells me I can follow her.

When I enter Ashley's room, I'm surprised to find only one nurse. Ashley is sitting up and her eyes are open, though tired.

"Hi Mama." She's quiet, but she doesn't seem afraid. I am afraid. Awake or not, she don't look good.

"Hi baby. Did you like your helicopter ride? That was something, wasn't it? How many girls in your class get to ride in a helicopter?" I try to pretend it was something special, that it's not because she's on death's doorstep that she traveled by medevac. My voice sounds fake cheery, but Ashley plays along.

"It was louder than I thought it'd be. And bumpy." She's still for a minute, and I think she is falling asleep. Then she says, "Am I dying, Mama?"

"Lord a mercy, no! Don't go saying such a thing!" I look to the nurse for affirmation, and she gives it.

"You're going to be just fine, honey."

"The doctor says she has diabetes," I say, in case she don't know it and is just playing along with me, too.

"Lots of people have diabetes," she says, tucking in the blankets tighter around Ashley's legs. "If you take care of yourself and do what the doctor says, there's no reason you can't have as healthy a life as any of your friends." She looks out the doorway to the empty hall and then back to Ashley. "I can't say that to all my patients. There are lots of kids who come in here and don't ever go home, or have to keep coming back." She pats Ashley's legs. "But you can go home in a few days, you'll feel much better, and hopefully we won't have to see you back here."

I feel relieved by this.

She leaves and I sit next to the bed in an armchair. The room is nice. There is only one hospital bed, so I figure Ashley won't have to have a roommate, which also means no other nosy parents knowing our business. There's also a daybed here, which I think is awfully thoughtful since when I birthed Logan, Travis had to sleep upright on a chair. There's a desk in the corner with a small vase of fake flowers and a postcard telling us we have free wireless. A little closet and a bathroom are on the wall across from a large window that looks out over the courtyard. It's like a little apartment, I think, and then realize it probably is to some families here. And then I wonder how long we'll be here.

"So what else did I miss?" I ask, scooting the chair closer to the bed.

"They made me change clothes," Ashley says, motioning to the faded blue and white nightgown she is wearing.

I reach out and touch it. "It's soft, anyway." Softness has always been important to Ashley. Before she'd even take a shirt off the rack, she'd feel it. I'm glad; if they're going to make her wear a flappy, breeze-in-your-south-end gown, at least it's soft.

"They took lots of blood," Ashley says, holding out her arm that is already bruising. The IV from our home hospital is still in, clear liquid still dripping down the tube and disappearing into the back of her hand. I hold it up. It's a feather in my hands, and I realize how much weight she has lost. She's swallowed by the bed: a hummingbird in a squirrel's nest.

She lays her head back and closes her eyes. "I'm so tired."

"You can't go to sleep." I stand and shake her shoulder. "They said I have to keep you awake. Do you want water? I'll get you water."

I reach over her small body and ring the buzzer for the nurse, who comes almost immediately. "She wants to go to sleep. Can I give her water or something? Doctor Benton told me she could go into a coma if she sleeps."

The nurse, whose nametag reads "Betsy," reaches behind the bed and rolls out a tray with a pitcher of ice and a cup. "Here's some ice chips. They'll help her mouth. She's getting plenty of fluids through the IV, but if her blood sugar is high it might take a few days to stop feeling so thirsty all the time."

"Is that what's in the IV? Water?"

She opens Ashley's chart and glances over it. "We're giving her fluids and insulin, along with a few other supplements she's probably lost over the last few days due to the hyperglycemia. I'll check if your blood sugars are back from the lab yet. If it looks like they're going down, I think it's okay if she sleeps. We'll check her glucose levels every hour to make sure. The doctor should be back in a few minutes, too, and he'll have more information for you."

She smiles at Ashley, laying her hand on her head. "Is this all wearing you out, sweetie?" Ashley nods. "Then you go ahead and rest. I'll bet your mom won't leave your side." She looks at me and I nod, moving the chair closer to the bed so I can hold Ashley's hand. Ashley lets her eyes close, and the nurse leaves.

I lay my head on the bed next to her arm and listen to her breathing in and out, shallow breaths punctuated by rhythmic sighs, until I know she's asleep. I try to pray again, but praying has never come easy. "Thank you for letting her live," I say. Then, thinking about what the nurse said, I add, "Thanks that it isn't cancer." I consider praying something about what she does have, but I don't really understand what it is, so I stop there. I realize the adrenaline that has rushed through me since the minute I saw Ashley go down on the driveway has begun to ebb, and I'm exhausted.

Suddenly Travis is patting my arm. "Wake up, Babs."

I'm groggy. I feel like I've been asleep for hours, but when I look at the clock only twenty minutes has passed. Ashley is asleep, and I see the alarm on Travis's face.

"She's just asleep. The nurse said it's okay." I wonder if the same desperation I see in his eyes is echoed in mine. Other couples might reach out and hold each other at times like this, but we've never been that kind of clingy, so we stand in our spaces, each worried but too stubborn to say it.

He's changed from his work overalls to jeans and a polo shirt, which is about as fancy as he gets. I notice for the first time his hair is getting gray around the temples and small lines are forming around his eyes, which look old right now. I wonder if he's aged all this today.

"Where's Logan?" I say, and then he shows up in the doorway. Something flickers in his eyes when he sees his sister and disappears just as quickly behind the usual glaze. I don't know why I keep expecting the same kid I raised to show up when I call his name, but he hasn't been that kid since seventh grade, and it still takes me a moment to recognize him, especially since I barely see him these days. He is taller than Travis or me, passing his dad's six-foot mark his sophomore year, and not a pound heavier than a twig. His hair is shaved on the sides and the resulting Mohawk is died pink on the ends and stands straight up. Last month it was green. He knows I hate it, which is why he does it.

"What's wrong with her?" He tries to be casual, but I hear the fear.

"She's fine. She's just asleep."

"Don't be obtuse, Mom. She's in a hospital. She's not fine."

I hate when he uses words like obtuse. He knows I don't know them. I've taken to sneaking his SAT vocabulary book when he's at school just to keep from appearing stupid.

"I told you," Travis says, in an effort to smooth the ruffled feathers. "She has diabetes."

"What's that mean, though?"

"It means her body isn't making any insulin, and sugar is building up in her blood," I say, one-upping Logan in this stupid game we play where I am no longer the adult. "She's got the type 1 kind, not the fat people kind," I add.

"Obviously," he retorts. "She's not fat." I feel like sticking my tongue out at him, but I resist because I am the adult, even if I don't know more words than him.

"Truce," Travis says, placing his large, square body between us. He turns to me. "What did the doctors say?"

"I haven't seen one yet. I spent the first half hour filling out paperwork. When I finally got up here, she was already done with the labs. A doctor is supposed to come back when the test results are in."

"And they are," says Dr. Benton, joining us in what is quickly becoming a crowded room.

"What are you doing here?" I ask, surprised.

"I have privileges here. I did my internship in pediatrics here, and I've kept the ties. I called from the hospital and asked if I could come work with Ashley since you live in my town. That way, we can be consistent with treatment, here and at home."

I'm so thankful and relieved I could kiss him. "Let me have the nurse bring in another chair or two, and we can sit down and talk about what's going on with your daughter."

He leaves and Logan slouches over to the daybed and sprawls out, turning the TV on with the remote that's attached to Ashley's bed. I snatch it and turn it off. "Do you mind?"

"Actually, I do," he says. "If you're going to drag me away from school, the least you can do is let me entertain myself."

"This is not about entertaining," I hiss, because the door is still open, and I can't very well shout with a dozen doctors and nurses lurking in the hall. "This is about your sister, who nearly died today. And since when did you care about school?"

"Yeah, well you said she's fine." He yawns and scrunches the pillow behind him.

Travis clears his throat, and I throw him a "stay out of this" look when I see him looking at Ashley. I turn as Ashley's eyes flutter open.

"Daddy!" Her voice is gravely but cheerful, and I'm jealous of the warmth she shows him that I didn't get. For goodness sakes, she threw up on me, and he's the one who gets the smile.

He leans over to kiss her on the cheek. "How's my chickadee?"

"A little better," she says, and Travis and me laugh because this has been her standard answer after being sick since she was three. "I like your hair, Logan. That pink looks good on you."

"It's been pink a week now. Nice you finally noticed."

"It has?" She seems thrown off by this, but before I can ask anything else, Dr. Benton is back.

"Well look here, our patient is up and alert already! How are you feeling?"

"A little better," she says.

"That's good. We've got some good concoctions flowing through your veins. You should feel back to yourself in a day or two." He rolls a stool to the other side of her bed so he is facing all of us and puts a stack of papers and packages on the tray table behind her bed. He takes out the file that has her name in red along the edge.

"You feel up to talking?" he asks Ashley. She nods. "Good. Because today, right now, life is going to change for all of you. I want to help make this as easy as possible."

I see Travis from the corner of my eye shift in his seat. I kick him in the shin.

"Changes?" Travis sits on the edge of his seat, moving his legs out of my reach and running his hand over his scruffy goatee. "What kind of changes?"

"The good kind," Dr. Benton tells us. "The kind that will make your whole family healthier."

I think of Travis's doctor telling us it'll be good for us not to eat the biscuits and gravy every day—that finding out about his LDL was a good thing because now we could all be healthier. I'm not liking this talk any better.

"I explained that Ashley has diabetes," he begins. "We know that from her blood glucose results. Everyone has some amount of glucose—sugar—in his blood. Your brain needs it to think. Too little, and the brain seizes and can't think straight or send the right signals to the body. Too much, and the brain slows down and damage starts occurring to the organs. A non-diabetic—" he motions to us, "has a blood sugar level around 95 milligrams per deciliter of blood. Fasting, it might go as high as 125, but any higher than that and we start suspecting diabetes. It can go as low as 80, so those are the numbers we typically look for. Between 80 and 125." He pauses and opens Ashley's file.

"Ashley has a blood glucose reading of 865."

I think he wants a reaction, but I'm still not sure what that means. "That's high then, right?"

"Duh, Mom," Logan says, swinging his legs over the daybed and sitting up. "There's a 45 milligram variance in what's normal. She's 740 milligrams over the highest normal number. Her glucose is almost seven and a half times what it should be."

I have no idea how he does this kind of math in his head and can't bring home better than a C+.

"That's right," Dr. Benton says, looking impressed.

"But it's not unusual, though, right?" asks Travis, bless him.

"It's not unusual to see people who are dead at that level." He looks at Ashley. "You are a very, very lucky little girl. By all accounts, you should be dead right now." I can tell Ashley don't feel lucky. Her face is suddenly tight, and she looks like she swallowed a bee. But Dr. Benton puts his hand over hers, tubes and all, and squeezes it. "You've been given a new life today. You ready to start it?"

Chapter Five

I wasn't raised Baptist. My friend Janise and I, baptized in the Lutheran Church as infants, snickered at the Baptists across the way that sang of plunging in the blood of Jesus. We thought they were strange for not dancing or going to movies, and we rolled our eyes at the old men who chastised us for playing cards on our front porch. But Sunday afternoons, when my parents handed us cheese sandwiches and apples for lunch and told us to eat outside, we could smell the fried chicken and cherry cobblers through the open doors as their congregation spilled out onto the stairs, paper plates bending with the weight of food and tall cups of homemade lemonade bleeding icy perspiration.

On Halloween, when my friends and I would dress as witches and ghosts and tubes of toothpaste, they'd gather at the church for the Harvest Festival. I'd lug home my pillowcase of candy, and I'd see them riding through the streets on hay wagons, their faces wet from bobbing apples, arms looped through each other's, singing and laughing. They laughed a lot, even when we stuck our tongues out at them and called them holy rollers.

I thought they all just had the happy gene until I walked in on Donna Jean in the girls' bathroom in tenth grade. Though she'd barricaded herself in a stall, I could hear her crying. I almost backed out. I'm ashamed to say I'm one of those who don't deal well with discomfort, and hearing Donna Jean sobbing like a willow tree was uncomfortable. But before I could turn around and leave, she opened the door and froze on seeing me. I asked if she was all right, 'cause I didn't know what else to say, and she nodded and said she needed more toilet paper. She'd used it all up, and so I stood awkward as she got more from the next stall and blew her nose and tried to collect herself. I didn't know her that well. She was a grade above me, a flouncy cheerleader with perfect hair and the football wide receiver as a boyfriend, and a Baptist to boot. But she stood there sniffling, mascara black under her eyes, and I couldn't very well turn and leave or ask her to move so I could go pee in the only stall now that had toilet paper. So I asked her what was wrong.

"Jim broke up with me," she sniffed. "He said if I wasn't going to put out, he could find a dozen who would. He said he's tired of waiting around for me to be ready." She blew loudly. "He's already given his ring to someone else."

I wasn't about to try to give Donna Jean love advice, seeing as she was gorgeous and flirty and everything I wasn't. I'd never even had a boyfriend let alone come close to putting out. But I couldn't say nothing, her standing there all weepy, having bared her soul to me, so I said what came into my mind at the moment, which is hardly ever a smart thing for me to do. I said, "Don't he know you're a Baptist?"

She gave me a funny look, the kind adults give right before they say, "Well don't kids say the darndest things!" And then she smiled a little. "I guess he didn't." And she straightened her shoulders, threw her tissues in the trash, and fairly marched out of the bathroom.

I certainly didn't mean it as a compliment. Just that everyone knows if you want to get laid, it's not the Baptist kids you hang out with. But she took it as a compliment, and after that she always smiled at me in the halls and from the sidelines of the football field. I heard two years later that Jim got some girl knocked up right after prom, and they got married, had three kids, and are now divorced.

I remember that, not because it was some meeting of God moment for me or anything, but because in the bathroom that day I realized it meant as much to Donna Jean that she was Baptist as it did to me that she was a Baptist. Only in a good way. And I realized it never meant anything to me to be Lutheran. And I began wondering if there wasn't something wrong with that.

I stuck that memory away for awhile. After Logan was born I told Travis, who wasn't any religion at all, "I think I want to go to the Baptist church. If we're going to raise children, it seems they ought to know God." And he just shrugged. So that's how we became Baptist.

Which didn't seem important at all, until all them god-fearing folks from First Baptist start pouring into Children's Hospital with flowers and balloons and goldfish, assuring us that God would heal Ashley.

* * * *

Brenda and Yolanda are the first to barge in. They immediately push past Dr. Benton and right over to Ashley, the smell of wild flowers and Aqua Net hairspray filling the room. "Oh, Baaaaby, how arrrre you?" Brenda drawls, leaning over to hug Ashley and crushing her with her oversized bosom. "We got here as soon as we heard." She lets go and looks around for a place to tie the dozen Mylar balloons decorated with the face of some Disney teenybopper. When I read the word *officious* in the week-five vocabulary list in the SAT book, I thought of Brenda.

"Over here," Yolanda says, hip-checking the tiny table with the ice chips on it until it rolls to the corner where she sets a plate of brownies. "We know how bad hospital food is, so we brought you some goodies."

"She can't have any of those, now," Dr. Benton says. He maneuvers around the ladies, picking up the plate and handing it back to Yolanda. I can see her lip curl just a hair, and I know she's forming an unfavorable opinion of my favorite doctor. "Ashley's on a special diet for the next few days."

"Aw, a few brownies can't hurt her none," Brenda says, stepping in and batting her over-mascara-d lashes at him. She gives him her best sugary sweet smile, Marvelous Mango lipstick smudging her front two teeth. He doesn't fall for her flirting, and I love him even more for this.

"In fact, they can hurt her very much." He turns to Travis and me and says, "I'll let you all visit for a few minutes alone." To Ashley he says, "No food." Ashley don't look like she even cares about the brownies, which is a first.

Yolanda watches him leave, and then says, "He's a stick in the mud, ain't he?"

"I think he's cute," Brenda says. "Not everyone can be plied with your cooking."

"What's wrong with my cooking?"

"Maybe you should ask your husband. He seems to always be starved at the church suppers."

Travis clears his throat. They both stop suddenly and look at us.

"Goodness, look at us bickering and adding to your suffering 'stead of helping out like we should be."

"We aren't suffering," I say. "Why are you here?"

Brenda's eyes get wide and hurt. "We're here to see Ashley. We thought y'all might need some encouraging. The church always visits people in the hospital."

"That's why they call us the hospital-ity group." Yolanda jokes. I don't laugh, and she looks around to see if anyone else got it.

"We want to check on Ashley and see if there's anything we can do for y'all."

"I don't know," I say. "We ain't been here long enough to find out what's wrong. And now you done chased the doctor out, and who knows how long 'til he comes back and we find out."

Travis steps up next to me and puts his hand on my arm. "We sure do appreciate y'all coming all this way out here. It means a lot to us to know people in the church care that much." Yolanda don't look like she thinks we are that appreciative. "We'll probably be needing help later on, but we really don't know much yet, and the doctor was just about to fill us in. You understand." I can tell they don't at all.

"There's more of us coming," Brenda says.

"The committee wanted to be here for your family," Yolanda adds.

There's awkward silence. Then Travis says, "You know, I don't think Logan has eaten yet, and he's bored to death in here. Do you think you could take him to the cafeteria for us?"

Logan shoots Travis a look to kill, but Yolanda and Brenda don't see it, and they brighten immediately. Feeding people is their specialty.

"Gloria is bringing barbecue sandwiches. And Dot's got a fruit salad. We could set up a little feast for y'all, and you could come down when the doctor is done and get some nourishment."

"That would be a great time for us to fill you in," I say, warming to this idea, as my stomach is growling like a grisly bear at the smell of the brownies. They are both smiling now, our dismissing them forgiven.

Yolanda pats Ashley on the head. "I'm sorry, bunny. I wish the mean ole doctor would let us give you some."

Ashley, bless her heart, manages a smile and says, "That's okay. I'm not hungry anyway."

Yolanda tousles her hair like she's a stray dog, all pity. "You're such a brave girl." She leans over and whispers in her ear loud enough for all of us to hear, "We're all praying God will heal you quick. The God who heals the lame and raises the blind will make you healthy, too."

"Now," says Brenda, wrapping her ample arm around Logan, "let's go put some meat on those bones." She flashes a smile at me. "We'll check back with you in a bit."

I sink into the chair again. Ashley waits until they're gone before she asks, "The doctor says everything's going to change for us. You think God will make it so it don't?"

I think of Logan, and how the milk allergy just kinda went away and then about Travis, who still can't eat bacon and eggs. "We can pray, I suppose, but I don't know if it will do any good." Travis gives me a look to kill, and then puts his arm around Ashley.

"We should pray that God will get us through this however he sees fit."

"Can we pray he'll heal me? Do you think God will?"

I look at Travis, who looks back at me with something kin to a warning. "I don't know," I say. "He can, for sure. But just because He can don't mean He will."

"Why?"

"I don't know," I say again.

"Because," Travis says, "sometimes we become better people—stronger—by going through adversity."

A tear slides down Ashley's face. "I don't think I want to be stronger," she says. "I think I just want to be normal again."

I move to the other side of the bed and hold Ashley's head against me. "I know, baby girl. I want that, too."

* * * *

By the time Dr. Benton comes back, Ashley is asleep again. It's as if she's suddenly let go of trying so hard to be well and has given in to being sick. I wonder how hard it's been on her the last few days trying to stay functional if she's been this sick all along.

"It's all right," he says, looking at Ashley and then at his watch. "It's almost noon. I should get back to my own office and see my other patients. I'll drive back after the office closes and we can talk then."

"Your office? Don't you work in the hospital?"

He laughs. "No. I go in occasionally when one of my patients needs me, but mostly I work in my private practice."

"You're gonna drive all the way back home, and then back here tonight?" Travis asks.

"Sure. It's only about an hour." We don't answer that, but I'm sure Travis is thinking the same thing that I am: that an hour might as well be cross-country for us.

When he leaves, Travis and I feel alone in the room. There's some machine hooked up to Ashley that keeps beeping every few seconds, and her breathing is still more like a fish flung on the floor, but as we are the only two awake people in the room, the unquiet quiet feels unnatural.

Travis breaks the awkwardness by standing and making a big deal out of stretching his arms over his head, which expose his belly hanging over his belt. "Should we go see if we can get a Dr. Pepper or something?"

"I'm not going and facing *those* women."

"I thought they were your friends."

"They aren't. Just 'cause we go to church with them don't mean we're friends. I don't have the energy right now to deal with them, and if there are four of them down there by now, it'd take all the oil wells in Houston to get me enough energy."

He shrugs. "How 'bout a coke machine?"

We find the machine in the waiting room at the end of the PICU wing. Travis pulls a wrinkled bill out of his pocket and tries to feed it into the machine. The machine don't like it and spits it out. He smoothes it down and tries again. Again it comes out.

"For Pete's sake. You got any money?" I don't have to check my wallet 'cause I don't carry cash. At least, not the bill kind. I start pulling out everything in my purse to see if there ain't some change at the bottom when a lady thrusts a crisp, new bill at us.

"Here. I have a pocket full of them. I get them at the bank down the street. I ask for new bills there, because otherwise I might never get a drink here."

Travis thanks her, trades his wrinkled dollar for her starched flat one, and slides it in. It eats it immediately and deposits a can with a loud clunk. He pops the top and takes a long swig and hands it to me. I wave it off and thank the lady. "You visiting someone?" I ask.

She shakes her head. "My son's in here. He was in a bike accident. He fell down a ravine and hit his head and broke a few bones."

"That's awful," I say, but not meaning it wholeheartedly because right now I wish Ashley only had a few broken bones.

"What kind of bones did he break to land him in PICU?" asks Travis.

I elbow him to give him the signal he's been rude, but the lady tears up and suddenly I'm looking for the tissues. "He's in a coma. He slammed his head pretty good. It ricocheted his brain against his cranium and now…" She trails off, and I feel awful for thinking what I did about Ashley.

"Motorcycles are dangerous things," I say, trying to be sympathetic.

She stops sniffling a moment and looks up at me confused. "Not a motorcycle bike. A bicycle. He's eight."

My vision of a teenager careening down a hill comes to a halt. I think of Logan when he was eight, still innocent and fun. He'd stopped hugging me by then, but he still let me wrap my arms around him and tell him I loved him. To lose him in those years….

"I'm so sorry."

"Yes," she says, dabbing at her eyes. "Me too."

Chapter Six

"Inside our bodies we have lots of different organs that do different things," Dr. Benton is saying. He settles back down on Ashley's right side and is talking directly to her. "Take the heart. What does it do?"

"Pump blood," Ashley says.

"Right. And the lungs, what do they do?"

"Take in oxygen and get rid of carbon dioxide."

"And the brain?"

"It regulates the other organs and processes information."

Dr. Benton seems impressed. "You must be an "A" student." Ashley smiles back. It's a weak smile, but it's more than I've seen in a long time, and I hope maybe he's diagnosed her wrong.

"Do you know what the pancreas does?"

She shook her head.

"It produces a hormone called insulin. Insulin takes the glucose in your bloodstream and helps your body use it as energy. With diabetes, your body has stopped making insulin. Without insulin, your body can't use the food you eat as fuel. Even though you might eat, you feel tired all the time." I see Ashley nod, and I think of the last two weeks and how she slept all the time and how I thought it was all because of the flu.

"Then the glucose—the sugar—doesn't have anywhere to go, because your cells can't turn it into energy or store it for use later, so it builds up in your blood stream. Essentially, it's poisoning you. Everything you eat and drink, except for water, is poison to your body right now. Your body wants to flush the sugar out, so it craves water. The more water you drink, the more sugar gets flushed out of your body."

"But she's not eating sugar," I interrupt. "She's hardly had anything sweet in two weeks."

"The word sugar is a misnomer," he says, turning from Ashley to me and Travis. "Almost everything you eat has at least a little bit of it that gets turned into glucose by the body. Anything carbohydrate, like the bagel this morning, is primarily seen by the body as sugar. It doesn't matter if it actually has sugar in it or not."

He turns back to Ashley. "But even if you don't eat, your body is producing glucose on its own. You need insulin whether or not you eat, and you aren't making any insulin right now."

"Do I have to have surgery? My pappy had a heart attack last year, and they stuck a balloon in his veins."

"No," he says slowly, glancing at us. "There's no surgery for this. There is no cure."

I think these may be the worst four words I've ever heard in my life. "But the nurse said she could live a normal life. Like all the other girls her age."

"She can." He takes a small black pouch off the top of the pile of papers he has on his lap. He unzips it and pulls out the contents one by one: a small blue machine that looks a little like a calculator without all the buttons, a fat blue pen, and a container that looks like what my camera film used to come in.

"You now get to be your own pancreas. Since yours isn't checking the sugar levels in the blood and making insulin to cover it, you will do it yourself." He opens the top of the vial and pulls out a strip of black, shiny paper. "This is called a test strip. It will show you how much sugar is in your blood." He puts it into a slit in the top of the meter and the screen lights up. A few numbers flash across it, and then it settles into a picture of a blinking drop of blood. "That means the meter is ready," he explains. He draws an almost microscopic needle out of a pocket in the pouch and unscrews the cap of the pen. He places the needle into the pen and then lets Ashley look at it before screwing the top back on.

"See? Tiny. You won't hardly even feel it." He takes her hand and presses the end of the pen against it. "This is the lancet. You should put a new needle in it each time you test. Then, you place it on the side of one of your fingers and—" He presses the button on the side, and I hear a slight wiz of air. Ashley grimaces and then relaxes.

"Is that it?" She grins at us. "It didn't hurt at all!"

He squeezes her finger slightly and a dot of blood surfaces. He holds the test strip up against it and it sucks the blood right into it. The screen changes suddenly to a countdown. 5 – 4 – 3 – 2 – 1.

565.

I feel the color drain from my face. "That's bad, isn't it?"

Dr. Benton takes the test strip out and throws it into a red biohazard container. "Normally, yes. That's very bad. But it hasn't been that long since the medics started the insulin. She's come down almost three hundred points, and that's exceptionally good. Eventually, we'll get it stabilized around 100. Then, the trick is to keep it there."

"How do I do that?" Ashley is examining her finger.

"With insulin shots." She stops examining and looks up at the same time that Travis and I lean forward.

"Shots?"

"Yes. Testing is only part of the job of the pancreas. The other job is giving your body the insulin it needs to cover the glucose in the blood, or, in the case of a diabetic, the glucose they are about to eat."

"What about pills?" I ask.

"You can't take insulin in a pill," he says. "Insulin can't be absorbed by the stomach."

"I see them on the commercials all the time," I say.

"They aren't for type 1. That medication is for type 2. It helps the body use the insulin it is already making. But Ashley isn't making any."

"Do I have to get a shot every day?" Ashley is like a rabbit looking down a shotgun barrel.

"Several times a day. And let's be clear here, Ashley. This isn't your parents' job. They should watch you carefully, and help you out, but it's your body, and your life, and you need to be the one in control of it. That means testing your own blood, and giving yourself shots."

She couldn't have reacted with more horror if he'd just cut open his own chest and handed her his bloody heart. "I can't give myself a shot!"

Travis backs her up. "She really can't. Don't none of us like needles none, but it took two of us to hold her down for vaccinations when she was a young'un."

I hit him on the arm, but the doctor ignores him.

"You can and you will. And before you leave this hospital, it will already seem like no big deal." Neither Travis nor Ashley looks like they believed him.

He puts aside the meter and begins laying out papers on the bed, motioning for Travis and me to scoot closer. "Before we hand you a syringe, though, all of you have to understand how insulin works. It's a tightrope you have to walk carefully. Too little, you'll be back here." He looks gravely at us. "Too much, and she'll be dead."

* * * *

The nutritionist comes later with her stack of Xeroxed pyramid charts and fake plastic food. She explains that we need to measure everything out now, and know exactly how many carbohydrates are in each serving. Lean meat doesn't require insulin, but we should only eat four ounces, the size of a pack of cards, or the palm of my hand. We need to cut back on beef and other fatty meats. We have to worry about fat, because heart attacks occur at much higher rates among diabetics. Only a half a cup of mashed potatoes or a half-cup of rice, fifteen carbs. One cup of strawberries, fifteen carbs. One ounce of chips, fifteen carbs. Suddenly the entire pantry is reduced to cups and ounces and measurements of fifteen carbs.

"Do I really have to count how many Doritos I eat?" Ashley asks.

"It's important that you measure everything you eat before you eat it. That way you'll know how much insulin you need to cover it. If you're still hungry later, you can eat more, and take more insulin for it. The days of sitting on the couch eating chips out of the bag are over, I'm afraid."

She doesn't look afraid at all. Ashley, on the other hand, is getting paler, and her eyes keep closing.

"Are you tired?" I'm hoping she is so the doctors will leave us alone to digest all this information, which I don't think has any carbs.

She manages a "hmm," and a sigh, but don't open her eyes.

"I'll come back tomorrow, " the nutritionist is saying as she picks up her toy food. "I'll leave these pamphlets for you to look over. Here is a book that lists the nutrition facts about food sold at popular restaurants. You should keep that one in the car with you. And these other pamphlets—" She puts them on the pile of pamphlets Dr. Benton left us and stands to shake our hands. "I know this all seems overwhelming right now, but it will become second nature to you really quickly. You won't always have to measure everything you put on your plates. You'll be able to eyeball it soon, but for now it's important that it's done right. For Ashley."

As if it would be for anyone else.

* * * *

The sky behind the shaded window is dark. We survived our first day. Travis and Logan are with Ashley, who is asleep, and I send the hospitality brigade home. I barely touched their pulled pork and potato salad. All I can think of as I look at it is Dr. Benton telling Ashley, "Everything you eat is poison to your body." I try to remember what he said about fats and proteins and carbohydrates, but it all blurs together and all I remember is poison.

When I was a teenager, a girl I babysat got leukemia. Blood cancer. They gave her chemo and all her hair fell out, and she threw up all the time and couldn't hardly walk she was so weak. I asked my mom why she was so much sicker when they were treating her than before, and she said it was because they were treating her with poison. "It takes poison to kill the poison that's killin' her," she said.

    I wonder if insulin is poison. I wonder if Ashley will get worse before she gets better. I remember how casual the doctor sounded, and the nurse, and how all normal it seemed to them. But something in my stomach tells me different. A mother listens to these instincts. We trust them more than science. Sometimes more than God. Something tells me it's going to get way worse before it gets better.

Chapter Seven

I step out onto the balcony where the helicopter landed with Ashley several hours ago and look across the skyline of Austin, blazing with lights of people and businesses that are going about their lives as if everything is ordinary.

The door opens again behind me, and I turn to see Logan, his hair looking like a flame under the red exit sign. He hesitates and then walks towards me. He don't look at me but leans against the railing next to me and pulls a pack of cigarettes out of his pocket, tapping it until one slides out. He offers it to me.

"Logan T. Babcock, what in the name of all that's holy are you doing with cigarettes?"

"They're yours," he says without blinking, without looking at me. "I thought you might want them." He kept his eyes on the city lights. "I took them from your sock drawer before we left the house. I figured if we ended up staying overnight you'd need them."

If I ever thought my son could shock me, I didn't imagine it'd be like this. I stare at him, but he don't look at me, or withdraw the cigarettes. I take it slowly, and he pulls a lighter from his pocket and offers me a light. I take a long drag and exhale the puff into the night air. "How long you known?"

"A while." He says nothing more.

"Do you smoke, too?" I try not to say it accusingly, but it's hard to reign in the motherly tone.

"God, no. Those things will kill you."

"Don't take the Lord's name in vain," I say, then immediately regret it. I'm glad he don't smoke. "I only have one a day," I say, as if this makes it okay. "At night. Since I was about your age."

Logan don't act surprised, but he don't say nothing else either.

"I gave up a lot of stuff when we joined the church," I say, as if I can justify it. "I stopped drinking and cussing. I gave up immoral TV. Shoot, your dad and I even gave up going out to lunch on Sundays. But the cigarette..." I can't finish, because I know there is no reason. I just didn't want to give it up.

We stand next to each other until the cigarette is gone. I drop it and crush it with my shoe. He makes no motion to leave, so I stay too.

"Is Ashley really going to be okay?"

"Of course," I lie.

"But you don't know that."

"I know Dr. Benton says she'll be fine. And so did the nurse."

"But he also said she could die. She has to give herself insulin, and too much could kill her."

I think about asking for another cigarette, but I'm not sure I want to tick off God at this point.

"They also say millions of people live with this. If people were kicking the bucket the way they are with boobie cancer, we'd hear about it on the news. There'd be fundraising walks and ribbons on car bumpers," I say.

"Maybe it's like gang fights in LA. It's so common it doesn't make the news anymore."

"If it were that common, we'd know someone with it. You know any kids with diabetes?"

"No. You know any adults?"

"No." I'm dying for another puff. I find a rubber band in my pocket and twist it around my fingers for something to do. "Well, maybe a few. But I think they all have the second kind. They don't shoot up; they take pills. And they're all fat."

"Stop it, Mom."

"What?"

"The fat thing. You know how many times today you've talked about fat like it's some defect?"

"I don't talk like that. It's just a fact. If you can't see your toes and none of the clothes at Wal-Mart fit you, you're fat. Like saying Mr. Rodriguez is Spanish or Mr. Ruben is bald."

"Mexican, Mom."

"What?"

"The Rodriguezes are Mexican."

"Isn't that what I said?"

"No."

"Well, anyway, all the people I know who have diabetes can't see their toes, and they still eat whatever they want, and they don't worry about how many carbohydrates are in the food, and I've never seen any of them pass out." I stop, because all I can see now is Ashley bent over on the driveway, falling, falling. I pull so hard at the rubber band that it breaks and snaps my fingers.

"In a couple days we all get to go home, and they wouldn't let us go home if Ashley isn't going to be okay." I want to believe this as much as I need him to believe it.

"Okay."

"Okay what?" I'm expecting some backtalk, some sarcasm, but he just shrugs.

"Okay, if you say she'll be fine, I believe you." He hands me the pack of cigarettes. "I'm not going to be your supplier. If Dad caught me, he'd kill me."

He starts back to the door but stops short. "You know Ms. Brenda told me the church was praying that God will cure Ashley. She thinks she doesn't need any insulin or any special diet."

This makes me angry enough to spit nails, but I bite my cheek. "God is using the insulin to cure Ashley. Sometimes he does that—using drugs instead of healing outright."

"She says we just need faith."

"Next time she says that, you tell her we have plenty of faith. We have faith that God sent us Dr. Benton and the miracle of insulin, because without them she'd be dead."

I think he's going to talk back, but instead he takes the lighter out of his pocket and tosses it to me. "Only one a night, Mom."

I nod and watch the pink Mohawk disappear behind the sliding doors.

* * * *

The Ronald McDonald house is right across the parking lot, and they have one empty room all of us will have to crowd into. I don't know what I expected, but this ain't it. It's like a cross between a hotel and a house. There's a kitchen and a family room on the first floor, and when we walk in several parents are sitting around drinking coffee. One man comes over and shakes our hand and introduces himself all proper-like to us, and then introduces the others in the room.

"This is Jim and Amanda; they have a sixteen year old son that was in a car accident. That's Torren; her baby was born with hydrocephalus—water on the brain. And Dina has a two-year-old daughter who is having her third heart surgery." We awkwardly shake all their hands. "I'm Hank. My daughter has leukemia," he adds, like it's an afterthought. I'm uncomfortable with how we are all defined by our diseases.

"Our daughter has diabetes," Travis says.

"Oh," Hank says. "That's not too bad then. I don't guess you'll be here very long. It's just really an education thing, right?"

Travis feels me stiffen and lays his hand on my back. "It's our first day," he says evenly. "I'm not sure what all will happen, but since she went into a coma, I think it's a little more than just educational." He's being nicer than I would be. I can feel my teeth grinding. "I think we'll just get to bed. Long day, you know?" He presses my back with his hand and fairly pushes me out of the room before I can open my big mouth. Logan mutters goodnight and trudges behind us. I'm sure as sugar we've embarrassed him beyond belief but I don't care much.

Thankfully, upstairs our room is self-sufficient, with its own bathroom and necessities. I shut the door behind us with a distinct satisfaction hearing the bolt click shut.

"I'm not staying with these people here. There's no privacy. And can you believe how they looked down on us 'cause Ashley don't need a heart transplant?"

"I'm sure it just came out wrong," Travis says. "And anyway, we aren't going to be here long. I'll have to take Logan back to school in a day or two—he can't miss the whole week—and then you can stay in the room with Ashley."

"I'm not going to sit around with those pompous folks all week listening to how their kids are all worse off than ours, that's for sure."

"Wow, Mom. Pompous. That's a pretty big word."

"Oh, shush!" I throw my bag on the bed and rifle through it to find my nightgown. "It's past midnight. Can we all just go to sleep?"

Travis and Logan exchange looks that I pretend to ignore. Looking for my toothbrush, I pull every crumpled item out of my bag and throw it on the bed.

Travis takes his shaving kit out of his bag and hands it to me. "The toothbrushes are in there."

I grab it out of his hands without thanking him and slam the bathroom door behind me. I hear them talking through the door, their voices so low I can't make them out. I drop my nightgown on the floor and screw the cap off the toothpaste and proceed to scrub the enamel clean off my teeth.

* * * *

We take up just one room because in a day or two Travis will have to head back for work and Logan will have to go back to school, but even for one night it feels crowded in the room. Logan points out that we're living in a home sponsored by a restaurant whose food we are no longer supposed to eat. He calls it irony. There's a lot of iron in the burgers, but I think that's supposed to be a good thing, if I remember yesterday's lesson in nutrition right, so I'm not sure why Logan thinks this is bad. I checked the nutrition book for McDonald's for the fries and nearly apoplected over the carbs. Apoplexy is in Logan's vocabulary book: SAT list, week 3.

Ashley is asleep when we arrive back at the hospital, and the nurse tells us it may be days before she is back to her self. I don't know which self that is because I don't know anymore if she seemed different than usual because of puberty, or because of the diabetes.

We eat breakfast in the cafeteria. I notice smugly they serve bagels and orange juice and cereal and eggs. I'm not the only one killing people.

Afterwards, Travis gets a paper and disappears behind the sports section, and Logan sees a pretty girl he slyly follows into an arcade room. I spread out the pamphlets and charts we were given across the table and go through them again. I shuffle the papers mindlessly, the words on the pages confusing and without meaning. Words like glycated hemoglobin, basals and boluses, hypoglycemia, ultralene, and neuropathy. There are lists. Lists of possible complications. Lists of tests and medications. Lists of foods with numbers after them. And graphs and math way past the algebra I struggled through in high school before I dropped out.

I'm stupid about school things. I know this. And now I'm afraid it's going to kill my daughter.

I put my head in my hands, blocking out the quiet commotion of the cafeteria, and try to pray. I think I might've fallen asleep because when a warm hand falls on my shoulder, I look up, expecting Travis to be there, but he's gone. The woman standing over me is Betsy, the nurse on duty when Ashley was admitted. She's dressed in cheerful pink scrubs with Betty Boop bee-bopping around them, but her face is drawn and serious.

"Mrs. Babcock, you need to come with me."

"Is Ashley all right?"

"She's fine now. She had a bit of an episode, though, and I think she'd like to see you."

"What kind of an episode?" I'm shoveling the pamphlets into a canvas bag without bothering to fold or stack them.

"She's fine now," she repeats, and I feel the hairs on my neck grow hot.

"What's wrong with her?" I say this slightly too loudly and several people near us turn. Others pointedly don't, bless them. I imagine most in this room have said these words in the last three days.

"Her blood sugar dropped inexplicably. I'll explain as we walk."

I follow her to the elevator bank and then up a floor before she says anything else.

In the room Travis is already beside Ashley, helping her into a chair as two orderlies strip the linens off the bed.

"What the Sam Hill is going on?" I stare at Travis as though this is his fault.

"I just came up to see if she was awake," he says, his face white as rice. "She was shaking all over and sweating like a hog in heat, mumbling all kinds of stuff that made no sense."

"Often when a patient becomes hypoglycemic they are unable to talk, or are confused."

"She told me the orange juice was making too much noise."

"It made sense at the time," Ashley finally speaks, a meek whisper.

"How can that make sense?" I say.

Betsy shrugs and moves the tray away from the bed as the orderlies put new sheets on. "When the brain doesn't have enough glucose it does funny things. It makes it hard to communicate. Sometimes a patient can't speak at all, and sometimes it comes out all gobbledy-gook. The nerves are misfiring, and the brain wants to just shut down."

"Why did they change the sheets? Did she pee in bed?"

"Mom!"

"No, Mrs. Babcock. The hypoglycemia caused Ashley to break out in a sweat. We just thought she'd be more comfortable in drier sheets."

"When did this all happen?" I glare at Travis.

"Just now. I just now came up and saw her. I rang the bell and a doctor came and tested her and gave her a shot, and then Betsy went to get you."

"I thought shots brought her sugar down."

"This is a glucagon shot," Betsy says. "It gets sugar into her system fast."

"I thought we've spent the last 24 hours trying to get it down."

"Apparently we did that. A little too well."

"Shouldn't you be able to control that?"

"You'd think, wouldn't you?" Betsy doesn't even react to my anger. She laughs it off as though this is some kind of joke.

"Yes, actually, I would."

"Look, honey. This is what you are going to be dealing with the rest of her life. There's no magic solution here. No magic calculation. And until we know how she reacts to the insulin, we can only keep adjusting. Every diabetic is different. With some, one unit of insulin will drop them 200 points. With some, it only drops them 15. She dropped real fast. She must have a good sensitivity to it, but not everyone does, and we just can't know that until we try it out. It's the nature of the beast. If it were all predictable, it wouldn't be much fun, would it?"

I feel like kicking her in her patootie as she leaves the room. When I turn back to Travis, Ashley is leaning against him in the chair, already asleep on his shoulder. He picks her up, heaving a little even though she is so tiny, and lays her back in bed. I cover her with the blankets and use a towel to dry the drops of perspiration off her forehead.

"Can you believe the nerve of that nurse?" I ask. Travis don't answer and I look over at him. "Travis?"

"I thought she was dying." He sinks into the chair next to the bed and puts his head in his hands, the same way I'd been doing just a few minutes before. I wonder if it came naturally to us, or if one of us picked it up from the other. "I came in and she was shaking all over, like she had a fever of a hundred and eight, and she was talking, but it didn't make no sense, and it seemed like it was hard to talk at all. She talked real slow, and her words slurred together, and she looked at me like she was begging me to understand. And she was sweating all over and shaking, and I didn't know what to do."

"Well," I say. "It seems like you did the right thing. She's okay now, right?"

"Lord Almighty, is this what every day is going to be like?" He looks up at me. "I can't do this every day, Babs. How are we supposed to go home and live normal lives? How can we put her to bed every night knowing this could happen any minute? How in the name of all that's holy are we going to send her off to school by herself for eight hours a day?"

Since I saw Ashley go down on the driveway—it seems like days ago—I've been on the verge of a nervous breakdown. I've been holding back waiting for the right time to go psycho. But now Travis is freaking out, and if I've learned anything in marriage it's that only one of us can have a meltdown at once.

"God will give you strength." We both turn towards the door, and Pastor Joel, the preacher at First Baptist, is standing in the doorframe. "God is our refuge and strength, an ever-present help in trouble."

"Yeah?" says Travis. "I didn't see him here giving Ashley her glucagon shot a few minutes ago. Where was he then?"

And Pastor Joel and I stare, adequately shut up, as Travis storms past us and down the long hallway of the hospital.

Chapter Eight

Pastor Joel motions me to go after him, so I do, though I'm madder than a hornet at him. I catch up at the elevators, where he's pushing the down button so hard and fast I think he's going to break it.

"Stop it, Travis," I say, yanking his hand away like I might've if it was Logan doing that and he was three. "You want to explain why you went off like that?" What I'm thinking is how it's usually me thrashing out at God like that. It's Travis's job to hold it together in the God department and hearing him yell like that is like the floor dropping out from under me.

"No." He pushed the button again, just to show me he could.

"What is going on with you?" I say, which is a poor way of saying I need him to be strong. I know it's a poor way 'cause he don't even look at me. The elevator doors open and Gloria, Brenda and Janise step out. Travis storms past them, but I'm too taken back by all the sudden appearances. I hesitate just long enough for the doors to close.

Janise leans over and hugs me—one of those long, I'm-so-sorry-for-you hugs. She's the one person in the world that would really mean it when she said, "If I could take your place, I would."

She hands me a bag of cinnamon rolls. "I knew you'd probably be stuck with hospital food, so I brought you breakfast." The smell, which would normally make me drool, leaves my stomach a little sick. In Texas, food is the cure for everything. Everything except this.

"Thanks."

"Is Travis all right?"

"I don't know." I'm still staring at the elevator doors, wondering what's just happened. I shake it off. "Sure, he's fine. It's been a rough morning."

"With Ash?"

"All of it. Being here, not really understanding what's going on. It happened so fast."

I lead them back to the room where Pastor Joel is sitting in the chair that Travis already claimed as his territory. Ashley is still asleep and Pastor Joel has his Bible out and is reading to himself. I share the rolls with him, and we all talk as if Ashley ain't lying right next to us. Gloria has brought plans for the Memorial Day church barbeque, and they discuss that for a few minutes. I listen, but not really. The Ricardos can rent a party-size grill for the burgers and chicken, and the deaconate will man it. We need at least four families to bring coolers to store the ice and cokes. Gloria is making her famous lemonade, and we need to find one or two other women to make sweet tea. The church will provide the meat—Brenda is calling the order in to the market, and someone on the deaconate will pick it up on Friday. Families A-M will bring side dishes, and N-Z will bring deserts. I half-heartedly suggest switching that around, because frankly who enjoys making potato salad all the time more than brownies, but Brenda waves me off and insists it works better when there is consistency. She's a Williamson.

She drones on some more. I'd like to tune out completely. I'd like to not be here. I'd like them to not be here, talking like nothing is changed, like life's going on. To be talking about picnics sitting next to my daughter who might as well be in a coma at this moment is surreal. That's one of those SAT words. It's a good one.

Brenda moves on to the Pro-Life rally that's happening here in Austin next week, and which our church is participating in. A million folks descending on the capital steps to make sure people know it ain't okay to kill babies, or something like that. This has never been my thing. I'm just not that much of an activist, although Travis is pretty vocal, especially for a man. His mama was a single mom and almost aborted him. I think that hits a little close to home for him.

Ashley gets really into it, too. The youth group is pretty active that way, and so she's been planning on walking in it for the last two months. Now, of course, I'm not sure if I'll let her.

Brenda's yapping on and on about things that don't matter at all: details about the busses, and how many kids are going, and what kind of poster board will stand up to the marching, and how hot it's supposed to be. I realize she's talking and talking 'cause she don't know what else to say to me. She's here to help, but there's nothing to do to help. Nothing even Travis and me can do. Some of us ain't that good at just being there for one another. Brenda's one of those folks. Baking and cleaning and making phone calls, sure. But not so much of the just being there.

She's going over the agenda for the day and asks if she can put me down as a chaperone for the youth group bus, if'n we're out of the hospital by then and all. I guess she figures she's got me cornered 'cause who's going to say no to life when their daughter's hanging by a thread. I don't want to admit to her that I've never been comfortable with the way the church is involved in political issues. Seems to me a church should be about God and not so much the government. But it always seemed important to Ashley, so I say yes. I don't add the "if we're out of here" part.

Now she fishes around in her trashy gold bag and pulls out a stack of fundraising flyers and a box of envelopes and hands them to me.

"You've got lots of time here, I figured this would be the perfect job for you. You can stuff the envelopes and put the labels on them while you're sitting here all day. Ashley can even help if she's feeling better." She smiles sweetly, the kind of smile the wolf in grandma's clothes smiled right before he gobbled up Red Riding Hood.

She's talking about where to get the banner printed that the kids will carry in the march downtown when I see Ashley's eyes flutter open. I get up from this tiresome group and sit on the bed beside her.

"Hi, Ash. It's me. How're you feeling?"

The women get quiet for the first time, and suddenly, Pastor Joel senses Ashley's awkwardness and herds the small group out into the hall.

"Why are they all here?"

"Because they care about you."

"I think they're afraid you might not show up for church this week and ruin our family's perfect attendance."

"I'd say that's a certainty."

"What time is it?"

I look at the clock behind her bed. "Ten. You fell asleep after the shot."

"I was so tired. I woke up all sweaty and jittery, and I couldn't keep from shaking all over."

"I know. The nurse said you had a sugar low."

"I felt like all I wanted to do was sleep, but I was shaking so much I couldn't. She gave me a shot." She rubbed her arm. "It really hurt. Are all my shots going to hurt like that?"

She still has the IV in, and the insulin is dripping straight into her arms. She's supposed to get it out later today, and we'll start the shots for every meal. We're both scared. "I hope not, baby."

"I have to pee."

I help her out of bed. She's still shaky in the knees, so I let her lean on me. She drags the IV behind her and shuts me out when she can lean on the sink, instead. I do motherly things, like fluffing her pillows and opening the blinds and pouring the now-lukewarm water from the pitcher on the table into the flowers. When she comes out she waves me off and makes a bold but slow stride towards the bed.

"You want to play a game? Pastor Joel brought a few board games, in case you're bored. Get it? Board games for the bored."

"Ha ha!" She grins, though, so I pull the tray table over as she raises the back of the bed so she's sitting upright. Her eyes are more alert and her face looks newly scrubbed, and I think how hard this must be for her at this age to not be taking care of her looks. We've only recently allowed rouge, and the teensiest bit of mascara and lip-gloss, but she already fits into them like a glove.

I rub my hands together fiendishly, the way I do every time we play a board game, and cackle like a witch. "Okay my pretty, what is your poison today?"

"Apparently it's food." She says this with a broad smile, as though finally she has found the perfect comeback at the perfect time, but it wipes the grin straight off me.

"Don't say that, Ash."

"Why? Gosh, Mom, do I have to feel terminal all the time? If I can't joke about it, I'm going to have a really depressing life."

Because it's true, I think.

She gives me a goofy face, mouth twisted and eyebrows arched, her tongue lolling out.

I force a smile. "Okay, then, Miss Cheerful. What'll it be?"

She looks through the games and picks Monopoly, which promises a good, long diversion. She is the banker, because I can't do math in my head fast enough, and I line the properties up by rainbow color order rather than board order along the foot of the bed.

She picks the shoe. She always picks the shoe. I sort through the rest, less certain. I hate the water so the ship is out. I'm allergic to dogs, and horses scare the bejeebers out of me. The use of the thimble is beyond me. I choose the hat. I put it on my head the way I did when Ashley was young. It still makes her laugh. I'd give all the monopoly money in the world, and all the change in my own account, to hear that every day.

She charges around the board buying up every property she lands on until she's near broke. I only buy the bigger payoffs. She never lands on them, but I'm forking over two's and five's like nobody's business.

About six turns around the board Logan sticks his head in the door. He looks unhappy, which ain't unusual, and nods down the hall. "The church people want to know if everything's all right." This is code for they want to know what's going on. Ashley scrunches her face because she knows the code, too.

"Don't tell them all of it, Mom."

"All of what?"

"You know, the personal stuff." Suddenly she's the self-conscious twelve year-old.

"I'll only tell them about the throwing up and the dragging the IV to the bathroom with your gown flying open in the back. How's that sound?"

She sticks out her tongue at me, and it means something faraway different than when Logan does it.

"Can you do the go round for me," I ask him, nodding at the game.

He shrugs but, God love him, he don't roll his eyes. I kiss Ashley's head, and Logan takes my place in the chair, sizing up the board and his loot with an expressionless face.

In the hall down by the nursing station the ladies are sitting in the waiting room. I can't tell if they're praying or gossiping. Probably a little of both. I don't see Pastor Joel.

Brenda seizes on me. "Is everything all right?"

I stare because I can't believe the words coming out her mouth.

"No, Brenda, they're not all right." Janise steps in and puts her arm around me, more to keep me from lunging than to comfort me. I don't know what's wrong with me. I don't know why these women bug the heck out of me so much.

"We know this is really hard. What can we do to help?"

Suddenly, I'm tired of all this. I am tired of fighting these women who have driven all this way to be with me. I am tired of trying to make a wall between us when I've been on the other side so often. I look at their faces, and even though I want to see the false sympathy, there ain't nothing there but love. I feel ashamed.

"The doctor gave me lots of information I don't quite get. Maybe you could help me sort it out."

They all immediately jump on that, anxious to do something other than bring gifts we can't eat and plan church socials. I say I need to get all the pamphlets back in the room, and I tell them to meet me at the cafeteria.

When I get back to Ashley's room, I stop short at the door.

Logan's sitting on the bed with Ashley, and they're laughing so hard I see tears in Ashley's eyes. She's bunched up like she's got the stomach pains, and Logan throws out one-liners that make her gasp for breath.

I'm all at once standing at the doorway of Logan's bedroom when they were just young'uns, buried in the dark of night in Logan's bunk beds. Despite me painting a whole room of pink butterflies for Ashley, she still sneaked in every night to sleep with Logan. As I'd head to bed, I'd hear them giggling in the black, trading jokes that revolved around body sounds and stuffing the blankets in their mouths to keep me from hearing. Of course I heard, and I'd stomp in and demand Ashley go back to her room and the laughter to stop, because school was coming early in the morning. She'd slink past me, but in the morning I'd find her back in his room, curled up in the bottom bunk.

One night she stopped going in, and I wished I'd never sent her back.

I haven't seen them pass a word between them for barely a year other than to grumble at each other over the dinner table. I want to be happy they've found each other again. Mostly I'm jealous.

I back out of the room without a sound and return to the nurse's desk where I say I've lost some of the pamphlets Dr. Benton gave me. She flips through a file cabinet and produces another stack like magic.

I sit in an orange plastic chair like my middle school had in their cafeteria, and I go through the motions of explaining diabetes to women with blank looks on their faces. Already, I'm using words they don't know, like I've entered a private club with its own language. I'd be surprised by how easily the new words slip from me but I'm numb, and they're just words.

They stay about an hour, nodding and looking through the papers, asking polite questions like "Can she eat cherry cobbler?" and "How do you know how much insulin to take for a chicken potpie?" They arrange a list of people who will feed the fish until we get home and water the flowers. Since we're all here, there's nothing else to do at home, and they all realize there ain't much else for them to do here. So one makes an excuse to go, and they all follow. One by one they hug me and kiss my cheek and say goodbye.

"We're praying God will heal, Ashley," Brenda says.

"But what if he don't," I say. "Maybe it's not his will to heal her."

I might as well have let loose a string of cuss words for all the shock. "Why would he not?"

I don't know this answer. God knows I'm praying for the answer, because I don't think he plans on healing her. The peace that he *isn't* going to heal her sits like stone in my stomach.

When they leave I'm alone in a cafeteria full of other people who are alone.

* * * *

In the room, Logan's put away the monopoly game and is sitting in his totally-bored position on the daybed reading a book the size of the New York city phonebook. Ashley is chattering with Travis, who won't make eye contact with me.

"The game's over already?"

"Logan wiped me out in a matter of minutes," she said, her voice all bubbly. "Look what Pastor Joel left me!" On her lap lay dozens of homemade cards. "From the kids at church! The youth group and a bunch of Awana kids got together last night and made them for me." She is so excited she's nearly bursting. She holds a few out, and I take them and look through them. Some are just pictures, the kind Ashley and Logan drew before they realized that nothing they drew looked like what it was supposed to. Some are obviously from the youth group, with scripture verses handwritten in everything from chicken scratch to calligraphy.

"I'd say you look pretty loved," I muse, opening each one and pretending to read and admire them, though I can barely see through my watery eyes.

"Especially Brian Lee." This comes from Logan, who, although he don't even look up, manages to smirk behind the pages of his book.

"Shut up, Lo!" Ashley's cheeks flush, and I'm irrationally relieved to have the two like cats and dogs again.

"Brian Lee made you a card?"

Brian Lee is in the grade above Ashley, which makes him a high schooler, and I've heard her giggle on the phone with her friends about him when she thinks I'm not listening. I suspect he's the one that instigated the interest in lip-gloss.

"The whole youth group did. Not just him." She sticks her tongue out at Logan, who buries himself further in his book. "I'm sure they all had to," she adds lamely.

I hand the cards back to her, and she shuffles them in the pile on her lap and begins to go through them again.

"So," I say, "Pastor Joel brought them by?" I try to sound innocent but Travis knows me well enough, and he suddenly finds some need to wash his hands in the lavatory. He washes for a long time. Ashley murmurs something akin to consent but is now lost to me for conversation.

Ash with her cards, Logan with his book, and Travis avoiding me with his near-to-godliness hands. My entire family is in one room, and we might as well be blind and deaf for all the interaction.

Travis comes out drying his hands on a paper towel and, without looking at me, says, "I talked to Joel. We're good."

This is as much as I'm likely to get from him. I'd bet anything they didn't actually talk. Girls talk. Men nod curtly at each other, slap each other on the back and ask how the Rangers are doing this season.

Still, they'll be some hearty praying at the deacons' meeting tonight with Travis's name attached.

* * * *

In the afternoon Ashley is officially unhooked from her lifeline of insulin and saline, and Dr. Benton presents us with our very own box of syringes. There are enough to draw all the heroine addicts in Austin to our small room. Logan tries to sneak out, but the good doctor tongue-lashes him into a chair and tells us we all need to know how to do this. He produces an orange and a vial of saline, which he says will neither harm Ashley nor the orange, and proceeds to show us what he assures us will become second-nature.

Pull air into the needle. Put air into the vial. Turn vial upside down and draw medicine into the needle. Pull needle out of vial.

This part is simple, even for me.

He holds the syringe like a dart, and I have a sudden visual image of Logan using them for target practice on our dartboard in the garage. I give him my best "Don't even think of it" look, and he gives me that "what in the world are you talking about" look, and even though we are in a hospital holding needles, this strikes me as so terribly normal I start to laugh. I turn it into a cough and nod for Dr. Benton to go on.

Quick as lightening he stabs the orange and depresses the plunger. Then he hands it to Ashley.

She forgets to fill the syringe with air and has trouble getting the saline out. "It's pressurized," Dr. Benton says as she struggles to pull the plunger back. "There has to be a certain volume in the vial. If you don't put air in first to take the place of the insulin you take out, it gets harder and harder to get the insulin out. Try again."

She does it right the second time and triumphantly holds up the full needle. "Now the orange," he says. She holds it like he showed her, but she's scared of stabbing it too hard, though I'm not sure she's scared of hurting the orange and more likely she's scared of doing this to herself. She places the tip gently on the skin and tried to press it in slowly. The needle bends.

"You gotta do it quick," he says, taking it from her and putting it in a red plastic jar with skull and crossbones on it. "Slow is painful. Fast is fabulous." He winks at her. "Again."

She does it again, and then again, and then once more before she passes it to Travis. Over the next half hour we all manage to mangle a handful of syringes and destroy the orange to a holey pulp and pop Ashley's illusion that we can be her backups if she finds herself unable to poke herself.

When lunch arrives, we're required to calculate the carbs and insulin, and Dr. Benton passes the syringe and the real vial of insulin to Ashley. Something akin to panic flickers but disappears behind her resolve. She takes the needle and draws out the insulin, looking to Dr. Benton who nods his consent, and then she plunges it, eyes closed, into her abdomen.

We're all holding our breaths. Ashley opens her eyes and looks around. "Is that it?"

Dr. Benton laughs. "That's it."

She smiles wide. "It didn't hurt at all."

Dr. Benton moves the tray over her bed. It's no country fried chicken and cornbread, but for the first time in days Ashley looks famished. "Go ahead and eat," he says, handing her the fork. "It's not going to kill you."

He tousles her hair and winks. And she, who blushes at a card from Brian Lee, winks back.

Chapter Nine

When I was eight I spent a lazy Saturday lying on my front porch watching a spider spinning his web across the threshold. He climbed up the frame a foot or so and dropped, catching the breeze across to the other side, glimmering silk flowing out behind him. Dropping to the bottom, he attached another strand and then climbed back up, 'til he had a lopsided triangle. He did this over and over, each time adding new thread and attaching it with a quick little hook of his back leg. In less than ten minutes, he had himself a fair home waiting for a bug to fly through for lunch. What he got was my mama throwing open the screen door and asking if I was going to fritter away the day like some privileged kid or go weed the garden like she'd asked me twice.

I never took much time to reflect before now, but all these hours in the hospital without laundry and dishes and chauffeurin' people around, I got lots of time to think. For some reason that comes to mind several times. I think we all ain't nothing but spiders, spinning a web across a doorway. All we see is the living we're building for ourselves, not realizing that at any minute the world might throw open its door and walk right over us. And all we've made is lost.

And what I think is I never noticed how fragile life is before this drive home. I'm suddenly waiting for the inevitable wrecking of my life. We're one crazy driver away from a crash. We're one Luby's away from a gun-wielding lunatic. We're one flu away from disease, one miscalculated donut away from death.

Even with the hospital in the rearview mirror, I can't believe we're going home. I can't believe we passed the tests. For three days we calculated the carbs in Ashley's food. We figured the insulin needed. We learned how to put new lancets in the insulin pen Ashley will use for three of the four shots a day. We successfully poked the orange. They patted us on the back, handed us a fistful of prescriptions, and sent us out the door.

Still, I'd have stayed in the hospital another year for the security of knowing someone would be there if 'n we messed up.

I let Ashley pick out the music, and she enjoys the freedom of sitting in the front seat and flipping through the stations. She finds one playing country and settles back to listen, staring out the window all quiet-like. The dry grass fields pass like a memory, and we drive without talking, aware of our tentative hold on life.

She breaks the silence with a question. "If I'm on a plane that goes down over the ocean, you know, like on that TV show, I'm going to die aren't I? Because I need insulin. I won't even have the chance to eat bugs and build a fire to try and survive, will I?"

I've been expecting the reality of living with this disease to hit her eventually, but this ain't the question I expect. I expect something along the lines of, "Can I still eat pizza with the kids in the band after football games?" I expect, "If I don't eat the mashed potatoes, can I have the Oreos, 'cause they're the same amount of carbs." I don't expect no plane crash.

"I think that's the silliest thing I've ever heard," I say. "If you're on a plane that goes down over the ocean, you got bigger problems than insulin."

"But what if I do?"

I want to point out that livin' in the middle of Texas with no water closer than Town Lake ain't likely to get her over the ocean, but I realize she's seen her web too close to the door, too. "Well," I say, twisting my face into a serious expression, as if I'm really considering this. "If you go on a plane trip, maybe you make sure you take extra insulin on board with you. That way, if you go down, you'll have enough until you're rescued."

This seems to satisfy her for a few minutes. She watches the fields fly by out the window. Then she says, "What if I want to be a cheerleader?"

"You hate cheerleaders."

"That's not the point. What if I decide I want to be one? Can I do that with diabetes?"

"Do you want to?" I look at her sideways and wonder if the disease has affected her brain. Will she be a different person now? Has this changed who she is?

"No way. They're all snotty and stuck on themselves." She looked out the window instead of at me, which is good because I almost snort in relief. "But if I did. If I changed my mind."

My heart aches with the squeezing of her life into something smaller than the world she knew a few days ago. "Dr. Benton said you could do anything you wanted."

"But he also said I have to be very careful about exercising because it can make my blood sugar go really low."

"Do you really think cheerleading is exercise?"

This makes her smile a little, and so I decide to play along. "Then you make sure you have a juice box with you all the time."

She grows quiet again, and I wonder what other obstacles she's building for herself.

When we turn onto our street, cars crowd the curb so we can barely squeeze between them and into our driveway. Balloons are tied to our mailbox, and a homemade banner hangs from our porch. "Welcome Home Ashley."

Ashley looks wide-eyed at me and grins. "For me?"

She jumps out of the car before I turn the ignition off, and she's running up the sidewalk as her friends burst out the door at her. I see her running, and I think of the morning hardly more than a week ago. I keep hoping the doctors are wrong. I hope it's a fleeting thing. But I see her now, all pumped full of insulin, and she's normal again. Well, at least, a new kind of normal.

Janise comes to help me get the bags after the girls have all disappeared into the house, giggling and gossiping.

"Thanks," I say, but not for the luggage help. I nod towards the sign and the now wide-flung door. "It's the happiest I've seen Ash for awhile."

She gives me a hug. "You know I'd do anything for y'all." A dark look passes over her face. "Morgan isn't here." Morgan is Ashley's best friend since kindergarten. "Her mom was afraid she might 'catch it' if she got too close."

I feel the blood rush to my cheeks. "You can't catch diabetes. How ignorant is she?"

"The same as all of us. None of us knew any better a week ago," she says, but not to rebuke me, because she is *my* best friend since kindergarten. I know what she says is true, but I can't help being angry.

"Just call her. She wants to understand. We all want to understand."

I just pick up our bags and carry them in myself. In the dining room I see the girls gathered around our table looking at something. When I peer over them I see a sheet cake decorated with thick icing and yellow roses. *"We're glad you're better,"* it says.

"Can we have some," Ashley says, looking expectantly at me.

I press my lips together and look over at Janise. She clearly don't see the problem. "I bought paper plates so you wouldn't even have to clean up," she says, missing the point.

Travis picks this time to exit the kitchen with a fist full of plastic forks. "I found them!"

"What are you two doing," I seethe. The girls are all looking at me now. I tell them to go play Wii until we're ready, and I wait until they scramble off like prairie dogs before whaling on the two people who should have my back.

"Are you crazier than a rabid coon? She can't have that stuff! It's loaded with carbohydrates!"

"What are carbohydrates?" Janise asks, as if she hadn't spent the last three days in the hospital with me.

"Flour," I practically scream. "Sugar. Milk. Apparently anything white and edible. Doctor Benton says she can't have more than 45 grams in a sitting for the next few weeks. Ten Doritos got 15 grams. That cake is more than 45 grams."

"You have a scale in the kitchen," Janise says, trying to be helpful and missing the mark entirely. "We could weigh out 45 grams for her."

"It's not like that. You have to know how much flour and sugar and stuff is in it, and I don't." I think about the nutritionist and her plastic food. "If a bagel's got 60 grams, that cake's got about a bazillion."

"What if we did know?" Logan is standing in the door so quiet I don't hear him until he speaks. "Did you make the cake or buy it?" he asks Janise.

"Made it," she says indignantly, because she's never served a store-bought cake in her life.

"Then tell me what you put in it." He disappears into the kitchen and comes back with a calculator and a pen and a scrap of paper. "It's not that difficult. We can do it."

So Janise lists the ingredients, which she knows by heart because this is the same cake she makes for every church function and every birthday. Logan asks how much of each until he has the recipe written down. Then he crosses off the baking powder, salt, eggs, butter and vanilla and Crisco. "These don't have carbohydrates in them, so we don't have to worry about them." He circles the flour, sugar and sour cream in the cake and the powdered sugar and milk in the icing and disappears back into the kitchen.

He comes back with the sacks of flour and sugars from our pantry and the tub of sour cream that I know is expired. He looks at the labels on the side. "See? This tells you exactly how much is in each."

Janise looks over his shoulder as if seeing the bags for the first time.

"Jiminy. What's all that mean?"

"It tells you what's in them. You know—how much salt, protein, fat, and carbohydrates. See? The sugar has four grams of carbs per teaspoon."

"Well, ain't that grand! That's not so much then, is it?" Janise is ready to call the girls when Logan gets out the calculator.

"That's per teaspoon. You have two cups in this recipe." He crinkles his forehead like he did when he was two and trying to figure out some cosmic question like why God gave some animals tails and some got none. "Let's see. Three teaspoons in a tablespoon. Sixteen tablespoons in a cup. That's 48 teaspoon in a cup. 48 times four is 192. And you have two cups, so that is 192 times two, which is 384." He doesn't even type the numbers into the calculator. He writes 384 next to the word sugar.

He moves on to the flour, and then to the sour cream. He totals the numbers in the cake column and circles it. 596.

He begins the column with the powdered sugar and milk from the frosting. It's even scarier. 772. He adds the two. The grand total is 1368. Janise's face falls, and my own heart sinks knowing not just this week, but never will she be able to eat cake again.

"That's for the whole cake though," he says, quickly writing more numbers. You don't eat the whole cake. You just eat a piece. So if you cut the cake into, say, twenty pieces, that's 1368 divided by 20. That's about 68 grams per serving."

Janise's face gets even longer, but suddenly I see what Logan is getting at. "Try twenty-four pieces," I say. "How many grams is that?"

"57."

"What about 30?"

Logan taps it out on the calculator. "45.8!" He grins, and I could kiss that pink Mohawk.

"45! She can have that, then. We'll cut the cake into thirty pieces, and she can eat it!" I'm so excited I could spit.

Travis is already beside me, cutting even pieces, and Janise is at the stairs yelling at the girls that cake's on. Logan makes himself scarce before the girls can overtake him, and I don't even have time to kiss him on his pretty pink Mohawk head. Travis gives each kid a plate with a small piece of cake and not one complains. They grab it and head back upstairs. I take Ashley's arm and pull her into the kitchen before she can escape up the stairs as well.

"We've gotta give you a shot," I whisper.

She nods, but she's still flush with joy, and it don't seem to phase her.

"Check your blood first," I say, digging the meter out of my purse. She does it like a pro while I'm putting the needle on the insulin pen.

"It's 130."

I beam at her. "Thata girl! 130's a good number!" I find the sliding ruler that the hospital gave us that tells us how much insulin she should take. "One half unit to every twenty carbs. So forty grams is twice that, so one whole unit." I frown. "What about the other five grams?"

"Can't we just round?"

"Maybe. I guess. Do you think, Travis?"

"Why don't you just scrape off some of that icing," he says, licking yellow frosting off a fork.

"Okay. That sounds good." I give the insulin pen to Ashley and watch her dial it to one. She looks at me for approval. I nod, and she lifts her shirt, closes her eyes, and stabs her stomach, squeezing the top of the pen until all of the insulin is in.

She opens her eyes and smiles at me. "That's it?"

"I think so." I'm breathless. She hands me the pen and rushes out to find her friends. I look at Travis, who is grinning like a Cheshire. "We did it," I say.

"Yup."

For the briefest moment it feels like we've beaten life.

* * * *

At dinnertime she tests again and is within the spread Dr. Benton gave us. We measure out the rice and the green beans, which I substitute for the usual fried potatoes and okra, and round it off with chicken I've broiled instead of taken out of a box. She uses the calculator and the sliding scale to figure her insulin while Travis taps his fork on the table, watching his food get cold. I can tell we may need a better routine. Logan and Travis stare at the plate a little too long, as though I've gone California fruit and nuts on them, but I ask Ashley to bless it and we all dig in. We try to talk as though nothing is different, but there's a shift I can't name, and we mostly eat in silence.

I excuse Ashley from doing the dishes, and she goes to her room to practice the flute. Logan goes out to the garage, and Travis settles in his chair and turns on the ball game. I clean the kitchen. It's all so normal, but it don't feel that way. It's as if a stranger came into the house to live with us, and we're on our best behavior, waiting for it to leave.

Except I know this stranger will never leave.

At bedtime Ashley tests again. I stand over her, making sure she does it right, and we both gasp when the number blinks 332. Her eyes get wide. "Do I need to go back to the hospital?"

I call Dr. Benton, who gave us his cell phone number when we left and told us to call—day or night.

"What did you have for dinner?" He asks. I tell him, including the amounts of insulin. He does quick calculations in his head. "That sounds right. Did she eat anything this afternoon?"

My stomach sinks thinking about the cake and I almost lie, except I really need God on my side now, and lyin' ain't going to get us nowheres good, so I fess up. I tell him about Logan doing the math and making sure Ashley didn't eat more than 45 carbs. Then I remember that we checked before dinner and she was fine, so I add that the cake can't be the culprit.

"That's it," he says, to my dismay. "The fat in the icing, with all that Crisco, delays all the sugar from reaching the body fast. It probably hit about the same time dinner did. It's not unusual for things like cake to not add up right, also. You think that the sum of the carbs would equal the insulin needed, but for some reason it doesn't always do that. Sometimes, even though the numbers say one thing, the requirement is totally different."

"Does that mean she can't eat cake anymore?" Ashley is hanging on every word and I see sudden desperation.

"No. Of course not."

I pat Ashley's hand that is clawing me.

"It's a balance," he says. "And a lot of trial and error. Write down in the logbook what she ate and how much insulin she took and what her blood sugar was, and next time she eats it, give her a little more and see if that helps. For now, wait another hour and test again. It takes the insulin some time to fully run its course, too. Then correct according to the sliding scale you have."

I thank him and hang up. I look at the clock and wonder how to test in an hour if Ashley is ready for bed now.

She gives herself the other shot, the one she takes at bedtime, eating or no eating, and then goes up to bed. Logan's still in the garage pounding away at his music. I tell him it's time to put the drumsticks away and get ready for bed. On the way upstairs I pass Travis, still in his chair, snoring.

I haven't tucked Ashley in since she was eight, but tonight I sit on the edge of her bed while she arranges her stuffed animals beside her.

"I'm going to have to check your blood in an hour," I say.

"Like in the hospital?"

"Yes, but not all night. Just in an hour. And if it's still high I have to give you a shot."

"Okay." Her eyes are almost closing, and I wonder if this is part of being twelve, or part of being diabetic. I may never know. The two are now the same for us.

I want to kiss her but instead I tousle her hair. "I'll be back in an hour."

"Mom?" Her eyes flutter open. "What if I die in the night?"

"What?"

"If my blood sugar goes low, and no one knows it because I'm asleep, I could die, right?"

"That isn't going to happen, Ash."

"But what if it does?" She sounds like the little girl who used to be scared of flying monkeys coming out of her closet to whisk her off to the witch's castle.

"Would you feel better if I test every hour, just to make sure?"

"Would you?" Her lids are heavy again.

"Sure."

"Mom?"

"Yeah?"

"Can you stay with me for a little bit?"

I turn off the light and sit on the bed again. I hum the lullaby I sang to her every night when she was a baby.

"What song is that?"

"Hush Little Baby."

"I forget the words. Can you sing it?"

And so I sing.

> "Hush little baby don't say a word;
> Mama's gonna buy you a mockingbird.
> If that mockingbird don't sing,
> Mama's gonna buy you a diamond ring.
> If that diamond ring turns brass,
> Mama's gonna buy you a looking glass."

I sing slow, almost in a whisper, and I feel Ashley curl up in a ball, her legs pressed against mine.

> "If that looking glass gets broke,
> Mama's gonna buy you a billy goat.
> If that billy goat won't pull,
> Mama's gonna buy you a cart and bull."

I think about her as a baby, all wrinkly and pink, tufts of blond fuzz sticking out of the yellow blanket the hospital wrapped her in.

"If that cart and bull turn over,
Mama's gonna buy you a dog named Rover."

Her breath slows, and I notice for the first time the heavy sighing is gone.

"And if that dog named Rover won't bark,
Mama's gonna buy you a horse and cart.
And if that horse and cart fall down,
You'll still be the sweetest little baby in town."

I hum a bit more and then stand to go. She reaches out and holds my hand. "The other one, Mama. Sing the other one."

I'd forgotten I used to sing a different one to her, also. It's been so long, it surprises me that she remembers. I lay my hand on her head and try to remember the words.

"Hush little baby, don't you cry;
Within your dreams you can touch the sky.
With you in my arms I feel whole,
Because you are my heart and soul."

She reaches up and squeezes my hand. "You'll check on me in an hour?"

"In an hour," I say and slip out of the room.

Travis nearly scares the bejeezus out of me, standing right outside the door. "I haven't heard you sing in a while."

I shrug. "We got no more babies." He looks like he'd like to say something and then don't.

After he goes to bed, I slip out into the backyard with a cigarette and stare into the sky, which is all black and dotted with brilliant stars sharp as the pin-prick ends of a thousand needles, a sky completely unlike the landing pad at the hospital in Austin.

I breathe in the smoke and let it fill my lungs slow and hold it there a second or two before blowing out real slow. I watch the smoke circle up into the darkness and fade away on the breeze. I take another drag, and another, willing myself to not think about tomorrow, or the next day, or the day after, but just this minute, this next test, this moment when we are all home and safe. I squash the butt end into the flowerbeds and cover it with dirt.

I check Ashley's sugar before I go to bed. She barely stirs when I prick her with the needle and squeeze out a drop. She rolls over when I let go, before I can wipe the blood, and I see it smear across the pillow. It's down almost 50 points.

I set the alarm for an hour, but I can't get to sleep anyway. I think about the prescriptions we have to get filled tomorrow, and the grocery shopping, and Logan's ball game, and the church car wash. When I check her again it's under 200. It has gone down so fast I'm too scared to sleep again, and I lie on the floor next to her bed another hour and check again. It stabilizes at 160.

I finally crawl back into bed at four in the morning, and wonder how I used to nurse the kids when they were babies. I did this hour thing all the time, and I don't remember ever being this tired.

When I wake, Travis is already gone. Logan's locked in the bathroom, and Ashley is deeply asleep. I stand over her, not wanting to wake her because it's been such a tiring week, but wanting to make sure she's still alive. Unlike the last month, her breathing is quiet and light. I'm thankful for these little things.

Chapter Ten

The second full day home is Sunday and tired or not, we all manage to haul ourselves out of bed and dress in Sunday best. Curious eyes follow us as we slip in a back pew a few minutes after the service begins. A few friends wave at Ashley and she waves back, obviously happy to be back. Logan whispers to Travis and then slides out to move up a few rows where his buddies are. Travis and Ashley pick up in the middle of the song easily, but I busy myself stowing my purse and finding a hymnal, even though the words are up clear as day on the screen behind the pulpit. When I finally can't postpone it anymore, I move my lips in time to the music, but I have no voice.

The truth is, although I was the one who told Travis we needed to come to church, I've just never taken to it the way the rest of the family has. I suppose it's natural for Ashley and Logan to feel comfortable here. They've never known anything else. Sunday after Sunday, since they was in diapers, we been here singing the same songs with the same people, year after year. The same groups of kids moved with them from nursery to preschool, graduating into the grade-school Sunday school classes, in AWANA and Girls in Action, and youth group. They done the same car washes year after year, went to the same summer camps, ate the same fried chicken and cornbread at the same picnics. It's no surprise they fit like red in a rainbow here.

I play the game, too. I bake my share of pot-luck dinners, and I learned where all the books of the Bible is. I nod like I understand when Pastor Joel speaks, and I pretend to write notes on the back of the bulletin and file them in my Bible to read later. Really, though, I'm writing grocery lists, 'cause I just don't get it all. The church is something of a social clique, and even after all these years I feel on the outside looking in.

I sing the songs, but I don't feel them the way Brenda and Yolanda do, who close their eyes and sway when the music gets loud and sometimes sing through tears. I read the words and just don't get why someone would cry over them. And then I fear God is going to strike me dead for not getting it.

It's not that I don't want to get it. Who wouldn't want to feel like there is some God out there who made the whole universe and still knows them, though they be a speck of dust, and loves them. I tried to pray a couple times that God would make it real to me like it is to them, but I feel like I am talking into space. I figure if there's a God up there he's probably just laughing at me. Or cussing me out for smoking, and maybe it's that one cigarette a night that's keeping him from talking to me. And I figure if I wanted him enough, I'd give it up, so maybe it serves me right.

Every time I walk through the church doors I'm a hypocrite, pretending to feel like God loves me, when I don't really even know if he's there. But I can't speak this to anyone, 'cause they all know God loves them. Even Travis, who coulda cared less when I first told him we should go to church.

I think God speaks to Travis because Travis sings like he means it. When everyone has their eyes closed for silent meditation, I peek over at him and his mouth is moving like he's talking without sound, and I think he's actually talking to God. I suspect he actually thinks God is listening.

Since we been coming, the service is always the same. Announcements, songs, prayers, offering, sermon, invitation. The invitation is the part at the end when the pastor invites those moved by the Spirit to come forward and pray for God to come live in their hearts and forgive their sins. I'd heard all that in the Lutheran church, except no one marched up any aisle in front of the whole congregation, so no one knew who was praying and who was just closing their eyes and thinking what to have for lunch.

One Sunday, not too long after we came to First Baptist, I felt Travis move next to me, a slight, uncomfortable kind of moving, and when the choir sang Just As I Am, on the second verse, he got up and walked all the way down that long aisle and right into the open arms of the pastor. And I sat all by myself in the pew, feeling the piercing stares of those around me, wondering what was going on.

Going forward meant you'd never been saved, and everyone figured we'd been saved long ago. I figured we had. We'd gone to church all our lives. Not Baptist, but Christian churches. We believed in Jesus and God and the Bible. Ain't that what saves you? But there was Travis, walking forward like the sinner repenting, and all eyes looked at me.

And after that Travis started reading the Bible, and getting interested in the men's group, and when he wasn't working Saturdays he went to prayer meetings. But he never said nothing to me about it, and I don't ask, 'cause I'm waiting for God to talk to me like that, too. Except he don't.

The sermon today is about faith in praying, and I feel like Pastor Joel is staring at me when he says God will give us anything we ask for if we ask believing in him, and I can't help but wonder if Ashley is asking God to take away her diabetes, and I hate myself for thinking it's never that easy.

After the service people crowd around Ashley like she's a celebrity, asking how she is and telling her how much they prayed for her. She takes the attention with grace, answering polite, and then skips off with the other girls out the back. Travis takes over the answering until Dot and Yolanda break up the group and turn the conversation to the pro-life demonstration this afternoon.

There's a potluck at the church but we go home to eat. It's simpler that way. For now. I figure as we get used to this, it'll be easier going out, but for now, home seems safer. We eat sandwiches, 30 carbs apiece, and carrots with ranch dressing. We can't do chips, but Travis discovers his pork rinds don't have no carbs in them so we munch on those instead. We skip dessert.

Travis and Logan beg off the pro-life rally this afternoon. I'd rather stay home myself, but Ashley pleads with me to go. The bus is leaving the church at two, so we barely make it there before it pulls out. Ash wants to go on the bus with the kids, but I want to take the car.

"I thought you were supposed to chaperone us. You can't do that from the car."

"Ms. Brenda said they got enough parents on the bus. They just need me at the march."

"Well, then you drive and I'll ride," she says, as though this is so logical I shoulda thought it myself.

"And let you go all by yourself?"

"No. I'll be with 45 of my closest friends."

"And what happens if..." I don't know how to say it. "You know, if something happens?"

"It's Austin, Mom. It's forty minutes away. What can happen?"

Oh, let me list the things, I think.

"They're waiting, Mom." I look at the bus and curious eyes are looking down at our conversation. "You are so embarrassing me. It's not like I haven't traveled on the church bus a thousand times."

"But not with—" I start to say diabetes, but then I bite my tongue. I want her to feel normal, but I don't want to treat her that way.

"I have my meter." She opens her purse and pulls it out. "And jelly beans." We settled on jellybeans as emergency food because they're easy to count, one carb apiece, and easy to carry.

"Okay," I say, thinking this may be the biggest mistake I've ever made. "But I'm following behind and walking in the march with you."

"Okay." She high tails it up the bus steps, and I watch her through the windows, waiting for her to wave at me. She don't even look back.

* * * *

The downtown in Austin is crowded for a Sunday afternoon. It takes a while to find parking, and I have to weave my way through blocks of marchers to find where folks from our church are gathering. When I find them, Pastor Joel and his humongously pregnant wife are giving instructions about the route we're gonna walk and where to meet up when it's over. When he offers to pray before we leave, everyone holds hands and bows their heads. I'd feel self-conscious but everyone downtown is from one church or another, so we ain't the only ones praying. He has to yell real loud to be heard over the commotion.

"Father God," he starts. "We know all life is precious to you. You have formed us in our mother's womb; you have created both our body, and the souls that inhabit them, and your word tells us they are precious to you. Before we are even born, all our days are written in your book."

I look around and see heads nodding. Ashley ended up standing next to Brian Lee, and now their hands are clasped. It makes me smile. I remember trying to figure ways to get close to Travis, way back when. Some excuse to talk to him, touch him, without it needing to mean anything.

That seems like a long time ago. And not so long ago.

Pastor Joel is finishing up, about how God has a plan for each of us, and he's quoting some part of the Bible that must be important 'cause lots of people are saying it with him, and then he's done and everyone says *Amen*. The group parts like the Red Sea, adults on one side and kids on the other. I'm wishing Janise were here. The Lutheran church in our town don't seem to be big into the politicking the way the Baptists are, and I miss that about being Lutheran.

Brenda unfurls the banner for the youth group. Ashley ends up holding up one side and Morgan's got the other. I look around to see if Morgan's mom is here to make sure they don't touch or breathe the same air or anything, but I don't see her. Brian Lee and his abnormally large football friends line up close beside the banner, and Morgan and Ashley giggle.

I try not to look at the ghastly photos of aborted fetuses some of the women are carrying on large posters as we meet up with other churches in town. Folks are handing out placards with the pro-life logo on it, too, and some with a picture of a very serious looking man in a doctor's coat who I assume must be some abortion doctor with a big red slash across his face.

"Doncha wanna carry one," a little girl asks me, holding out one of the pictures of a dead baby on a poster stuck to a stick.

"No, thank you." I say. "I think I'll hold out for one with just words." The little girl skips off to hand her poster off to someone else, who ends up being Ashley, who hands off the banner to Brian Lee in order to carry it. Three of her other friends take one as well, and they join the front of the crowd gathering to begin the march down Main Street. Although she is still skin and bones and her sundress is hanging loose on her, her skin is rosy today, and her eyes are alive and sparkling. Brian Lee leans towards her and says something that makes her giggle again.

"She's the picture of health, isn't she?" Donna Jean has fallen in beside me, natural as if we was best friends. I've never gotten over seeing her as the beautiful upperclassman cheerleader and even now, I feel frumpy and unnerved by her attention. She went off to college and married some handsome educated man and brung him back to our podunk town for some reason I will never understand. By then we was already going to First Baptist, and Donna Jean had the grace to shake my hand with a nice smile when she came back but not ask what I was doing there. She's married, but she never had kids. I find myself watching her sometimes to see if she don't like them or if she's one of those who wishes she had one but just couldn't.

Today, her expression is unreadable as she walks next to me handing out flyers to the few people who are out this afternoon.

"Tom and I have been praying for your family this week."

"We appreciate that." I appreciate that she don't say she's praying God will heal Ashley.

"How is Ashley doing?"

"She's okay." I glance at my daughter holding up her sign and chanting with her friends. "Better than okay. She's probably taking it better than the rest of us."

"Kids are so much stronger than we give them credit for."

"I suppose."

"I don't quite understand them, I admit."

"Who's that?"

"Teenagers. How some things are so important they might kill themselves over it. Like getting pregnant, or failing a class in school. And other things, like faith in God and being healthy, don't matter at all."

"I read in a magazine about that once." I try to remember what it said that made so much sense to me at the time. "The part of the brain that thinks about consequences, long term stuff, don't develop 'til they're mostly grown. They actually can't really think about what's gonna happen ten years down the line. Realistically, I mean." I glance at her in her designer pantsuit, and I feel like I'm sounding all big-shotty about talking to someone so educated like I might know something they don't, but she has this look of wonder on her face, like everything is now clear as day.

"Someone should explain that to teenagers," she says.

"They won't listen." I remember my daddy telling me the older he got, the smarter his daddy got. I tell her this and she laughs.

"It's better that way, anyway," I say. "At least for Ashley. Today she's fine. She feels good. She's not thinking about tomorrow and the next day, and the year down the road."

"What's down the road for her that isn't here today? Is it just that she's going to have to do this, the shot thing, every day?"

"Partly. I mean, today is one thing, but think about the rest of her life—that she's not going to get a break from this. She can't go on vacation from it. Every single day of the rest of her life. Shots. Counting carbs. She's not thinking about all the literature that says she's a higher risk for heart disease, and blindness, and amputation." I'm talking now like I haven't to anyone since she was diagnosed, and I want to stop, but I can't, because Donna Jean listens to me.

"Kids only see this minute, and look at her." Ashley is clearly flirting with Brian Lee, in that kind of comfortable way I never could. "She isn't thinking, 'I have to take another shot tonight, and then four more tomorrow, and four more the next day, and every day for the rest of my life.' She's not thinking that every shot she takes could be a tiny bit too much, and she could end up in the hospital again. She's not thinking every high is slowly eating away at her nervous system and her kidneys, and that she will never be able to eat the entire pan of brownies when it comes fresh out of the oven."

I've stopped and I'm crying beside the road, while the rest of the marchers pass us with hardly a glance. Donna puts her arms around me, and I'm crying into her shoulder, ashamed.

"Look at her," Donna says, turning me back to the parade. "Do we ever know what's in our future? Do any of us know what's in store for us? But today," she squeezes my arm, "today she is great."

We begin to walk again, and I use my hand to wipe the tears because I don't have any tissues on me.

"You know what Jesus says about diabetes?" She smiles at me like she's got a secret. "He says don't worry about tomorrow, because today has enough worries of it's own."

I find myself smiling back. "Ain't that the truth?"

For the smallest of minutes, I think God might just be talking to me.

* * * *

When we arrive at the Capital steps I find Ashley sitting on a curb, her head in her hands, with her friends gathered around her like she's a freak show.

"What's wrong," I say, pushing through them.

"I'm fine," Ashley says, clearly embarrassed. "I'm just really weak. I needed to sit. It's a lot of walking."

"Let's test," I say, and fish through her purse and find the meter, shooing everyone else away except Morgan, who is sitting with her. I take her hand to test, but she grabs the lancet from me, clearly agitated.

"I can do it myself," she snaps. Diabetes or being twelve, I wonder.

She has to prick her finger three times before she gets one deep enough to squeeze blood out of. She drops the test strip trying to get it in the meter. Her blood smears across the bottle as she digs a new strip out, her fingers shaking as she tries to get this one in. She squeezes her finger and more blood bubbles up and she touches the strip.

56.

I open her purse to find the jellybeans, but she snatches it from me. "I got it, Mom. You don't need to hover all the time." She finds the Ziploc bag we've put a handful in and counts out seven. Pure sugar. She tries to close the bag, but her hands shake and she drops the jellybeans. "Crap."

"Ashley!"

"Can you go away, Mom? I'm fine." Of course I'm not going anywhere. Morgan looks up at me.

"I'll count them out for her and make sure she takes them, Ms. Babs." I hesitate, then nod and stand up. I back up a foot or two and watch Morgan count out seven and put them in Ashley's hand. She puts them all in her mouth at once.

"It's the walking," I explain. "Dr. Benton said exercise could do that. We know now if you're going to exercise you should eat something extra, or take less insulin for lunch," I say to Ashley.

"Yeah. Okay. Go, please."

Morgan looks at me and mouths, "I'll watch her."

I nod and walk away, but not too far. I never walk too far away anymore.

They sit on the curb while the crowd listens to a man behind a microphone telling about the development of a baby. A few cells that have all the DNA necessary to make a human being, the organs and the body parts, every piece of the puzzle that makes a person an individual. Parts of the personality are already determined at four weeks, he says. What you will look like, who you will be, are already in the making before the mother even knows you are there.

I wonder if the part of Ashley's DNA that made her diabetic was already there. Waiting. Waiting for this flu, this moment of weakness. Waiting to change all the DNA that came before it, to change Ashley's life into this thing I don't know.

The speaker goes on and on, sanctity of life and all that. He talks about the damage abortion does to mother, too, and quotes some of the verses Pastor Joel used in his prayer. He moves on to embryonic stem cell research, and his words get too big for me. I understand the word evil and the word research and the idea that it kills unborn, but most of the rest is lost on me. It sounds like he's saying they can take some baby out of the womb and use its cells to make other things a person needs, like that scientist doctor on the poster is creating some baby factory to make babies for baby parts and then kill them, but that sounds like science fiction, so I figure I must be getting it wrong.

Donna Jean is lost in the crowd, and I edge closer to Ashley and the rest of the kids hoping not to lose them too.

"We need to send a message loud and clear," his voice is booming over the mic system, "that we will not tolerate the killing of unborn children for any reason. Not for convenience, or for the scientists who justify murder as a means to an end." People with the posters of the doctor start waving them and chanting.

The sun is hot on my head, too hot for May, and I'm suddenly so tired I sit on a curb, too. If the DNA was there at the beginning, it must have come from us, from Travis and me. I don't remember much of biology, but I know everything we are comes from what our parents pass down to us. We are the sum of their parts. Greater, maybe, and completely different as a product, but all the same, everything we are came from somewhere in them.

She came from me. I gave it to her.

People around me begin to cheer something the man has said. They are chanting something that sounds like nothing to me. I find Ashley in the crowd, jabbering with some girls. "I want to go home," I say.

"Now?"

"I'm so tired. I just want to go."

"I want to stay," Ashley says. She looks like she has recovered from the low without any side effect. "Morgan's mom will take me home."

"I didn't see Morgan's mom."

"Not here. From the church. I'll ride the bus, and she'll pick me up at the church."

"Did you ask Morgan's mom?" I try not to be snippy, but I know Morgan's mom won't let Ashley in their car until the health department clears her.

"No, but I'm sure she would. Or Sarah's mom. Can't I stay? We just got here."

"No. We've been here long enough. And I don't want you walking more and going low again. I'm tired and we've already wasted the whole afternoon. There are things I need to do at home more important than this."

"But why can't I stay?"

Because your blood sugar might dive, I think. *Because you might pass out. Because I might lose you, and I could no more bear that than sprout wings and fly. Because you have diabetes,* I want to say.

"Because I say so," I say out loud.

She pouts the whole way home, and I'm sure that is the twelve year-old part of her.

Chapter Eleven

When the kids are gone to school, I take stock of what we left behind a week ago. Two laundry baskets of dirty clothes sit in the hallway, and piles of clean ones needing to be folded are heaped on the couch. The wastepaper can in the living room is overflowing with Kleenexes from when Ash had the flu, and a stack of magazines lies on the floor. Logan has been ripping out pages with pictures that he deems a possibility for his first tattoo that he's getting over my dead body. There is an almost empty coffee cup. I don't even remember whose it was.

On the kitchen counter, Janise has stacked the mail from the last week on top of the papers the kids had brought home from school—the day before papers and school suddenly didn't matter.

For the first time in over a week, life seems back to normal. I throw laundry in the washer and straighten the living room, taking comfort in the routine of folding clothes and putting them back in the drawers. I tackle the stack of mail, separating into a throwaway pile, a to-file pile, and the bills, some of which are now overdue. When I finish the bills, I walk them to the mailbox at the end of the drive. As I head back up, I spot the bottle of Sunny D in the dry grass. The ants have swarmed and gone, and now it is sun-bleached and dried. I pick it up to throw it away, and a knot forms in my stomach.

For almost three hours I work and the house is quiet. By the time I go to dump jeans in the wash, I've got the radio on and am humming along. I dig through the pockets as I toss them in, putting loose change in the jar on the dryer and throwing out wadded up Kleenexes. When I come to Logan's favorite pair, I find a folded piece of paper in the back pocket. I set it aside until I get all the clothes in and shut the lid. I unfold it, thinking it'll be a note from some girl, or this week's baseball practice schedule, or the name of some pizza place the band is playing. Instead, it's a form from his coach saying Logan's been kicked off the team.

I scan it, stunned, and then take it to the couch where I sit down to reread it.

There was a brawl in the locker room. Logan and some other kid. Technically, no punches were thrown and both students were deemed to be at fault, so the coach chose to take the matter in his own hands rather than send it up through the ranks to the principal. Both students received detentions to be served cleaning the equipment closet and washing uniforms after school, and both were indefinitely suspended from the team.

I turn it over, but there's nothing else. There's no date. I try to remember the last time I saw Logan play ball. Two weeks before the hospital, maybe. Two weeks of deception. *How's the practices?* I've asked. *Same ole, same ole,* he says back. He didn't tell me he was flunking PE the first quarter when he kept forgetting his gym clothes. He lied about forging my name to the driver's ed permission form. And this morning he walked out of the bathroom with a royal blue Mohawk.

Enough is enough, I think. *This time, I'm gonna wring his neck.*

I scrounge through the junk drawer to find the coach's phone number, when the phone rings. It's the middle school.

"Mrs. Babcock? We need you to come down to the school."

Instantly, I forget about Logan. "Is Ashley okay?" Suddenly my world is dropping out from under me.

"Not really. We need you to come right now."

I already have the keys in my hands, and I'm hunting for my purse. "Did you call the hospital? Has the ambulance come? Should I just go there?"

There is silence at the other end of the line for a minute. "Ashley's fine, Mrs. Babcock."

I stop my flight out the door. "You just said she wasn't."

"She's not sick or hurt, if that's what you mean. She's in trouble. We need you to come pick her up." And in case I was wondering she adds, "The expulsion kind of trouble."

I'm so relieved Ashley ain't lying dead somewhere that I'm in the car before the word expulsion registers. I've feared this call but never expected it to come for Ashley. Logan's a different matter, of course. He's clashed with school since eighth grade when he created an explosion in chemistry class that sent the entire school into evacuation mode. Then there was the protest he began over the quality of cafeteria food, complete with a sit-in that resulted in a school-wide ban on recess for a week. Not to mention this year's adventures. If there was any form of authority, Logan was there to rebel against it. Trouble always follows him.

But never Ashley.

I'm between scared and mad by the time I march into the office and demand an explanation. Ashley sees me from the corner where she's been banished and lunges at me, throwing her arms around me and bursting into tears.

The principal's door opens, and she motions for us to go in. The secretary makes a point of not making eye contact with us.

"What in the world is this about?"

She motions to a chair. "Have a seat."

"No, I will not have a seat, Laura. What is going on?" Ashley's leaning on me still, shaking hard and digging her nails into my arm. I pry them off and notice how sweaty they are.

"Ashley's brought drug paraphernalia to school." She lets this sink in and then deals what she thinks is the final blow. "You know the school has a zero tolerance policy. That is automatic expulsion."

This is so absurd I laugh.

"I assure you this is not funny, Mrs. Babcock."

"Jiminy, Laura, call me Babs. We've known each other since grade school."

She opens the desk drawer and pulls out the insulin pen, the needle still attached. "Did you know she had this in her backpack?"

I am no longer laughing. "As a matter of fact, I put it there." Suddenly, I know Ashley isn't shaking because she's scared.

"Did you take the insulin?" I'm in her face, holding her damp hair out of her eyes and gripping her head. She nods. "How much? How much did you take and did you eat anything?"

She shook her head. "One and a half units, I think. Then they made me leave the lunch room."

"Where is your lunch?" I'm now completely ignoring Laura, who's telling me to calm down and sit. "Where's your lunch? Is it in your back pack or still in the cafeteria?" As I'm asking, I'm hunting through my purse, throwing items on the desk until I finally just dump the entire contents searching for a tick tack, a life-saver, something with sugar. "She needs food. Where is her lunch?" I grab a can of Coke off the desk. I pop the top open and hand it to Ashley. "Drink it." I don't have any idea how many carbs are in the can, or how much she is drinking, but I'll worry about that later.

"Is this a drug reaction?" Laura is suddenly backing against the wall, eyes wide over Ashley's gulping of her drink.

"Yes. It's called insulin, and she needs it to live. But she needs to eat when she takes it or she dies. Do you get that? You'd let her sit here and die while you made your smug little point about zero tolerance?"

I snatch the insulin pen off the desk and hold it close to her face. "It's prescription. Does this look like it's dangerous to you? Does this look like some illegal substance? It's got a drug company logo on it. Do you people not read the notes I send in? She's got diabetes. Why do you think she was gone all week?"

Ashley is wide-eyed, but I can't stop. All this anger at what is happening to our lives rushes out, and I can't stop. Is this what her life is going to be now? Shots and tests and accusations and near-death experiences?

And while I'm ranting more, the door opens and I feel a hand on my shoulder. When I see it's Travis I burst into tears, and he wraps his arms around me. Laura, smartly, leaves.

When she returns, the contents of my purse are not spread around her desk anymore, and the can of coke is empty and in the trashcan, and Travis has pulled up a chair between me and Ashley. Laura looks at us coolly as she sits behind the safety of her desk. "Do I need to call security or can we resolve this now?"

Travis leans over, resting his hands on the desk. "Do you have any idea..." His voice trails off with a tremble. I expected him to smooth us out, but instead he stands and opens the door, nodding for me and Ashley to leave.

"This isn't over," Laura says, raising her voice enough to follow us into the hall. "Prescription or not, Ashley brought drugs to school. And a needle. That's serious, and the school board's going to be on my side."

Travis walks back to her, his face inches from hers, and lowers his voice. "If you think for one second you, or your school board, is going to keep us from keeping our daughter alive, you are in for a long fight."

On the way out I watched him put his arm protectively around Ashley, and a weight I didn't know I carried fell off my shoulders.

* * * *

We call Dr. Benton, who's with a patient and whose nurse tells us we need to get us something called a 504 and refers us to a lawyer who will help us if we need it. I say we should wait 'til Dr. Benton calls back, especially since we got insurance to cover the doctor but no lawyer insurance, but Travis calls anyway. The lawyer seems overly eager to talk to us. I think he smells a lawsuit, but by now I just want Ashley back in school.

She's gotten over the fear of being in trouble and now is complaining about the way they hauled her out in front of her friends and made a scene at the school. She's afraid she can never show her blush-cheeked, lip-glossed face again.

This drama is new, so I test her blood, hoping it's the diabetes, but I'm disappointed when the meter shows 132. I realize it's just being twelve.

"At least twelve goes away," Travis says, tying on a tie I haven't seen in a month of Sundays. "If the diabetes causes this kind of moodiness, we'd never get her married off."

I point out a salsa stain on the tie, and he takes it off. He rummages through his drawers trying to find his only other tie, a white one with small blue and pink handprints Logan and Ashley made for him one Christmas back when their handprints fit on something as small as a tie.

"You sure you don't want to go with me?"

"I wouldn't know what he was saying anyway." I spit on my finger and rub it across the salsa stain trying to figure if I'd washed it already and it's set in for good.

Travis stops fiddling with the knot and looks at me. "You think I do?"

"You know better than I do."

"I don't understand half of what anyone has said the last week. You were the one who understood what the doctors were trying to say. Carbohydrates, basals, hyperglycemia. I got no idea still what any of that means."

"Logan explained it all to me," I say, finally dumping the tie on the heap of dirty laundry on the bed.

"Maybe we should send Logan to the lawyer." We look at each other as if we're actually considering this, and then he pecks me on the cheek, which I can't remember the last time he done this, and says goodbye.

Ashley is flopped melodramatically across her bed and moaning that since everyone is at school, she can't even text them. I toss her book bag at her and tell her to catch up on all her make-up work or help me fold clothes. She chooses the schoolwork.

When Travis comes home the house is some semblance of back to normal, and I'm in the kitchen broiling chicken again 'cause I don't know what else to fix. He lays a folder on the table and grabs a Dr. Pepper from the fridge before sitting down.

"Is it fixed?" I ask, joining him. "Can she take the needles to school, and more importantly, can we fire Laura?" This last comment is joking, but only partly, 'cause I'm still mad.

"Yeah, yeah, and no. At least not yet." He shoves the folder across the table at me, but I don't open it because I know it'll be full of legal jargon.

"Just tell me."

"It's called a 504. It's a federal civil rights law, so it applies to everyone in the country, including us."

"Ashley ain't black," I say, because civil rights brings flashes of bus protests and diner brawls to mind. I don't get where this is going.

"Not civil rights like race. It's a disability law."

"She ain't disabled either."

"According to the law she is. She needs special rules for her because she's different, the lawyer said."

"She's not different." I get up and pull out pans for chitlins and then realize I have no idea how many carbs are in them, so I put them away.

"I don't mean she's different. I mean, she has different needs. Put that away and come sit down and listen, 'cause I can't take days off work every time there's a problem at Ashley's school. You gotta handle this, too."

I sit, but I don't look at the papers.

"It just means she's got rights. It's good stuff, Babs. Look at this." He pulls out a paper with a list with those dotty things in front of each item, but I push them back to him.

"I don't want to read them. Just tell me."

"Okay." He settles for this and glances at the papers. "A 504 is a law that says Ashley's got the right to feel safe at school, like she's not going to pass out and die and nobody will know what to do. The law says there's gotta be people at the school who know what diabetes is, and know how to give her shots if she needs it, or test her blood, and they gotta know what all the numbers mean, too, so they know if she needs to eat or call a doctor or something." He looks at the list again. "All her teachers got to know she has diabetes and what it looks like if she goes high or low, and what to do if it does. They gotta let her go to the doctor anytime she needs to and it's excused. And she gets to go to the bathroom or water fountain anytime, too. They can't keep her from doing that."

I think about how Ashley came home crying the day right before she passed out, because the teacher wouldn't let her go to the bathroom, and she thought she was going to pee her pants in class. She was so embarrassed. And I told her to stop drinking so much.

"She gets to eat whenever she needs to, and," he looks at me triumphantly, "she gets to carry her needles and insulin."

"Really?" All I can think of is, *We got Laura!*

Travis puts the papers back in the folder and drains the Dr. Pepper. "But we got to fill out all the papers first. To make it legal."

"Well, let's do it." I get up to get a pen when Travis stops me.

"We can't do it ourselves. We have to do it with the school, with the principal and the administrative people, and the teachers."

"I'm not doing this with Laura. I won't sit in a room with her again and listen to her smug educated talk and her big words and her talking down to us."

"But we're right." He's quiet when he says this, like he's calming me down, but what he's really doing is offering me a weapon to bludgeon Laura. "We were right, and she was wrong, and now we need to go get her to put that on paper."

I look at the papers in my hands and nod. "I'll call and make an appointment tomorrow."

But we never make it.

Chapter Twelve

I don't notice Ashley's itching right away. By the time I see her scratching at her stomach with the fervor of a dog with fleas, she's scratched a good few layers of skin off, and fingernail size streaks of blood are seeping through her clothes. She winces giving herself a shot for dinner, and I see the red blotches across her white shirt.

I pull up the shirt enough to see her abdomen is dotted with angry welts. I recognize them right away as hives. I'm no stranger to hives on my kids. Logan got them when he drank milk as a toddler, and every time he rolled down a hill of Saint Augustine grass. Ashley got them when the local pool dumped too much chlorine in the water and when I use bleach that smells like flowers. But we haven't been to the pool in months, and I stopped using bleach the day Travis accidentally used it instead of detergent on a load of his work jeans.

I run through the list of suspects in my head. Laundry detergent: the same. Bath soap: the same. Her shirt: cotton, and old. She hasn't used any lotions or perfumes that I know of. I ask. She denies.

"When did it start?"

"I don't know." She pulls away and cleans up her testing supplies and needles, unconcerned.

"Think."

She does. "Right before we left the hospital."

Well, that makes sense. Maybe it's the hospital sheets, or gowns, or the disinfectant that they use. I give her calamine lotion and she dabs it across the welts before going to bed.

Her blood sugar at midnight is 103. A good number. I test again at three in the morning and it is 174. I blink at the number on the glowing green screen. Ashley is asleep immediately although she never fully awoke. I am seeing double with exhaustion. In a fog of awareness, I decide I've done something wrong and go back to bed without checking her again.

In the morning the meter reads 260.

"But I didn't eat anything bad, " she protests, scratching the palms of her hands something fierce.

I grab them and see they are covered in a rash.

"When did this happen?"

"I don't know. Since last night. This morning I guess."

"Do I call the pediatrician, the allergist or the endocrinologist?" I ask Travis, who is in the garage looking for a new package of drill bits for his toolbox.

"Dr. Benton."

It's my thought too, not because I think it's got to do with diabetes—who's heard of a rash with diabetes?—but because I like Dr. Benton best.

"What do you think it means?"

"I don't know, Babs, but you have to take care of this. I can't take any more time away from work. Just call and make an appointment this morning. I'm sure it's nothing."

I know it's not nothing because by the time we arrive at Dr. Benton's office the hives are on her arms and neck.

We've never been to Dr. Benton's office, and it's much smaller than the pediatrician's. There's less than half a dozen chairs, and the only people in the waiting room are two old people. The receptionist takes one look at Ashley and tells us to come on back.

The room is small, two chairs and one of those examination tables crammed together, and the walls are white and the window has white aluminum blinds that are open to the oak tree behind the building.

It takes only a minute or two before Dr. Benton comes in. He shakes our hands and makes small talk before asking Ashley to get up on the table. He looks at her neck and arms first, then her hands and stomach, which by now are raw and scabbed.

"When did this start?"

"Right before we left the hospital."

"Can you remember the day?"

Ashley thinks before answering. "Maybe the night before we left, but maybe even the day before that. I don't remember exactly." I want to ask her why she never told me.

"That's okay. Do you remember if it was before or after you started taking the shots?"

"After. I'm pretty sure."

He sits and looks at a folder, which I am guessing is her file from the hospital. "Where on your body did they start?"

"My stomach." He nods as if this means something.

"And then where?"

"Then my hands, then my arms, then my neck. But those all just started today."

"We didn't know what doctor to call," I add. "She's had hives before, but since her blood sugar was so high, we figured you would be our first stop." This is not entirely true, but true enough.

He looked up with his eyebrows arched high. "What's going on with the blood sugar?"

"It's high," I repeat, not knowing what else I should say.

"But I didn't eat anything," Ashley adds. "It just went up. I took my shots and everything."

"Do you have the records of your food, insulin amounts, and meter readings?"

I have forgotten to bring anything, and I'm about to apologize for this when Ashley pulls it out of her purse, the pocketsize book she got at the hospital to record everything she eats and how it affects her. Dr. Benton looks through it, eyebrows scrunching at the last page.

"Is it an allergy?"

"Maybe." He stands and pats Ashley on the knee. "I'm going to copy this off and then you can have it back. I'm going to send you to the hospital for a few tests."

"Children's Hospital?"

"No, just the one here. I want to run a few allergy tests. I'll be right back."

He disappears and I watch Ashley fidget with her purse. "I'm sure it's nothing," I say to calm her, even though I'm lying as I say it. That feeling I had in Austin last week—the feeling that things were going to get worse before getting better—is getting stronger.

Dr. Benton returns with the logbook and a dose of Benadryl. "Take this and see if it helps the itching some. I called the hospital and they're expecting you. They're just going to take some blood and run a few tests on it for me to rule out some things."

"What do you think it is?"

"We won't know until the tests come back." I can tell he's hedging, and this is very unlike the doctor who was so straight forward with us last week. He holds Ashley's hands as she hops down from the table. "It's probably something simple, like a reaction to the insulin we put you on. We may just have to switch brands, and that's no big deal. You won't even notice a difference. Except the new one won't make you look like you've got the pox." He smiles and punches Ash lightly on the arm as he leads us out and tells us he'll call us with the results as soon as he gets them.

* * * *

"Four hours," I say, yanking open the drawer with the pots and pans, and then slamming it again. "They shot her up with a bunch of stuff, and then we have to sit around and wait to see if she goes into ana ... ana-something."

"Anaphylactic shock," Logan says, not looking up from his homework. I'm starting to regret telling him he has to do schoolwork in the kitchen instead of locked away in his room with his music blaring.

"What's that?" Travis asks.

"It's when she has an allergic reaction that kills her," I open the refrigerator, then switch to the freezer, which I also slam. "Can you believe that? We can replace someone's heart with someone else's but the best way we can tell if someone has an allergy is to inject them with it and see what happens. Is there nothing in this house we can eat but chicken? If I have to eat one more broiled chicken, I might choke to death."

"What about spaghetti," Travis suggests.

"You trying to kill her?" I pull out the box from the pantry and slide it roughly across the counter at him. "Look at the carbs in that."

"So did they find anything?" He slides the spaghetti back to me.

"No. Now we have to wait two days and see what happens. Meanwhile she's scratching herself raw. I guess we'll have chicken."

"We can't eat broiled chicken every night, Babs."

"What about tacos?" Logan unfolds his lanky body from the stool and goes to the pantry, pulling out the box of shells and handing it to me without looking at it. "21 carbs for three shells. Minimum for the meat and cheese, maybe four for tomatoes."

"What about the beans?" I'm not trying to be troublesome, but I'm pretty sure beans are out.

Logan shrugs and takes his place behind his books again. "Make a salad."

I look at Travis who also shrugs. "Anything but chicken sounds good to me."

"I'm done." Logan shuts his textbook and notebook and shoves them in his backpack. "I'm going to Jim's to practice. His band has a gig Saturday, and they asked me to stand in."

I open my mouth to say no way. I don't like the band. I don't like his drumming. It's a school night. But I think of the tacos, and the cake, and the monopoly game, and I just nod.

"Back by six-thirty," I say.

"No prob," he says, and he's gone.

"Is this serious?" Travis asks when we're alone.

"I don't think so." I take a seat at the high stool next to Travis. "Dr. Benton seems to think if it's an allergy to the insulin, we just switch. In fact, he already gave us a vial of a different brand."

"The long acting one or the meal one?"

"The meal one."

Laying the paperwork from the hospital on the counter, I go through the tests with Travis. I don't know how to pronounce most of the words, and even though the allergist explained what tests he was going to run, I couldn't remember well enough to explain them.

"What's a serological test?" Travis asks.

"I think it just means blood test. They did a scratch test, where they kinda pricked the skin on her back with different things that might cause allergies, and then they took blood to test, too. I think."

"This says they are testing for carrier proteins and additives. I thought they were testing for insulin. Could it be something else?"

"The allergist said there are things in the insulin, you know, additives and stuff, and that maybe she's allergic to that and not to the insulin itself."

"Can you take that stuff out?"

"I think so. He said something about trying purified insulin."

"What do they do, run the stuff through a Brita filter?"

I can't tell if that's a joke or he's serious. Actually, I'm not sure that's not how you get purified insulin. I gather the papers and put them in the file of Ashley's medical history that is growing. "So we just have to switch insulin?" he asks.

"He said that may be all it takes." I go back to cooking so he can't see my eyes. After twenty years together, he'd see that I don't believe this. And if he asks enough, he'd find out Dr. Benton didn't seem to believe it either.

The light in the kitchen is fading as the sun moves to the other side of the house. We don't talk, but I know he's thinking the same thing I am, that two weeks ago we were chowing down on enchiladas and jalapeno cornbread without the slightest idea what insulin was, or that there were different kinds, or that one small, common virus could change our lives so drastically.

* * * *

I forget about the baseball paper until after Ashley is in bed and Travis is dozing in front of ESPN. I go out to the garage where Logan is banging away at the drums and lay the paper in front of him. He stops banging and looks at it, and then at me.

"It's no big deal. I don't even like baseball that much anymore."

"It *is* a big deal, Logan. What in the Sam Hill are you fighting about?"

"Nothing. It wasn't even a real fight." He moves the paper and starts to pound again, but I grab the sticks.

"Stop it."

He stops, but he won't look me in the eye. I don't remember Lo ever not looking me in the eye, even if it is some *I dare you* kinda look.

"You're not the fighting kind. What happened?"

"Troy said something, and I shut him up. That's all."

"You shut him up?"

"Yeah. Or shoved him up, more like it. Up against the lockers. But it shut him up, too."

I try to visualize my skinny beanpole boy shoving anyone against a locker, but I don't see it. I find a five-gallon paint can and pull it up to sit on. "Why?"

He sighs, like he knows he ain't getting out of this one. "He said some things. They weren't right, so I had to straighten him out."

"Straighten him out?"

"It's really annoying how you repeat everything I say when you're mad."

"I'd say I'm allowed to be a little upset that my son got in a fight, got kicked off the sports team we was relying on for college scholarships, and then conveniently forgot to tell us."

"You know, Mom, you'd like everything to be my fault, wouldn't you? Did it ever occur to you that maybe I'm not as bad as you and everyone else would like to think?"

I look at his spiked hair and ripped t-shirt, and I can't see the good kid under there at all, but I know he's there. "I don't think you're bad," I say, getting off my makeshift chair. "I think you work really hard trying to make people see you that way, and for the life of me I can't figure out why."

I start to go but Logan fires back. "Well I guess that apple doesn't fall too far from the tree, does it?"

I turn slowly. "What do you mean?"

"I mean, you do a lot of trying to make people believe something about you that isn't true, too."

Red creeps up my neck, hot as a branding iron. "You watch your mouth, Logan T. Babcock. You may be taller than me, but I'm still your Mama."

"What're you gonna do, punish me? I'm already off the team. What more do you want?"

"I want you to stop embarrassing this family by acting like some kinda rebel and start taking some grown-up responsibilities around here. You can start by putting up that drum set and taking out the trash before bed."

I'm almost in the house when he says back, real quiet, "Don't you want to know what the fight was about?"

"It don't matter," I say, not turning back to him. "Fighting's fighting, and it's wrong."

Even through the shut door I can hear him banging even harder on those stupid drums, and I wonder where I went so wrong with him.

* * * *

We don't have to wait two days to find out the results of the allergy tests because by morning Ashley's shoulder where they tested her is beyond swollen, the hives on her arm and neck hidden under the puffy redness that's overtaken the right side of her.

On the way to the hospital I call Travis, who was gone when we woke, but I only get his voicemail. I call Dr. Benton's office, which isn't open yet, and get an operator who promises to get him the message. I don't call the school. I don't know if they think the expulsion is proceeding, but I got other bullhorns in the rodeo right now.

I'm no stranger to the hospital anymore, and I greet the receptionist with a howdy as I pull down the shoulder of Ashley's shirt. She immediately shows us to a curtained room and tells us she'll get the doctor right away.

Ashley's been quiet all morning. Quiet, in fact, since we got home from the hospital last night.

"You okay, Babe?"

"Yeah, I'm fine."

A nurse I've never seen comes in with a clipboard. She barely looks at us. "The doctor will be here in a minute. I need to get your information. Which one of you is the patient?"

"The one who looks like her arm is a helium balloon," I say. I get a look for that. "Ashley Babcock." I think of Logan's SAT list week 5: acquiesce. I don't know how to pronounce it, but I know it means what

I have to do to get Ashley help.

"Age?"

"Twelve."

"And what is she here for?"

I point to her bloated arm and neck. "I'm afraid she got in Willy Wonka's secret stash of gum last night and things went terribly wrong when it came to the cherry pie part." Ashley giggles, but the nurse gives me a look to kill. Clearly there's no sense of humor in the ER. "She had allergy tests yesterday, and this is what happened."

"Is she taking any medications presently?"

"No."

"Benadryl," Ashley reminds me. "I'm also taking insulin: aspart and Lantus."

"Except for dinner last night you took the lispro instead of the aspart," I remind her. I look at the nurse, whose pen is hovering over the page waiting for us to decide. We're the medical equivalent of Laurel and Hardy. "She's taking aspart, lispro and Lantus."

"Are those insulins?" She doesn't think we're funny. I don't think it's particularly funny that she don't know what aspart, lantus and lispro are.

"Yes." She writes that down. Just "insulin."

"Anything else?"

I look at Ashley and she shakes her head. "No."

"Any allergies?"

I think she must be joking, but there's no humor here, so I point again to Ashley's arm. "Clearly she's allergic to something."

"And do you know what that is so I can write it on the chart?"

"If I knew that I wouldn't be here, would I?"

"Ma'am, I'm just trying to do my job. There's no use being snippy with me."

"I was thinking the exact thing." We stare like two dogs in a fight before she looks back at her paper.

"So no known allergies?"

"No." I sigh.

"And are you the parent or guardian?"

"I'm the parent."

"And your name?"

"Babs Babcock."

"I need your official name, please."

"That is my official name."

"I mean, your given name, not a nickname."

"That is my given name."

"Babs Babcock?"

I can feel myself getting hot under my collar. Ashley still has the giggles. "Yes. That is my given name. Actually my given name was Babs Deanne Walker, but then I got married and my name officially became Babs Walker Babcock."

"Your parents named you Babs?"

"Short for Barbara, except my mother was Barbara and they didn't want people confusing us. Is this important to my daughter's condition?"

"And you just happened to marry someone named Babcock?" She has stopped writing now and her eyebrows are so puckered they almost touch.

"Is a doctor coming soon? I'd like someone to see my daughter before her arm blows up. Is that possible?"

She seems not at all pleased with me and scoots out her chair with a loud fingernail-across-the-blackboard scraping and holds out her hand. "I need your insurance card, please."

"Of course." At last something that's relevant. "We wouldn't want to leave without making sure you know where the money's coming from, would we?" I hand it to her, and she snatches it from me and leaves.

Ashley bursts out laughing. "Willy Wonka? Do I look that bad?"

"Well, you ain't pretty," I say, trying to smile. But as I look at her wiping happy tears off her cheeks, I think just the opposite.

Chapter Thirteen

Dr. Benton shows up a few minutes later, his hair still wet, wearing running pants and a black t-shirt. He could be some model in a Calvin Klein ad.

"Sorry it took a while to get here. You caught me at the gym. So you gave Nellie a hard time?" The twinkle in his eyes told me I wasn't the first to get her goat. "What have your blood sugars been the last 24 hours?"

I hand him the logbook where Ashley's writing down everything she eats and the time and amounts of her shots. He glances through it. "Is there any reason you know why your readings have gone up in the past day? Anything you ate that is hard to calculate? Any snacks you didn't write down?"

Ashley shakes her head.

"I know your mom is here, but you need to tell me the truth. It's really important. We need to find why your blood sugar has gone up 250 points when you haven't eaten anything. Did you miss a shot?"

I think Ashley's going to cry when she shakes her head. "Honest. I didn't eat anything."

He looks at me and I nod.

"Okay, then, I'm going to look at where the allergist gave you the shots. It won't hurt. I just want to see which ones gave you the most trouble back here."

He examines her without any other words. When he finishes, he just says, "I'm going to find the allergist who did the shots. Can you wait a few more minutes?"

He don't wait for an answer because we aren't going anywhere.

"I don't think he liked what he saw," Ashley says.

"Nonsense. He sees stuff like this all the time. It's just an allergy. We'll find out what it is that you're allergic to, and then we stop using it."

It takes a long time before he comes back, the doctor from yesterday in tow. They both look again, without talking, and they leave again.

"Something's wrong," Ashley says. "He's always really nice. He always jokes with me. What do you think is wrong?"

"Nothing's wrong," I say, but I don't believe it. I see the same thing Ashley does, and it ain't good.

When he comes back, he's alone. He pulls up a swively chair, and the twinkle is completely gone.

"What is it?"

"Well, it looks like I was right. Ashley has an allergy to insulin."

"So we just switch, right? That's not too bad, right?"

"It's not that easy. She doesn't have an allergy to just aspart or lantus or any of the others. She has a systemic allergy to all of them."

I search his face for some sign that he's kidding us, but there's nothing. I feel Ashley stiffen beside me. "But I need insulin. Don't I? Don't I need it to stay alive?"

"Yes."

"But I'm allergic to it?"

"Yes."

"Then there's something else, right? Something else I can take?"

"No. There's nothing else."

Ashley looks at me wide-eyed and scared. I'm out of my body, watching this like a scene out of a movie, because this cannot be happening. People who need to take insulin to stay alive don't become allergic to it. God wouldn't do that to people. God wouldn't do that to Ashley.

"This happens. It's really rare, but it happens. You have a systemic allergy. That means it's not just one part of your body, like the place where you give yourself a shot, which reacts. Your whole body is reacting to the insulin."

"Does she have to take medicine on top of the insulin then? Something that keeps her from rejecting it?"

"That's a start, but it isn't that simple. If we keep giving her this amount of insulin, her body is going to continue to reject it, and more forcefully. Already, in just a small timeframe, she has hives all over, and the insulin itself isn't even working. That's why her blood sugar is so high."

"Am I going to die?" Ashley's voice is freakishly high.

"Of course not," I say. Dr. Benton doesn't say this. What he does say are the words I don't want to hear.

"We need to admit her into Children's Hospital again." He stands and lays his hand on Ashley's good shoulder. "We need to get on top of this quickly. There are a couple avenues we can take. The first is to get you on some stronger antihistamines, to see if we can't get your reactions under control. Also, we're going to take you off the shots and put you on a subcutaneous insulin pump."

"A what?"

"An insulin pump. It's a little machine the size of a cell phone that will deliver insulin through a tube directly into her abdomen."

"I'm going to have to be hooked up to a machine?"

"A very little machine."

"For how long?"

"If it works, forever. The good news is you'll be done with shots. The pump will act in place of the shots, kind of like your own pancreas. It will give you a lot more freedom eventually to live a more normal life, too."

"How can it be normal if I'm hooked up to a machine all the time."

"A very small machine. I guarantee almost no one will even notice." When Ashley raises her eyebrows at him, he lifts his shirt and pulls a black gadget off his belt clip and holds it out to her. A tiny tube runs from the bottom of the pump and disappears into his sweats.

She holds the pump, small enough to clamp in her fist, and stares at Dr. Benton. "You have diabetes?"

He nods and takes the pump back. "Since I was three."

"Why didn't you tell us?" I ask.

"Is that the first thing you want people to know about you?" A look of understanding passes between them "I need to shuffle my appointments around today and take care of a few things at the office before I get to Children's Hospital. I'll phone them and let them know you're coming and have them get a room ready. You need to prepare for at least a few days. Can you do that?" I nod. "Okay, then. Have you eaten this morning?"

"No," Ashley answers.

"Don't eat. Can you do that?"

"Yes. I'm not really hungry anyway."

"The high blood sugar will do that to you. You do need to drink as much water as possible, though. And throw out your aspart, but keep the lispro, okay? Lispro is less likely to cause allergic reactions, so that's the one we'll try in the pump."

"What about the Lantus?"

"Throw it out too. The pump uses only one kind of insulin. That will help, too, with the possible allergic reactions. Any other questions before you leave for the hospital?"

"Will this work?" This is me asking, but I see the question in Ashley's eyes, too.

"Maybe." Dr. Benton sits down again. "It might work, but it might not. I told you this is pretty rare. The combination of antihistamines, some good immunosuppressants, and the pump take care of the problem in about half the cases."

"Half? What about the other half?"

"Then we move on to something else."

"What else is there?"

"Maybe we should take it one step at a time. Let's see if this works. If it does, there's no need to worry about what else."

"I want to know," Ashley whispers. "What are the other options?"

He seems to study us before answering, as if he is trying to see if we can take the news. "If it doesn't work, we'll try something called desensitization. It's the same kind of thing we do with people with hay fever and grass allergies. We give shots a little at a time of the substance, increasing the amount until you build a tolerance to it."

"You're going to keep giving her the stuff that's making her look like this?"

"Yes. But not in these quantities. In much smaller quantities, so she doesn't have quite the reactions."

"But won't her blood sugar be really high if she's not getting enough to begin with?"

"Yes. Which is why we'll need to keep her in the hospital. We'll have her on a special diet, probably mostly through an IV, and watch her very carefully."

"Does that usually work?" It seems to me if that would take care of the problem we should start there.

"Sometimes. Sometimes not. I'm not trying to be a wet blanket here. I just want to be honest."

"Has anyone ever died because nothing worked?" This is Ashley again, and I'm surprised she can ask the hard questions I can't make myself ask.

Dr. Benton doesn't answer for a minute. He looks like this is as hard for him to answer as it is for her to ask, and I know before he opens his mouth what the answer is going to be.

"Yes." He takes a deep breath. "But very few. Rarely. Very rarely. And I'm not going to let that happen to you, okay?"

I know he can't promise this, but Ashley has complete trust in him, and I let the sentence rest in air.

"Go pack your things. I'll see you this afternoon in Austin. We're going to get you better, okay? This is just a blip on the radar screen. Next year you'll look back on this as just another page in your diary. Or in your scrapbook. Or wherever you ladies keep that information these days."

When he leaves, I expect Ashley to cry, but she don't. She's quiet until we get to the car, when she suddenly blurts out, "The youth group is having a movie night on Saturday. Do you think I'll be back in time to go?"

This is twelve. I know, because I remember it, and it's so normal it makes me laugh out loud. Ashley frowns at me like I'm making fun of her, but I'm mostly just amused at the equal level of importance she gives her health and a social gathering.

"Well?"

"Probably not, sweetie. But there will be others."

She pouts a bit on the way, and for the first time since puberty struck, I'm enjoying it.

Chapter Fourteen

After a few days it becomes clear the first course of treatment ain't working. Ashley's reactions worsen, and she starts the funny breathing thing she did before she was diagnosed. She gets a little to eat—chicken and broth and sugar-free jello; even fruits and vegetables have too many carbs. She's hooked up to an IV too, for extra fluids and vitamins, but she whittles down to nothing but bones under skin stretched thin. The hives break out in other places than her arms and belly, and none of the medicine they give seems to help her itching. For the first day or two she's restless at the hospital. She reads a bit, and uses my phone to text her friends, and discovers the addictiveness of daytime soaps. She wanders down to the arcade, but most of the kids there are siblings of sick kids, and she feels self-conscious about her looks, so she ends up in her room most of the time.

By the third day she's sleeping a lot. I don't know if it's boredom or the blood sugars they just can't seem to get down. She's running in the three hundreds regularly now, and hospital workers stop acting like this is common.

Travis can't get off work much anymore. His boss let go all the other workers because business is so bad and needs Travis there every day. We're thankful he's keeping Travis on, for the money of course, but mostly for the insurance. He drives in at night for a few hours every day and then drives back home. Logan stays at home during the week since it's so close to the end of school. He's got finals coming up. His visits, when he comes, are the only thing Ashley don't sleep through. They sit together and play games and talk while Travis and me get something to eat in the cafeteria.

I call Pastor Joel and tell him to tell the women at the church not to come by. It's not that I don't appreciate their efforts and all, but it's more work to have them here. And I don't want to plan any more functions.

Travis tells me Brenda organized a committee of women to bring breakfasts and sack lunches every morning to him and Logan. She connived a few teens to mow and water the lawn and weed the garden.

Ashley perked up a bit when she heard Brian Lee was the first to volunteer. Janise began a magazine drive to gather "fun and useless" magazines to send with Travis for Ashley and me, and Donna Jean has taken over the job of dealing with our insurance company, which has turned into a full time job in itself. "You have enough to deal with without worrying about where the money is coming from," she told us.

Saturday morning, she calls and asks if the youth group can meet at the hospital for the movie night. "They want to do this. They are so worried for Ashley. And my guess is it might be good for Ashley to have some friends around. If she's feeling up for it."

"I don't know." I take stock of the tiny room. "We might fit about seven kids in here, maybe one or two more, but not the entire group. And we don't have a DVD player in the room."

"I already called the hospital," she says, not a whit of apology in her voice. "They said we could use their recreation room, and there's a DVD player in there along with plenty of couches and floor space for the entire group." She pauses, and then adds, "And they said it should be fine for Ashley to go."

I'm dumbfounded silent by this.

"Please let us do this. Pastor Joel says we can bring the church bus, and all the kids are already counting on it."

"I don't know if Ashley'll want to see 'em. She's so embarrassed about her looks right now."

"I bought her a new outfit. A shirt, really lightweight, but long sleeves, to cover the swelling. And some Capri's. Very trendy. And I'll bring some make-up and do her hair before anyone gets there. She'll feel like a princess."

I have run out of excuses. "Okay."

"Okay?"

"Yeah."

"I'll see you in a couple hours then. The kids are planning to get there about seven. Maybe Ashley can invite some of the other kids from the hospital to join us."

"Sure," I say. "Donna Jean?"

"Yes?"

I want to tell her how much this means to us. How much it'll mean to Ashley. How I don't know how we would've made it through this week without her. But I can't find words that do it justice.

"Thanks."

"You're welcome, Babs." There is a second silence before she hangs up the phone. I think of the bracelet Ashley wore last year, the leather strap with the letters WWJD engraved into them. What Would Jesus Do?

He would do this, I think.

* * * *

While the kids gather for movie night, Travis and I decide to go somewhere for dinner where we aren't eating off plastic trays. Even though Travis done plenty of back and forth, I've barely left the hospital since we got here, and I'm feeling like a caged cat.

Dr. Benton gives us the name of a restaurant, and we drive down towards the river, across the bridge, and down a winding road until I make Travis pull over so I can check the directions again. By the time he finds a place to pull off, we're in a lot packed with cars thick as flies under a neon light that says "Chuy's."

"We're here," he says.

The place is crowded and noisy, so loud we have to scream to the hostess who takes our names and asks us if we want to sit inside or out and tells us we're welcome to wait at the bar. I blush to think what Pastor Joel and the ladies of First Baptist would say if they saw us here. In the bar area there are a bunch of kids playing pool under pink and blue lights, and the Pepto Bismal pink walls and ceilings are lined with velvet Elvis paintings and hubcaps. I'm starting to reevaluate my opinion of Dr. Benton.

For forty minutes we wait while young college kids swirl around us. We don't talk much, 'cause we can't hear each other anyways, and we sip at our sweet tea, lost in our own thoughts. When the hostess takes us to a table outside, my ears are ringing and my stomach growling.

Normally, a deck in Texas summer is not the place to eat, but tonight the stars are out and the breeze is blowing enough to keep us cool. I'm glad not to be inside where everyone's happy and drinking and being normal when our lives are turned upside down. A perky waitress brings us chips and salsa and flashes her outlandishly white teeth at us and takes our orders. I watch trucks come and go from the parking lot and nibble on the chips until I finally blurt out what both of us is thinking.

"Ashley'd sure love this place."

"We'll bring her here when she gets out. Like a celebration." He uses his napkin to wipe up the salsa he's dripped all over the table. "She's gonna be fine. You know that." It's a statement. Which don't make no sense to me, because I know no such thing.

"Sure." I shrug and look down at my hands, and I break the chip into tiny pieces.

"Babs?"

"What do you want me to say, Travis? You want to hear I don't know that she's gonna be fine? That I sit in her room all day watching her waste away planning what songs she'd want at her funeral while you and Logan are going 'bout your normal lives back home?" It's unfair. As soon as it's out I know it's unfair to say that.

I see him lean back in his chair and look up at the string of colorful lights above us, hurt in his eyes. "I'm sorry."

He don't look at me, so I add, "I know you'd be there if you could. I'm not angry at you. I'm angry at this whole thing. I feel like I'm all alone in this."

He still don't answer me, like he crawled into himself again and shut me out. I'm so tired of this by now. I don't know when it happened, this quiet between us. Sometime when the kids were small and loud and demanding attention, and I didn't notice that we stopped talking. Or rather, that he stopped talking back. And by the time I noticed, he'd buried himself in work and that dang chair and ESPN.

I'd thought for awhile, right after Ashley came home from the hospital the first time, we were doing better. We were talking more. He kissed me more. I'd almost forgotten how much I'd missed that. I thought maybe there really was a silver lining from all this. But now we hardly see each other again, and it's all changed. Or it hasn't.

"How's Logan's finals going?" I change topics.

"Okay. He don't talk about them much. But he studies a lot, so I think he's doing all right. He told me about the baseball team."

"Oh?" I try to be nonchalant. That means casual, which is hard to do when you feel guilty for keeping a secret.

"He said you gave him a tongue-lashing for it."

"Yeah. He's lucky I didn't ground him for a month of Sundays. A fight's a fight, whether there's fists involved or not."

"Do you even know who it was with?"

"Does it matter?" I ask, laying out the pieces of the chip on my napkin and putting the small bites into my mouth one by one so it takes forever to eat it all.

"It was Troy Donegan."

I suddenly know why Logan got in a fight. Troy is this small, bony boy with a chip on his privileged little shoulder.

"What was it about?" I finally ask, chewing very slowly.

"He was talking trash."

"About Logan?" It's not hard to imagine someone talking trash about Logan. He draws it on himself.

"About Ash." I stop chewing, a stabbing pain in my heart replacing the hardness. "You and Logan are so alike you can't even see straight," he adds.

"We are not," I protest, and then immediately wonder why I'm protesting being like my own son. I think of Logan telling me the apple don't fall far from the tree.

"Give the kid a little slack now and then." He signals the waitress for another drink. "What I don't get," he says, "is why you didn't tell me about it in the first place."

I shrug and hunt out a blue tortilla chip from the basket. "Why didn't you tell me Bob's company is going under?" Bob is his boss—that company is our lifeline. I've had this information for awhile now but haven't said a word about it until now. Like by saying it out loud our lives might come crashing down. It's not that I'm angry so much as really worried.

He stares at me, not blinking. "How did you know?"

I shrug again. "People in the church talk. A lot."

"I was gonna tell you. When Ashley was better." He puts down the chip that's halfway to his mouth, and looks down. I can tell he's embarrassed. Or ashamed. "We still got the insurance. For now. And he's trying to find me work with other contractors. The housing market ain't what it use to be, Babs. He just don't have work for me, but I'm getting other stuff."

"We got no security, Travis." My voice comes out high and tight, more mad than what I feel. "What happens when he can't pay his bills, and we got no insurance? It's probably costing us a thousand dollars a day to keep Ashley in this fancy hospital, for who knows how long." I'm scared. I want to roll back time a week to when Travis might have reached out to take my hand, to squeeze it and tell me everything will be all right. I'd even take having him tell me to trust God. I need him to tell me God will provide, even if I don't agree. I need to hear that.

But Travis slams his hand on the table instead. "I'm looking, Babs. What do you want me to do? I can't make people buy houses they can't afford just so I can build them."

We sit for a few minutes not talking, listening to the music blaring through the doorway and watching the young kids without a care in the world drinking and flirting and playing pool.

I push the salsa and chips aside. "Are we going to be all right, Travis?"

"Of course. We got some money tucked away. And we can sell some stuff if we need to." The food comes, and I wait until the server is gone to talk again.

"I'm not talking about money. I'm talking about us. What happens if Ashley don't make it?"

He uses his knife to make a barrier between the rice and the beans so they don't touch: a habit that drives me nuts. "We've got to trust God will heal Ashley."

It's what I wanted to hear, but now that it's out there, I can't help but answer, "And if he don't?"

He freezes for a second, then takes a breath. "And if he don't, we've got to trust that it's his will, and he'll give us strength."

I don't like that answer. I don't know what I wanted him to say, but this isn't it. I'd be mad at him except he's got that pinched look on his face, and he won't look at me, and I know, even though a place in him believes it, it hurts to say it.

"How could Ashley dying be his will? It just don't make any sense to me that he'd do that to a little girl."

"He's not doing it to her, Babs. It's not like he's sitting up there on his throne and says, hey, lets kill off one of my kids."

I flinch. "Whether he's doing it or not, he could stop it. Why won't he?"

He pushes his food around more, not eating. "I don't know, Babs. Pastor Joel says sometimes God makes great things come out of tragedies. Greater things than could come without them."

I stare at him hard. "I don't want great things. I want Ashley."

"Me too, Babs." He sighs and looks at me, finally. "I'm not against you. I just don't know. I just know we have to trust that God is in control, and whatever happens he'll work out for the best."

"I don't want to trust God." There. I said it. I expect Travis to react, but he don't. He just lays his fork down and then looks up at me. His eyes mirror the Christmas lights above us.

"What do you want to trust in, Babs?"

"Us," I say. "You, and me, and Logan, and Ashley. And Dr. Benton. And science. I want to believe in things I can see and feel and know work."

"Just because you can't see God don't mean he's not real."

"I know that," I say exasperatedly. "But God... I can't depend on God. Sometimes when you pray, he answers, and sometimes he don't." I have a vision of my own dad suddenly in front of me. Not the dad I knew and loved. The dad all wasted away with cancer, breathing through an oxygen mask, eyes empty. Travis and I sat by his bed day and night that last month, pouring out prayers that if he had to die, he'd do it quickly and painlessly. It was anything but quick and painless.

I shake the vision off. "Sometimes he makes sick people better, and sometimes he don't. Sometimes babies that should live, die, and old people that should die, live. You can lay it all in God's hands, but it don't mean it will work out. Medicine works. You have a headache, you take a pill and it takes the headache away. It don't care whether or not you believe in it. It don't care if it will make you stronger if you have to brave through the headache. It don't care if you been a good person or a bad person. It just works. You can't trust God to work."

He thinks about this as he takes a stab of enchilada and chews it. "You think you're the only one who thinks about this stuff, Babs? You think I haven't asked myself those questions too?"

I actually didn't. His faith seems so sure of itself. Then I think of him in the hospital yelling at Pastor Joel. "How do you do it, then? How do you keep believing?"

"I don't know. Maybe because it's easier than not believing."

"So it's like a crutch?" I try not to be bitter when I say this, but his answer is the most useless answer ever.

"No. It's not that." He's frustrated, I can tell. I've asked him to explain something personal. He don't do well with explaining or personal, but I need to know. I need to know how he can not be angry that Ashley is so sick.

"You know what Pastor Joel told me the other day?" he says.

"What?"

"He told me you can't always know what God is going to do or why, but you can always trust that it's the best thing."

I put down my fork, not that I'm eating anyway. "You telling me it's best for Ashley to die?"

"No!"

"Then what does that mean?"

"I don't know, okay? Maybe it means we see just the little picture. Today and tomorrow and maybe a few days down the road. But God knows it all. He sees the future all the way through the end."

"And the future is better without Ashley?"

"No, Babs. You're twisting my words." He puts his fork down and pushes his plate away. "I don't know all the answers. It just seems like trusting God is more a sure thing than trusting science. I don't know how you can trust pills more than God. Especially after medicine isn't exactly working for us right now. I gotta go to the bathroom." He stands suddenly, pushing his chair so fast it starts to fall over and walks into the restaurant.

I'm alone again. In the middle of a crowd. I push the food around on my plate, but I can't bring myself to eat it. All I can think is how many carbs there must be with all the rice and beans and tortillas and how if I can't trust God or science, who can I trust?

Chapter Fifteen

"Enough is enough," Dr. Benton says on the fifth day of our second settling in at Children's. "It's time to move to plan B."

"The desensing thing?"

"Desensitization. Yes." He lays a graph across Ashley's lap. "This is a day-by-day guide to what's going to happen over the next few weeks. We're going to keep you on the pump, and the lispro insulin, but we'll back way off your dosage. You'll start with a miniscule amount. Not enough to do anything to your blood sugars—not enough to do anything to cause your immune system to react, but hopefully enough that your body will accept it. Once it does, we'll up the dosage. A little every couple hours."

"How long until I'm able to eat again, and take regular amounts?" Ashley is tired of the intravenous "food" and is asking for something substantial. She's lost so much weight I can pick her up, which I've had to do twice when she couldn't walk to the bathroom by herself 'cause she was so weak.

"Six months, if things go well."

"Six months?"

"If it goes well."

"And what if it doesn't go well?"

"Then we move on to plan C."

"I thought there wasn't a plan C."

Dr. Benton takes the graphs from Ashley's lap and puts them back in his folder. "There is always a plan C. We don't give up until we've won."

For the first time he sounds tired and not at all sure. I follow him into the hall, out of earshot of Ashley and ask, "Do you know what plan C is?"

"I'm working on it."

"Do you think the desensi-thing —"

"Desensitization."

"That. You don't think it will work?"

"There's no way to know, Mrs. Babcock."

"Are there odds?"

"There are always odds. But those odds don't count much to the one who falls outside of them."

"So it's bad, then?"

He runs his fingers through his hair. I can tell he's frustrated with me, but I can't let up. I'm like some pit bull that's got her jaws around a neck and I can't let go.

"It's bad if it doesn't work. It's good if it does. That's as certain as I am. This works, Mrs. Babcock. It works most of the time. More often than not."

"But?" There isn't certainty in his voice. He isn't talking like a doctor talks who has a better than odds-on chance.

"I just like to have a back-up."

"And we don't?"

"I'm working on it."

I let him go. He walks down the hall and disappears around a corner. I watch way past when I can't see him. I stand in the hall while nurses walk around me, and parents move in and out of rooms, and dinner trays are collected. I think how tired I am, and I think how Dr. Benton must feel responsible for keeping Ashley alive, like I do. For the first time, I wonder if he has a wife and kids at home. How can he run his office when he's down here in Austin 7 days a week? I realize it's Sunday and he's here, even though it must be his day off.

When I go back in the room, Ashley is asleep, her breathing like loud, punctuating sighs. Travis was called as a fill-in on a remodeling job today, and Logan is practicing for a gig with the band next weekend, and I'm alone.

I try to read, but I can't concentrate. I don't want to turn on the TV and wake Ashley. I think about going to the cafeteria, but the thought of food makes me nauseous. I finally decide it's as good a time as any to pray, so I close my eyes and wait for the words to come. But I don't know what to say. "Help us," is the best I can do. I wait for God to speak to me. But he don't.

And then Donna Jean walks in.

"Am I interrupting," she whispers.

I'm so glad to see her—anyone—that I want to throw my arms around her. I take her down to the family resource center, which is empty tonight, and pour us both a cup of coffee. We sit on the couch.

Immediately, she opens a black bag she is carrying and pulls out a laptop. "I convinced my company to donate this to you. It's old," she says, shrugging off my protests. "It was just gathering dust in a supply closet, and it seemed like something you might be able to use to help you. Or at least maybe occupy some of your time."

She opened the laptop and turned it on. "I thought you might want to research other options. You know—if the desensitization doesn't work."

I feel such a rush of gratitude that I don't even hate her for knowing the word.

"I took off all the work programs, but there's still word processing and Internet. Also, I put on some games. And it has a DVD player, if Ashley wants to watch something in the room." She opens up the Internet. "Do you have an email account?"

"Travis has one. And the kids. I don't. I just never had time." What am I? An 80-year-old codger? What forty year-old don't have an email?

"We can set one up for you if you want."

With a few clicks she signs me up, then hands me the laptop and a notebook. "Here are a few sites I thought might be interesting. And a few keywords to Google. Let me know if there's anything else you need."

"Are you leaving already?"

"Bible study starts in an hour and a half. I'm leading the ladies group."

I don't know if I should hug her or something. She stands, ready to go. With the laptop on my knees, I try to stand but it nearly slides off. I barely catch it before realizing my feet are caught in the cord. I clumsily fall back onto the chair.

"It's okay." She laughs, handing me the pen that rolled off the couch. "I can see myself out. Call later, if you want. Let me know how it's going."

I watch her leave out the glass doors and disappear down the hall before turning back to the computer.

I start with the websites she's written for me. One is a message board for parents with diabetic children. I don't know where to start so I click on the first post: "Anyone heard of Apidra?" There are ten responses to "kaylasmommy," and I learn that Apidra is one of the newer insulins on the market. I write the question in the notebook: "Have we tried Apidra?"

The second post is from "findthecure" and is titled "Nailing the 504 to the school room door." There are 123 responses. Seems like I'm not the only one having trouble with a school that doesn't get how dangerous diabetes is.

The third post is from "mike315." "Endo from hell!!!!" *"Our family moved last month and I am having a hard time finding a new* endo for my four year old son. The only one in our town wouldn't give us an appointment for six months. When we called and said it was an emergency, because we couldn't get Evan's numbers down under 200, he told us not to worry unless they stayed above 300 for more than a week. Also, when we asked if we could start the process for getting Evan a pump he told us it was a waste of money and that people on pumps get lazy about controlling their BS. Anyone here know of a good endo in the southern eastern part of Georgia?" There are 97 responses.

Before I know it an hour is gone, and I'm still working through the forum. I've learned schools are far from perfect, families routinely fall apart fighting over how to deal, people are firmly on the side of pumps or shots, but not both, insurance is the enemy, and we should thank God for Dr. Benton, because I don't see anyone who has a endocrinologist as good as him.

The door opens. I look up and see Ashley, her hands on her pencil-thin waist. "How long you been here?"

"A while. How did you find me?"

"Betsy said she saw you and Miss Donna Jean come down this way. What are you doing?"

I pat the couch next to me, and she sits and looks over my shoulder. "Where'd you get the computer?"

"Miss Donna Jean. Look what I found." I show her the message board and then back out to the list of forums. "They have a whole bunch of groups. There's one for kids your age with type 1."

"Are any of them allergic to insulin?" She's always known how to cut to the chase.

I hand her the computer. She types quickly. I watch her fingers flying over the keyboard and wonder where she learned her way around the computer so well. She don't find anything in the message board, so she backs out into Google and does a search for "insulin allergy." One million eight hundred thousand results pop up.

The first one looks like just a definition, but the second one is Insulin Allergy Successfully Treated. She clicks on it as fast as a fish on bait.

It's a university study profiling some kid a little older than her. She skims through the medical jargon and slows on the description of the kid. His symptoms sound like hers. They use the same method Dr. Benton is starting Ashley on. The story is extremely vague on specifics. It don't tell us how he survived for six months on barely-there insulin levels, or how much weight he lost, or when in the process the hives went away, but it did end with him getting off steroids and taking further insulin without problems, and that's all Ashley needs.

"See? This'll work!"

"Let's see what else is out there. Just in case. Let's see if there are any plan C's."

The next was a case where a type 1 woman was treated with a mix of insulin and steroids, just like Ashley had the last few days. The next few were more explanations about what it is and how rare it is. One was a medical study about the causes of it and how the different kinds of insulin provide alternatives. The last of these mentioned that many people who have allergic reaction to human insulin are fine with beef insulin.

"Insulin from a cow?" Ashley stuck out her tongue and bit it. "Ewww!"

"You'd rather have pig insulin?" I suggest, reading further.

"How do you think they get the insulin out of a pig?"

"I'd think the pig would need it's own insulin. Don't you?"

"Maybe they found a way to increase how much it makes, and they can take out the extra."

I consider this, as outlandish as it sounds. Maybe they could do the same with me. Maybe they can make me produce extra, and I could donate it to her.

I write the new options in my notebook:

Beef insulin?

Can a relative donate theirs?

On the second page there are several "ask the doctor" sites where people write in and ask the doctor to diagnose them based on email. None of these is what we're looking for, although one doctor does say how rare it is to be allergic to insulin. We find this not at all helpful.

We slog through another page or two of websites, Ashley getting more discouraged with each page until we find the one we didn't know we were looking for. It's a science magazine article with the headline "Mice Cured of Type 1 Diabetes; Humans to Follow."

"A cure?" Ashley is brimming with hope, tapping the down arrow furiously as I try to keep up with her.

"Slow down," I say irritably, trying to understand the words on the page. It's a vaccine. A simple vaccine that's already being given for other diseases. It's been shown to stop the immune system from attacking the pancreas. "It cured them." The words wash over me.

"I'll do it," Ashley says, her eyes glued to the screen. "I'll try it. It's safe, right? If it's used for other diseases, it has to be safe to use."

"Why hasn't this made the news," I add, not wanting to admit that just two weeks ago I would've turned the channel on the news if that tidbit came on. Who cares about field mice being cured of some disease you know nothing about?

I write down the web address in my notebook and a few sentences to remind me about it, not that I could forget. I'll show them to Dr. Benton later and ask if he can find out more about it.

"That's the answer! I know it!" Her eyes are shining again. "God's gonna cure me!"

My heart sinks to my knees. "Baby, don't go getting your hopes up..."

"Why not?" Suddenly she's a tempest whirling on me. "Don't you want me to get better? Don't you want this whole thing to go away?"

"Of course, I do—"

"Then stop acting like God can't do it. If we believe, and we ask, God will do it. That's what the Bible says. Believe and ask."

"It's not that easy, Ash."

"It's as easy as believing. You don't have faith. That's your problem."

She's right. Lord Almighty, she is right. I have no faith. I seen my father waste away from cancer even as he was praying for God to heal him. I seen people lose their farms when the rain didn't come, even though they prayed on their knees for God to send it. There are starving kids in Africa, suffering Christians in China, soldiers in battle all praying for God to save them. Our church folks gather every Wednesday to pray for God to answer these prayers. And he don't. Least ways, not all of them. How am I supposed to believe he'd hear us?

"Life is more complicated than that. It's more complicated than throwing your wish list into some God-wishing-well and thinking everything will come out roses."

"No, it's not." She stands, unsteady but ready to leave. Tears are filling her eyes, and there's more hurt than fire there. "It's just that easy."

As she starts out of the room, she stumbles and grabs the door to keep herself up. I'm at her side in a blink, but she pushes my hands off. "I want to go alone. You stay here and find us a plan C."

"Ash, baby, I'm sorry." Just as suddenly as it came, the fire dies in her.

"It's okay." When she touches my arm, it feels like a feather. "I'm not mad, Mama. I have faith enough for both of us."

* * * *

It don't take long for me to become computer-savvy. That's what Dr. Benton calls me, but I'm not sure he always means it in a positive way.

I'm the bulldog. He's the neck.

I admit I can be overbearing. "It just ain't right for the woman to wear the pants in the family," my own mama used to say. But if I became my mama, Ashley'd die lying here in this hospital with people just twiddling their thumbs around her. Travis is either working or trying to find business for Bob; he oughta get paid twice for that. I want him here, but that's not possible now. Without his job, we have no insurance; without no insurance, we got no way to pay for all this. So Travis works all day, every day, and is hardly at the hospital, which I don't hold against him, but he has his job, and Dr. Benton has a job too, with lots of patients and an office, and if I'm not here to fight for Ashley, ain't no one else to do it.

I keep copious notes—that's what Logan calls it—about everything I find on the Internet, and I tear the pages out and give them to Dr. Benton when he comes at night. He looked at the mice experiment and shot that down. "It's a great idea, but it's a long way from being anything significant. They're still testing it. Right now, in mice, it only works a little, for a short period of time. Like it reverses the disease partway, for a few hours. Then it's back. Maybe in a few years this would be an option." He hands the paper back.

I keep at it though. Day after day, new things. Every time I Google the same things, and the same 1.8 million hits show up. I slog through them, page after page, thinking something has to be there. Out of 1.8 million web pages, there has to be an answer somewhere.

"There's an insulin you can inhale, like one of those asthma things. You think we should try that?"

"They took it off the market."

"Why?"

"Not enough money in it."

"How can there not be enough money in it? People got some kind of emotional attachment to sharp needles?"

"How about this one," I say a couple days later, handing him yet another paper. "This says diet and exercise can completely reverse the disease in some people."

"That's for type 2," he says, handing the papers back to me without even looking.

By the sixth set of notes in my awful chicken scratch, he brings in an old printer and sets it up on the desk in Ashley's room. "Now you have your own control center," he says. "This way you can spend more time researching and less time writing."

I print everything I come across: pharmaceutical evaluations, newspaper articles, message board posts.

My own message board post remains mostly empty. There are over five hundred hits on it and a handful of replies that read, "How terrible! I've never heard of this. We'll be praying for you."

Ashley has made a few friends on the "kids with type 1" forum. Their posts are the kind of normal I'm now hoping for Ashley. "Cut myself cutting up an orange today. I decided 2 test, since I was already bleeding. Hate 2 waste blood! lol" "Found sour apple glucose tablets! yum! much better than fruit punch!" "Anyone know how 2 hide pump under prom dress?"

I read some of them to Ashley when she's not up to reading them herself. Sometimes she wants me to write back, so I write what she says and add at the end, "Written by Ashley's mom. Ashley—12, dx t1 may, dx insulin allergy june."

One day she receives an email from a girl on the forum. "Check this out!"

It is a link to a newspaper article somewhere in Europe. I skim it, then go back and read it again. And then again. And I print it out and run down to the nurses's station.

"Do you know when Dr. Benton will be in?"

She shakes her mile-high hair and keeps clicking at her keyboard. I thrust the printout in her face. "Have you read about this? Do you know anything about it?" She glances at it and hands it back.

"Sounds like some kind of scam to me."

"It's real. It's from a real newspaper. It was online."

She shrugs without looking up. "There's lots on the Internet that's not real. People make this stuff up for kicks."

"It's not." I take the paper back, but now I'm not so sure.

I go back to the room and read it again. Then I Google it, but I can't find anything else except the article. Maybe it's a fake.

By the time Dr. Benton arrives, I'm more nervous and less excited about giving it to him. I've learned hope can be scary because at the end there's usually disappointment.

"What have you found for me today?"

I hand it to him real slow. "I'm not sure it's anything. It's probably not even real."

"I'd be disappointed if you didn't have something." He smiles as he takes it, but as he reads his face grows serious. "I've heard about this. A year or so ago. I'd completely forgotten about it."

"So it's not a hoax?" My heart starts beating faster now.

"No, not a hoax." I let him read more, biting my lip to keep from interrupting.

"Can I keep this?"

"It's true? That British doctor really cured diabetes with baby teeth?"

"Yes, it's true." He seems distracted suddenly, folding the paper and putting it in his pocket and checking Ashley's vitals with barely a word. Ashley sleeps through it all, which is what she does most of the time, now.

"I got her baby teeth. All of them. I can bring them in. Can you cure her?"

"No. I can't do that."

"Could he? That doctor in the article?"

"No. I don't think so."

He's not looking at me so I pull on his arm. "Dr. Benton, look at me." His eyes meet mine, but I can't read them. "What does this mean?"

"I don't know."

"But it means something?"

"Yes." He runs his fingers through his hair in that way Travis does when he's figuring how to pay the bills. "It means something very big. Possibly. But possibly not."

"Are you kidding me?" His eyes seem to focus on me, like he suddenly realizes I'm in the room.

"I'm sorry. I mean, I don't think that baby teeth are going to help now, but it may be the lead on something even better. I don't know for sure. I have someone I need to call, and I need to look into a few things. So no, it isn't the answer, but it might lead to the answer." He grabs me into a hug, a very undoctorly thing. "You keep looking, Mrs. Babcock. This is good stuff. We might get there after all."

* * * *

When I talk to Travis on the phone he don't get it. "What do you mean they cured diabetes with baby teeth?"

"I don't know how. I ain't no doctor. The article just said the doctors took something in the baby teeth and made them grow new insulin cells. And the kids aren't diabetic anymore."

"And Dr. Benton thought he could do that?"

"Not exactly. But he seemed to think it meant something. Like, it was something he never thought of before."

"But it's not our plan C?"

"It sounded like it might lead us to plan C." I hear him sigh on the other end of the line. "It means something, Travis. It does. If you could have seen the look on his face."

"Okay. How is Ashley today?" And we stop talking about cures and shift to the day to day we're comfortable with. He found his company two new jobs that'll take him through the summer. Logan is job-hunting for the first time and is weighing the choice of fast food or gas attendant, not particularly thrilled with either. Life is going on as normal at home, and it seems like a world away from where I am.

Chapter Sixteen

The stretches of boredom are broken by bits of news called in from home. Pastor Joel's wife had her baby—a healthy girl they name Mary Ashley. I am both touched and horrified. It ain't like Ashley's dead already, but since they mean well I try to lean more to the touched.

Brenda calls to say her cinnamon brownies won second place in CinnamonFest. Yolanda's new pool hit a snag when the diggers hit granite and had to bring in dynamite to blow it out. The paper had a typo in one of the ads, and HEB had to sell all their brisket and t-bones at 80 percent off instead of 30 percent.

Despite the mundaneness of these news bits, I look forward to my cell phone ringing, if only to hear a voice that's not a doctor or nurse's. But when I hear the voice of Logan's principal, I know no good can be coming.

It's not just that it's her, although that alone sets my teeth on edge, 'specially since school's been out a month already. It's mostly the way she says my name, like a squeeter got caught in her throat and she's trying not to swallow it.

"It's about Logan."

"I didn't expect you'd call about anyone else," I say, taking the phone into the bathroom so's not to wake Ashley and not to expose the hospital staff to what I'm sure is about to be a very unsavory conversation.

"The school janitor has made a very unfortunate find in Logan's locker."

"A moldy PB and J sandwich?"

"A test, Mrs. Babcock." I've always hated the way teachers and principals use my formal name to emphasize they are serious, the way I use Logan and Ashley's first and middle to get their attention.

"Oh my. A test. In a school locker. Shall we report this to the police, because I'm quite sure there has been some great crime committed here, Mrs. Gianuzzi." I can do it too.

There's a pause and I can almost hear her teeth grinding. "A standardized test, Mrs. Babcock."

"Should I know what that is and why this is a crime?"

"It's the test the state gives students every year, part of the requirement for federal funding. Logan and his classmates took the test at the very end of the year. No one in the school should have had a copy of that test. Every copy was kept under lock and key until distributed for testing, and then every one was numbered, handed out, and collected."

"If they were all collected, how does Logan have one in his locker?"

"That's what we would like to know."

My completely fine stomach suddenly feels completely not fine. I sit on the toilet and push the door closed all the way. "What is it you're trying to say, Mrs. Gianuzzi?"

"That we believe it's possible Logan got a hold of a copy before he took the test and used it to prepare."

"Was it an answer key?"

"No."

"So you're afraid Logan found out what was on the test and studied to make sure he got the answers right?"

"Yes. That's called cheating, Mrs. Babcock."

"You can stop using my name like that. I know who I am. What I don't know is why a school would be so worried about a student studying to make sure they do well on a test." I've never liked the principal, mostly because it seems to me like she has never liked Logan. From the first day, she tried to force him to change his hair, except there ain't no rule in school about hair cuts. I swear she made a judgment about what kind of student he was the moment he stepped off that bus looking like some punk rocker, and she ain't never looked far enough to see differently.

She don't like me none either, which I gather is mostly because, while I don't like Logan's hair none the better, I don't make him change it. And I don't have past a tenth grade education, and she ain't the kind that can understand that.

"Don't you find it strange that Logan barely makes Cs in class, and yet he scored almost off the charts on the standardized tests?"

"I find it strange that he makes only Cs in school and yet can translate everything the doctors tell us about his sister into language we all can understand. That, and he's like some rainman of nutrition facts 'cause he can calculate the carbs off the side of a box faster than you can whip out your calculator. I find it strange that you would call me, worried that he did well on some test you should be hoping he does well on instead of calling his teachers asking why he ain't making better grades."

There's more silence on the other end, but I don't get the feeling she's considering me so much as taking time to load her weapon. "The fact that he had the test in his locker is enough for us to bring him in for questioning."

"Bring him in for questioning? What are you, Law and Order? I still don't see no crime."

"Having a copy of this test is a crime."

"How do you even know it was him that had it? If you didn't find it until after school was out, how do you know it was his locker, or that he put it in there?"

"We know it's his locker because we have the records of which student had which one from last year."

"Do you know where I am right now?"

"I'm not in the mood for a game," she snaps.

"I'm in the hospital." Well dang if that don't shut her up. "In case you didn't know, my other child is real sick, and our family is spending every minute of every day trying to find the cure that's gonna bring her home. Right now, I don't give a hoot about your test. All I care about is keeping my daughter alive."

"I didn't know. I'm very sorry to hear that." She does, actually, sound sorry.

"Look, Mrs. Gianuzzi. I'll talk to Logan, okay? I'll ask him about it, and if he took it I'll make him come by and personally apologize."

"It doesn't work that way. This is very serious."

I sigh, because this ain't getting nowhere. "I'll make him take the test over again, then. How about that? Will that make it right?"

"It's not a matter of the scores. This is going to go before the school board. Logan may be facing expulsion."

The word expulsion is just getting funnier and funnier. "You're gonna have to wait in line. I gotta see the board about my daughter first. Her crime was trying to take the medicine she needs to stay alive."

"The school board meeting is the end of the month, Mrs. Babcock. You and Logan will have to show up then to present your defense."

"Yeah," I say. "I'll just make sure my daughter is all better by then so we can make your issues our priority." I hang up without saying goodbye. A moment later the phone rings again. I turn it off without answering. I try to collect myself before leaving the bathroom.

Travis and Logan are there already, looking at me strangely as I exit the loo so gracefully. Travis looks at the phone in my hand. "Trouble?"

"Apparently Logan swiped some big test at school, and the principal has her panties all in a wad." The color drains from Logan's face and Travis turns to him, the mood in the room suddenly chilled.

"Logan?"

"It wasn't mine. I swear."

"So you know about this?" I ask, angrier than I have a right to be now. "I just told your principal you couldn't possibly have been involved." I didn't, but I'd been wanting to say that to her. I'd been thinking it, and the fact that Logan so easily cops to the crime makes me feel betrayed.

"I wasn't involved. I didn't take the test. I didn't even look at it."

"Then how did it land in your locker?"

"Another kid stole it."

"Who?" demands Travis.

"I can't say. He stole it, but he didn't use it either. I found him sneaking out of the counselor's office with it when I went in to..." He trails off a minute and before I can ask why he's going to the school counselor he finishes. "I saw him with it and told him he needed to give it back or he'd be in real trouble."

"Real trouble? As opposed to..."

"Failing the test."

"I thought it was one of those state tests. That doesn't even affect his grades does it?" I know it can't, 'cause Logan got hugely good scores, but his grades didn't go up an iota.

"If he failed, he couldn't graduate."

"Doesn't he have another year to take it?"

Logan flops onto the daybed. "He's a senior. He flunked it last year. This was his last year."

Travis sits in the chair across from him and leans back, folding his arms across his chest. "So you took the test and he failed?"

"No. I told him he needed to return it, and I'd tutor him."

"You?" I realize I have snorted at this idea, and I cover it by pretending I am sneezing. As good as his test scores are, I can't imagine Logan teaching anyone.

"Except by the time I convinced him I could help, the counselor was back and he couldn't get in to the office to return it. I took it, cause I didn't want him being tempted to cheat, and I thought I could put it back when..." He breaks off again, and then adds, "later."

"So?" Travis says.

"So what?"

"Did he pass?"

Logan grins that cat-in-the-fish tank kind of grin. "Yeah."

"That don't excuse it," I say, frustrated at the situation he's just put us all in. "Now, you're the one in trouble. They want to expel you."

This wipes the grin off his face, and he pales again. "But I didn't do anything wrong."

"You have a test in your locker you shouldn't have. That's all they care about."

"But it's not even the test I took."

"What?" I stop pacing and stare hard at him.

"It's not my test. They give a different one to the juniors and to the seniors."

"Well, there's your defense," Travis says, as if that settles that. He gets up and walks to the door. "Anyone want a Dr. Pepper?"

When he's gone I sit down across from Logan, who picks up a magazine and flips through it just to not make eye contact with me. "Logan, put that down." He does, and sighs heavily.

"I was trying to do the right thing, Mom."

"Why didn't you just take the test back to the counselor, or tell your friend to?"

"Obviously if he took it back, he'd get in trouble. And if I took it back, I'd get in trouble."

"But, like you said, you didn't do anything wrong."

"You think they'd believe me?" I look at his hair, his clothes, the way he hangs over the daybed like he's been draped there. I think about his grades and the way he's more likely than not to say exactly what's on his mind the moment it pops into it. And I know he's right. And like a flash I realize the two of us is just peas in a pod.

"Okay," I say.

"Okay what?"

"Okay, I'll take care of it."

"Take care of what?" Ashley says in that groggy voice we've come to know as her usual voice.

"Doing what I do best: cleaning up after the two of you. I'm going to go see what happened to your dad."

I close the door behind me and lean against it. I have no idea how to fix this. Stolen tests. Contraband needles. Unfist-fights. Even in doing right, they did wrong. Right now there's just too much of life to battle, and I am tired.

Chapter Seventeen

In my room at the Ronald McDonald house, the last resident had left a calendar. It's a diary of sorts, the small boxes that are supposed to represent days filled with appointment reminders, medicine changes, drug reactions, simple facts of life with a dying child.

Meagan admitted, relapse, acute lymphoblastic leukemia.
chemo/radiation ruled out as options
cbc- white count 1500
Meagan falls getting to bathroom, breaks tibia, wheelchair bound
hip bone marrow aspiration, spinal tap done
m.d.b.g and g tested for compatibility. negative.
Meagan put on bone marrow transplant list

The notes are jottings of facts, but I wonder how many tears were shed writing them.

The notes end abruptly. I don't know how to interpret the facts of the last few days to know if it ended well, but I tend to think not. If'n it were me, I'd take the calendar home and put it in the baby box where I keep Ashley's treasured things, so that one day I could pull it out and show her and say—

But I don't know what I'd say. *See how God answers prayers? See what a little faith can accomplish?* Or will I say, *See how miraculous science is? See what the persistence of doctors and the will of a family can accomplish?*

I sit on the bed fingering the pages, the glossy photos of Texas wildflowers. I find a pen and turn back a month, just two days after Meagan's last treatment and write, "Ashley admitted, diagnosed type 1 diabetes." I fill in as many days I can. First low blood sugar. First shots: lantus and humalin. Leave hospital. And then I stop to decide if I want to fill in the days we are home and decide not to, merely drawing a line though them with the word HOME on top,

Next I fill in our current stay. I end with today. *1 month anniversary. Dr. says desens a failure.* It is all that will fit in the box but it says so little about what is going on.

Travis walks out of the bathroom as I'm hanging it back on the wall. "The shower was cold tonight."

"Visiting hours are over. Everyone is coming back to clean up for dinner." Dinner has come to mean less of a meal and more a time of day. No one here eats much.

He looks at the calendar where I've written and points at a blank one at the end of the month. "One day we'll write, 'took Ashley home' on one of those squares," he says.

"Not take it home?"

"No. We should leave it for the next family. So they know."

"About Ashley?"

"Yes. And hope."

I don't answer, so he takes me by the shoulders and turns me around. "You have to believe, Babs."

"In what?"

"Just believe—that Ashley will get better."

But that makes no sense to me. You can't just believe without believing in something. And right now neither God nor science is pulling through for me.

"Did Dr. Benton tell you what he's going to do now?" Travis asks.

"No," I answer.

Travis lets go of me and picks up his towel to rub his hair dry. "He said he has someone flying in to talk to us tomorrow. Where are you going?"

"Back to the hospital. Do you want to come?"

"I thought we were going to spend some time together. I just got here. I ain't hardly seen you in weeks."

"Then come with me."

"We can't talk there. Not in front of Ashley."

"She's asleep."

"Exactly. Now's the perfect time to go out. Let me take you out for real food, Babs."

It's been three weeks since our last eating out disaster, and seeing as how that one didn't end so well, I'm not anxious to repeat it. "I'm not hungry."

"It's not about the food."

"So why go out?"

"To be together," he insists. I want to remind him that our last togetherness thing ended with me alone at the table and him fuming in the bathroom until his enchilada got cold.

"We can be together in the hospital."

"This conversation's like a dog chasing his tail." He grabs the remote to the TV and throws himself in the one chair we got in the room.

"What?"

"Just go." He punches buttons on the remote. A baseball game appears.

"Are you coming with me?"

"No."

When I get to Ashley's room she's asleep, and I sit in the dark watching her chest rise and fall. Her hair has thinned, and she is ghostly white.

I should be at the house with Travis. We've barely spoken in the weeks since Ashley and I packed up and moved our lives to Austin. He drives back and forth every night and we talk on the phone, but mostly when we talk it's about his roofing job and TV shows and Logan, who is now out of school and working at a music store selling guitar strings and clarinet reeds. The conversations are clipped; we are both exhausted. If we speak about anything truly important, we argue, so we don't.

It's not because of Ashley, though. It's been years since we've had more than these surface conversations. I don't know when we stopped having the real conversations that newlyweds have: the kinds that are about what you hope and dream for your life and for the world in general. It must have been when I couldn't see no further than getting through the piles of laundry and how to make dinner with no cheese or ground beef in the house. Sometime around when Travis gave up running his own contracting business to work for someone else so we could have insurance and afford to fix the brakes on the truck.

Brakes and insurance are important things, but not much of a conversation starter.

The monitor hooked up to Ashley's heart is beating unbearably fast. Tiny bleeps across a black screen. I move over to the bed and sit beside her. Brushing her hair back, I can tell her head is hot, like she's running a fever. I feel like she's slipping away from me.

"Can't we do a transplant?" I asked Dr. Benton last week. Pulling out my notebook and flipping to the pages full of examples of islet and pancreas transplants, I ask again, "Why aren't we doing this?"

"I'm not ruling it out. But she's going to be hard to find a match, and on top of that, the success rate is about 64 percent. The likelihood that her immune system would attack the new pancreas is high. It's just delaying the decision we have to make now."

"But it might buy us time, right? Isn't that all we need? A little more time? Then maybe that mice vaccine thing might be working."

"We don't want to trade one very serious problem with another. There's a risk of death with the surgery, along with a long list of complications that could have Ashley needing to come back to the hospital several times a year. And whether the new pancreas works or not, Ashley would have to be on immunosuppressant drugs for the rest of her life."

"We'd be trading one poison for another?"

"In a sense. There's also a good chance, a very real chance, that the transplant would only be partially successful."

"How can it be partially successful?"

"The body accepts the new pancreas. It works, but not well enough that the diabetic can stop taking insulin altogether."

"What about the baby teeth thing?" I say, switching gears easily.

"We can't use her baby teeth. I've told you that. But it might lead to something else. I'm still researching."

"When?"

"I can't tell you when it will be, or if it will be something at all. I'm trying here just as hard as you, Mrs. Babcock."

As I cool Ashley's head now with a washcloth, hopelessness fills me. Every road is a dead end.

* * * *

I lost Logan when he was four in a Wal-Mart. We'd gone to get the kids' Christmas pictures taken, and Ashley was in the cart in a red velvet dress. Logan walked up and down the aisle with me hunting for ingredients to make sugar cookies. While we were sorting through the cookie cutters choosing shapes, I noticed Logan had a plastic candy cane in his chubby fist—one of the big clear things full of red and green chocolate candies.

"Where the Sam Hill did you get that thing?"

"Can we buy it, Mama?"

"No. Where'd it come from?"

He pointed to the end of the aisle. I swung the cart around to return it, and Ashley reached out at the same time to grab an angel cutter. The entire display cascaded to the floor. Ashley squealed and clapped her hands as I looked at the dozens of brightly colored shapes around the cart.

"I'll pick 'em up. You go put that back. Straight there and back, you understand?"

Logan nodded solemnly and took off for the display. I sighed and knelt to put the cookie cutters back in their box. When I finished I stood and looked for Logan. He was gone.

"Dadburnit. Now where'd he go?" We high-tailed it to the end of the aisle. There was a cardboard display with 24 holes for the plastic candy canes. Not one was missing.

I looked around but he wasn't there. I kept walking, looking down each aisle but he wasn't there. My heart started beating a little faster as I reversed direction and went the other way. Still no Logan. I started calling his name, quiet at first to not draw attention to us, but then more loud. Customers stopped to ask if I needed help and they, too, fanned out, looking. Someone brought me the store manager.

"Is there a problem?"

"I lost my son. He was right here, and then he wasn't. He's four, about this high, brown hair, brown eyes. He's wearing black pants and a red sweater with a reindeer on it."

He spoke into a walkie-talkie, sending employees to the toy section and the front doors and soon lights were going off and the intercom was announcing a Code Adam and everything shut down.

They found him in the shampoo aisle, frightened and wondering how he'd gotten turned around.

For months after that I had dreams about losing him, waking with that awful pit in my stomach. Even though I knew it was a dream, I'd sneak into his room in the middle of the night and put my hand on his back to feel him breathing, just to make sure.

The dreams went away before he turned six, and I stopped checking that he was breathing every night. And in those little acts of negligence, I lost him all over again.

Chapter Eighteen

I started having the dreams again, except in the new ones it's Ashley I've lost. She's in a hospital gown, and I take her into the store to find medicine and she disappears on me. No matter which way I go, she's always just out of reach.

I fall asleep in Ashley's room and a nurse wakes me up.

"Mrs. Babcock?" I feel her hand on my shoulder and I'm suddenly alert.

"What happened? Is Ashley okay?"

"I think you were having a nightmare. You were calling for her." I feel my cheeks get hot, but she goes back to Ashley's chart without blinking at my discomfort. "Lots of people talk in their sleep. Especially around this place."

She's new on this floor, and I haven't quite gotten used to her briskness. Her name is Ingrid, and she speaks with a heavy German accent that I sometimes have trouble understanding. She takes Ashley's vitals a little roughly. She takes her temperature and blood pressure and writes them on the chart. She pricks her finger. Ashley murmurs in her sleep and then is quiet.

"What is it," I ask.

"465. Holding steady the last few days." I don't tell her I already know this, that I know every number the last two weeks. "You should go get rest," she says. "She'll sleep all night, and it looks like you have a big day tomorrow."

"What's tomorrow?" I have a sudden mental picture of them yanking the pump off Ashley with the same ceremony of pulling the plug on a coma patient.

"I don't know what's going on, but your doctor left a note in the chart." She hands me the paper.

Tell Ashley's mom to go home and get sleep. Tomorrow is a big day. We start plan C.

My heart beats faster. I laugh at the thought that Dr. Benton knows I am here and that the McDonald house has become home, but mostly

I laugh because there's finally a plan C.

After hours of questions, thousands of Google hits searched, an entire notebook full of ideas, Dr. Benton has found a plan C.

"Can I keep this?" I hold the note up and Ingrid grunts. I kiss Ashley on the head and whisper into her ear. "Hold on, baby. Tomorrow we find the cure."

I've got no idea if plan C is a cure, or if it will even work, but I don't let myself think about this as I cross the parking lot.

There are a few families in the common room sipping coffee and chatting. They could be anywhere, friends trading stories over Folgers decaf. I wave but don't stop.

Our room is dark already. The blinds are closed, the lights out, and I see Travis's body under the covers. I slip out of my clothes and into pajamas and slide into bed next to him. It is only the third or fourth time we've slept down here together in the last month.

We have always kept an invisible line down the bed. His side. My side. We each needed that space of our own, but tonight the space is too big. It's been too big for a long time.

I scooch over and rest my arm alongside his. He stirs, so I turn on my side and whisper, "Are you awake?"

"Sort of."

"We have a plan C." It sounds ridiculous when I say it out loud, like we are secret agents planning some covert operation, but immediately he turns towards me and props himself on his elbow.

"What is it?"

"I don't know. Dr. Benton left a note for us at the hospital." I am so excited my voice is shaking.

"Do you think it's the doctor that is flying in tomorrow? It must be that. Do you know anything about him? What did the note say?"

"Just that tomorrow starts plan C."

He considers this. "You can't get your hopes up too much about this, Babs. We don't have any idea what this is."

"But it's something. It's something, and something is a good thing."

"Maybe." I can tell he isn't sure. Anger flashes through me.

"What do you mean, maybe? Anything is better than nothing, and nothing is what we've got now."

"I don't know, Babs. You've researched everything. Dr. Benton has talked to every expert in the field. There's no known answer. No sure thing. This don't happen enough for there to be any kind of precedence." The big word slides out of his mouth like he's comfortable with big words and trying to show off.

I know the word precedence. It's in the SAT book. It means this hasn't happened before. I know that ain't right. I know at least two people have died because they were allergic to this insulin, and no amount of science could change that. I know this, but I haven't told him.

"Then Ashley will be the precedence. She will be the one in all them medical journals, and parents will read about her and it will give them hope."

"I'm just saying you don't know what it is. Whatever it is, they haven't proven it will work. Maybe it's dangerous. Maybe it's experimental. Do you want our daughter to be some doctor's guinea pig?"

"She already is." I'm out of bed now and scrambling for my jeans. "I don't get you. You give me this holier-than-thou lecture about having faith and believing, and when I finally find something to latch onto, you tear it down."

"I just don't want you to be so desperate you'll cling to anything, even if it's going to put Ashley in jeopardy. Do you have any idea what some of these experiments are like?"

I pull my t-shirt on over my pajama top and pat my hand over the dresser to find the keys. "We *are* desperate, Travis. And she's already in jeopardy, which you'd know if you spent more than an hour with her a couple times a week." I grab my pack of cigarettes out of the drawer, stuff them in my pocket, and slam the door after me. I know I've hit below the belt on the last comment, but I'm angry and I don't care so much.

The families in the common room look up and smile like they didn't hear anything. It's like that here. There's a lot of hushed arguments and tears and slammed doors, because there's just no leaving the stress at the hospital. All of us drag it back and aim it at the only ones who care enough to be here with us. We try to act normal, but it's no more than a house of shattered lives, and every one of us knows it.

The back yard is quiet. Quiet meaning there's no one there, but not that it's silent, because the city is moving all around us. Though there's a fence and several lawn chairs, it don't feel like a backyard to me. Beyond the fence is the parking lot of the hospital, and too often there's the siren of an ambulance blaring through the night. Other hospitals are close by as well, so we're surrounded by tall buildings whose lights blaze all night. I sit in a chair and light up a cigarette. The ritual calms me, and after a few deep draws my hands stop shaking and my shoulders let go some of their tension.

I miss my own house. I can't even begin to count the amount of things I miss there. I've only been back twice, and it felt like walking into someone else's life. My house, my clothes, my bed and kitchen, but not my life. When Ashley is back, I think, it will be home again. I don't let myself think of any other possibilities.

A helicopter flies over and lands on the roof of a nearby hospital. I wonder who it is in there, and why they're in need of Medivac, and who might be speeding through the streets of Austin to arrive in time to see them. Without thinking I'm praying, *God let them all be safe and well*. I wonder if I'll ever see a helicopter again without sending up a prayer and reliving these weeks.

When I finish the cigarette, I crush it and bury it with my shoe in the flowerbeds before going back inside. I'm not ready to face Travis again, so I pour a cup of coffee and join the two ladies in the common room. We've met briefly before; one is cancer, one is heart problems. This is how we know each other. I am diabetes.

"Hi," cancer says as I sit. "Rough night?"

"The same," I say. The two women hmm, because here same is not necessarily good. "How is your son?"

"Good. If good is throwing up and losing your hair and losing weight. Which apparently with cancer is good. We keep telling him that."

It takes poison to kill the poison that is killing him, I think.

"Is it working? Do the doctors think it's helping?"

"Oh yes. We should be going home soon." She crosses her fingers like a child does. "We hope this will be our last overnight visit to Children's. It's looking good. He won't be able to play basketball in the fall, and he's more worried about that than anything, but I think this time it's going to be gone for good. There's plenty years of basketball left, I keep telling him. Plenty of years."

"Have you been here a lot?"

"Two years, on and off. He was only twelve when he was diagnosed. Isn't that your daughter's age? Anyway, it feels like two years of childhood stolen right out from underneath him. You'll understand. It goes by so fast. Even without the cancer, it goes by too fast to waste precious time in the hospital."

"Did you know a Meagan? She was here not too long ago for leukemia. Her parents stayed in our room."

Cancer sips her coffee. "Un uh. But I didn't stay here every time Jason was admitted. I stayed with my aunt for awhile. But there's only so much you can intrude on family. They have their own lives, and they don't really understand. They want to, mind you, but they just can't. And then it's just easier not to try to make them feel comfortable with the whole thing." She drifts off a bit into her coffee and stares at the wall.

"And your son?" I ask cardio.

"He's on the waiting list for a new heart. He's at the top of the list now. The doctor's are really hopeful there will be one soon." She seems hopeful.

"How old is he?" The coffee is horrible.

"Three."

We fall into silence again. We sit drinking bad coffee until other parents begin trickling in, then we say our goodnights and go our separate ways.

When I climb in bed again, Travis is snoring. I stay on my side of the bed and stare at the ceiling until the light from the moon between the blinds moves across the room and disappears.

* * * *

In the morning Dr. Benton leaves a message on my cell phone to meet him for lunch downtown. He gives me the address for a Mexican restaurant. Travis and me leave the hospital around noon. The restaurant is a small, out-of-the-way place not far from the university. My first thought is that Ashley would love it, with its bright colors and tinny music. A string of colored chili pepper lights runs from one side to the other, and impossibly big sombreros and lively sarapes cover the walls. A few college-aged kids sit in a booth in a corner, but otherwise it's empty.

We stand for a few minutes by the fountain, waiting. I watch fluorescent orange fish swim around in the blue mosaic tile. The colors make my eyes hurt, and the trickling of the water makes me need to go pee.

"Are you sure you have the right place?" Travis asks, which is the most he's said to me all morning. The door opens behind us, and Dr. Benton enters, a thin man following.

"You beat us! Jack's airplane was a little late and traffic was a bear!" Dr. Benton leaned over and kisses me on the cheek in such a natural way I blush. He shakes Travis's hand and introduces us to Jack.

"Mr. and Mrs. Babcock, this is Dr. Jack Van Der Campen."

There's something familiar about him. His eyes. I swear I've seen him before. I shake his hand and glance at Travis, but he don't show any recognition.

A small woman in a multi-colored skirt and white ruffle blouse motions us to a table and hands us sticky menus. Once we have chips and salsa and drinks in front of us and have ordered, I lean forward.

"Do I know you? Have you been on TV or something?"

The doctor smiles a barely-there smile. "I doubt it. We scientists aren't that famous."

"Jack worked at Johns Hopkins for many years. He's been on the leading edge of diabetes research for the last decade and has some very promising results in curing type 1 diabetes."

At the word "cure," I reach over and squeeze Travis's hand under the table. He wriggles it out and uses it to pick up his Dr. Pepper and take a drink before saying, "Why has it taken so long to find him, then?"

"I've been out of country," Jack says, not at all acting offended. "I've just finished up a series of operations in the Netherlands, and I'm applying to start a clinical trial here in the U.S. I'd like Ashley to be a part of it."

"Like a guinea pig?" Travis says. I stomp on his foot.

"Not exactly, Mr. Babcock."

"Travis."

"Travis. What we want to do has already been proven effective and safe, both in animals and in humans. We did the surgery on 35 teenagers and young adults in the Netherlands, and a year later, 27 of them are insulin independent. The rest are significantly more stable and use far less insulin. None had any adverse reactions."

"So, why is this the first time we're hearing about this?"

"Because the United States doesn't take much stock in medical trials in other countries. They have to have all the paperwork in order here. They want the government agencies to oversee the process to make sure every patient is adequately protected."

"When can we get Ashley the surgery?" This time Travis stomps on my foot.

"We need to know more about what it is," Travis says.

"Of course you do." The enchiladas arrive, plates steaming and heaped with rice and black beans. For a minute no one speaks as we shuffle the chips and salsa and tortillas and drinks to make room for the plates, but we quickly fall into eating and talking resumes.

"Even if this is something you all decide to do," Jack continues, "it's not going to happen tomorrow. Setting up a clinical trial takes a little time. Everything's been filed, but we're still waiting for the FDA to approve it, and there's no way of telling when that would be."

Travis stabs at his food. "What exactly is a clinical trial? It sure sounds like just a fancy names for using humans as guinea pigs."

"I assure you it's much safer than that."

"A clinical trial is federally regulated," Dr. Benton adds. "All of the ethical and legal codes that apply to all medical practices apply. There is a carefully controlled protocol—"

"A what?"

"A study plan. The doctors and researches have to know exactly what they are going to do and follow it. The entire thing has to be approved and monitored by an Institutional Review Board, which includes physicians not involved in the research, as well as statisticians and community advocates."

"That sounds like a bunch of gobbeldy-gook to me," Travis says, still not eating.

I'm mortified, but Dr. Benton laughs and even Jack smiles a little while shoveling a tortilla smeared with beans in his mouth. "It just means there are a lot of people looking out for the participants."

"How many people were cured?" I ask, trying to get back to what is important.

"27 of 35 received complete independence from insulin. In essence, they are cured."

Travis picks up his fork again and begins to separate the rice and beans. As he spreads guac and sour cream over his food he says, "I'm not real good at math, but that don't seem like much better odds than a transplant."

Dr. Benton motions to Jack to answer. "It's slightly higher, actually, but the trial in Holland gave us great information in how to modify the process. We fully expect the success rate on the U.S. trial to be much greater."

"And the risks?"

"I won't lie. There are some serious risks. Part of the treatment involves the killing of Ashley's entire immune system. For awhile she'll be extremely vulnerable."

"You're killing off her immune system?" Travis's voice is loud enough to draw the attention of the boys in the booth.

"The problem of transplants," Dr. Benton says, leaning forward over his plate towards us, "is that the reason Ashley has type 1 is because her immune system attacked her pancreas and killed the islet cells. If we just transplant a new pancreas, or even new islets cells, we have the same issue all over again. The dead islet cells are the symptom, not the disease. With this treatment, Ashley will basically heal herself, but we have to make sure we stop the immune system from putting us all back at square one."

It strikes me at this moment that I've understood everything he said. I don't know how to set the clock on my DVD player. I can't understand my oven instruction manual to set the time-bake, but I understand every word a doctor says about pancreas and islets and immune disorders. This makes me laugh, not the funny kind of laughing but the kind that turns into choking and coke coming out my nose and soon turns into tears and I have to excuse myself in utter embarrassment.

Travis follows me out, more not to be alone with the doctors than to be with me, I suspect.

"What's going on?"

"I don't want to know what he's saying," I sob, aware this is making no sense. "I want to be stupid again."

God bless him, though, Travis understands. He puts his hands on my shoulders and hunches enough to be eye to eye with me. "There ain't no going back, Babs. And Ashley needs you to be just this smart. Smart enough to know if this is the thing that's going to save her or kill her. That's our responsibility, and no one can make that decision but us."

I sniff and wipe my nose on the napkin I've carried out with me. "What if we make the wrong one?"

The air outside the cantina is stifling. Marimba music floats out the door. Travis lets go of my shoulders and straightens. "We won't. We go in and ask all the questions to get all the information we need to make the right one."

I realize I've felt like he and I are on different sides, fighting each other more than the disease. He takes my hand, and we walk in together and sit back down.

Dr. Benton and Dr. Van Der Campen act as though nothing happened. We eat for awhile, gabbing about Texas heat and European winters, and NASCAR, which, it turns out, both Travis and Dr. Benton have an affinity for. We eat until there's nothing left but a few crumbs from the chips. I haven't eaten so much in over a month. If I hadn't lost weight lately, I'd be unbuttoning my jeans under the table. As it is, I feel faintly sick.

The waitress clears the plates and brings a platter of sopapillas dripping with honey and cinnamon, and the men all order coffee. When the cups are full and the waitress is gone, Travis breaks the light mood.

"So," he says. "Tell us about this miracle treatment."

Chapter Nineteen

We get a steady stream of visitors, and I imagine somewhere in the narthex of the church is a sign-up sheet labeled *Babcock visitations*. Little by little the kids have stopped coming, which is probably a good thing as Ashley is well beyond lip-gloss and blush and hardly is up for entertaining, but the women try to make it down at least three times a week.

Brenda always brings food. Pulled pork sandwiches and coleslaw. Peach cobbler. Biscuits and honey butter. Baked beans. She hands them over with apologies, knowing food is an ironic gift but the only way she knows to show her pity. If Logan is here, he sneaks it down to the cafeteria and polishes it off, and if he's lucky, makes a few friends with off-duty nurses.

Yolanda brings DVDs and board games. Gloria brings flowers from her garden. Janise brings pictures. She must spend hours every day following Ashley's friends around town and taking their pictures. She brings them in and hangs them around the room, so that when Ashley is awake she's surrounded by the people who care about her.

Donna Jean brings books; mostly books she thinks Ashley will like, and I spend hours sitting by the bed reading to her. I feel like she's five again, when we used to curl up on her bed and read for hours, her begging for more and me just trying to get her down for a nap.

There are other books tucked down in the paper bag, too. Ones for me to pass those long hours when Ashley is asleep and Logan and Travis are back at home, working, and I've got nothing to do but imagine every awful possibility.

When I come back to the hospital after lunch with the doctors, Ashley is semi-sitting up, the bag of books spilled over the covers. She's running her hands across them, shuffling them, trying to find something.

"Do you want me to read to you?" I ask, picking up the books and putting them back in the bag. Some are on the floor and I've got to get on my knees to find them.

"There's one about faith," she says.

"I don't know that one. I'll find you more of Lois Lowry," I say, rummaging through the bag.

"I want the quote book," she says, her voice airy and wispish, like she's nothing more than a ghost.

"How about Anne of Greene Gables? That was always one of your favorites."

"I want the quote one, Mama."

"I don't know that one." I try to persuade her and wonder if she's hallucinating. "How about we finish up *A Wrinkle In Time*?" I find the raggedy copy that's ours, the one she's read so many times the cover is hanging loose and the pages falling out. Ashley gives in, and I open to where she dog-eared the page. It's nearly finished.

I usually try to steer her away from this one. It's full of strange words; long ones I don't know and made up ones I can't pronounce. But today I'm relieved to be in a world so different than the one we're in.

Ashley lays back and closes her eyes, but I can tell she's listening. Like when she was a kid, she's in the book, in the imaginary world, playing the part of the main character. It's fitting that there's an untouchable, unknowable villain in this story, one that weakens and takes over the people that come to it. I almost tear when I get to the part where Meg's dad tells her, "But I wanted to do it for you...That's what every parent wants." I stop here, a lump in my throat. *God*, I pray, *if it could be me in that bed instead of her*. Ashley opens her eyes. She knows what I'm thinking, but she whispers, "Go on."

I read through another page, until I get to Mrs. Who's advice for Meg. I can't go on. Ashley, who knows this part by heart, begins to say it in her wavering, thin voice.

"The foolishness of God is wiser than men; and the weakness of God is stronger than men. For ye see your calling, brethren, how not many wise men after the flesh, not many mighty, not many noble, are called, but God hath chosen the foolish things of the world to confound the wise; and God hath chosen the weak things of the world to confound the things which are mighty."

I've heard Pastor Joel read this very thing in church before. I look at Ashley, not able to get herself to the bathroom, and think about how she's confounding science. And I wish God wouldn't have chosen her.

"What did Dr. Benton say?" It's the first she's asked, and I close the book.

"He says there's a new possibility, and it's up to Daddy and I to decide if it's right for you."

"What is it? Are we going to do it?" I see the hope flickering in her eyes, and I want to say *yes! Yes, we start tomorrow and this is all going to be over before you know it!*

"We're considering it." That's a generous statement, seeing as how Travis stayed for ten minutes of the explanation at lunch and then stormed out the moment stem-cell replacement was mentioned.

"You can't possibly be listening to them," he said outside the restaurant as I begged him to come in. "Did you hear them? They want to do stem-cell research on her!"

"I want to hear what they have to say at least before I say no."

"Do you know who he is?"

I don't. I been trying to put my finger on it all lunch, and the fact that Travis knows him makes me feel like I'm not going out of my mind.

"He's one of the pioneers of stem cell research." When it's clear I don't get the meaning of that, he added, "Embryonic stem cells. He takes aborted babies and uses them for science." When I don't react strong enough to that, he continued. "He lobbied congress to make it okay to use eggs fertilized for invitro treatments to grow into embryos and kill them for research."

Suddenly it dawns on me where I seen him. The posters at the rally. The ones with the scientist and the red slash through him: that was Dr. Van Der Campen.

"It don't matter," I said. "He's not killing babies today. He's trying to keep Ashley alive, and that's what matters."

"So that's what you want to do? This is nothing more than two-steppin' with the devil."

"Doctors are not the devil, Travis. The devil is diabetes, and in case you haven't noticed, it's winning this war."

He looked at me with something kin to venom. "Nothing's ever been more important to you than babies and kids. That man kills babies." He was angry, but I was angrier.

"Those babies were already dead. And if it saves my daughter, I want to hear."

"Then you're gonna have to hear alone." He stormed out and left me alone, again.

But Ashley don't know this, and she rests back, taking in the idea that Daddy and me are thinking on it. "Okay. I'm going to sleep a little."

"Okay." I pull the sheet up over her. A small book no bigger than a calculator slides to the floor. I reach down to pick it up, and she grabs my hand.

"Read this one. It's really good."

I hesitate for a moment and then take it because she wants me to. Kissing her on the forehead, I tuck her in and close the door behind me.

In the hall I look at the book. It's the book on faith she was talking about. Famous quotations about faith. When I was Ashley's age, I used to pray to God to show me something important, to talk to me. The pastor said the Bible was God's Word, so I'd pray God would speak to me, and then I'd open it randomly and point to a place on the page with my eyes closed. I usually opened to obscure books like Leviticus or Hosea and got weird verses like "If you don't run for you life, tomorrow you will be killed," or "A lizard can be caught with the hand, yet it is found in kings' palaces."

I pray the same prayer now and open the book to a page in the middle. On one side is a picture of the Grand Canyon, a miniscule person standing near the edge with his arms thrust out to heaven. On the other side is a poem by Patrick Overton. It says:

Faith
When you walk to the edge of all the light you have
and take that first step into the darkness of the unknown,
you must believe that one of two things will happen:

There will be something solid for you to stand upon,
or, you will be taught how to fly

I turn the words around in my head. What does that mean? The first part makes sense to me. I've never felt more like I'm at the edge than now. But what's the darkness? This endless hell of watching Ashley wither away before my eyes, or the possible treatment Travis thinks is of the devil? Or is it just not knowing which way to go? What's the solid thing to stand on? The cure? What's flying? Dealing with her dying?

"I'm too stupid to understand this stuff," I say out loud to no one. I shut the book and put it in my pocket.

On the way to the cafeteria I run in to Logan getting off the elevator. His hair is tinged purple at the ends of the Mohawk, and he's got an earring: something neither his father nor I would've approved in a million years. I stare at the gold hoop before I meet his eyes, but I say nothing. There are too many battles, and this one seems so inconsequential.

"Hi Mom." It strikes me that he's nervous as well as defiant. He is at once daring me to yell at him here in this hospital and scared that I will.

I'm so tired of fighting. "You know you'll have to buy your own. Ashley will never let you raid her stash of earrings."

He grins. "Is she awake?"

I nod toward the room. "Go check. She said she was going to nap, but maybe she was just trying to get rid of me. She's been asking when you're coming."

I watch him trot down the hall, all legs and arms and purple fringe. I'm ashamed that I wonder: if Ashley dies, will he be enough?

I call Travis and the phone rings until his voice mail picks up. "Call me. We need to talk." I consider telling him I'm not the monster he thinks I am; that Dr. Benton and Dr. Jack are not the monsters he thinks they are. But I fold the phone and put it away.

I push the button for the elevator and wait for it to open. I pull out the book again and close my eyes. I open and point.

"*'Faith' means not wanting to know what is true.*" Friedrich Nietzsche

I throw the book in the trash.

* * * *

Days that stretched out like a cat in the sun are now speeding by. The FDA approved the clinical trial and Dr. Van Der Campen and Dr. Benton have given me a handful of papers that detail the criteria, requirements, and process.

Ashley meets all the criteria. She's between 10 and 30 years old. She's been diagnosed with type 1 within the last six months. She's got complications difficult to control by other known treatments or drugs. She's kept records of testing her blood sugar at least three times a day.

Not that the testing does anything. It's high. It's high every time we test. All the different types of insulin and steroids in the world ain't changing that.

Already three people are signed up. They're only taking 20. Dr. Van Der Campen says it's just the first phase, and they'll take those results to tweak it further and then do another trial later with lots more people, but Ashley don't have that much time. It's gotta be now.

Travis has managed to show up only when I'm out, not sleeping in Austin and not answering phone calls. He sends Logan instead, who reads the paperwork and asks a billion questions I can't answer.

"How can you not know what Ashley's beta cell number is?"

"Why should I know? I don't even know what a beta cell is."

He shuffles the papers searching for her medical records and the last lab results. "Here it is. Jeez it's low, but she still has some. That's important. She has to still have some beta cells working or she can't be in the trial."

"What's a beta cell?"

"It's a miracle she has any after being so high for so long."

"You make it sound like she's a drug addict."

"She is."

I look at the IV drips that have become her fifth limb, the pump still on her stomach, the monitors with cords snaking under her flowered nightgown. "What's a beta cell?"

"Those things that produce insulin."

"I thought those were islets," I say, now confused; but Logan suddenly looks up at me as if seeing me for the first time. After years of eye rolling and attitude, there's something there other than disdain.

"Beta cells are in the islets. The pancreas holds the islets, the islets hold the beta cells. Like a sentence is made of words, and the words are made of letters."

"Oh." And instead of being jealous, I'm in awe of my son.

"How is the music store?" I ask.

"Good. There's a drummer who teaches there on weekends. He said he'd give me lessons for free. And the church said in the fall I can fill in with the worship band one or two Sundays a month."

"That's great."

"Well, I said I'd have to wait. You know, until Ashley is home."

Silence hangs in the air, the question of the future. I can't imagine not going home with Ashley, but looking at her on the bed it's hard to imagine life ever being the same as it was. God knows a part of me hated him for letting her get diabetes, but now I'd give anything to have her go home, shots and all.

We'd left the door to Ashley's room open, so I don't hear Travis walk in. He stands in the doorway and clears his throat.

"Hi Dad," Logan says, but I go on reading the papers.

"What are you up to?" Travis says, knowing full well what we're doing.

"Filling in the application," I say, trying not to be snippy and not succeeding.

"Behind my back?"

"It's a little hard to do it in front of your back when you're not here."

Logan looks from me to Travis, clearly uncomfortable, and I hate myself for putting him in this position. Travis and I may not be the most lovey-dovey couple, but we never fight. Until now.

Travis must think the same thing, because he pulls up a chair and sits heavily in it. "I'm here now."

Logan sizes up the situation before being the bigger one in the room and speaking up. "Mom didn't apply. She's just looking at whether Ashley qualifies."

"You'd be willing to sacrifice everything you believe for this treatment?" He isn't snide. It's this that almost breaks my heart. He can't believe I would turn my back on everything I've railed against for years. "I never thought you were one of them, Babs. Sure, it's easy to tell a young girl not to get pregnant when it's not your life that's changing. It's easy to protest stem cell research when you have nothing to lose by it not succeeding. But when your very own daughter's life depends on it... I guess this is where the true believers are separated from the social activists. Don't you believe God will provide without sacrificing his own morals?"

It's Ashley who answers. "Albert Einstein." Her voice is a ghost of itself, hollow, and so slight we think she is delirious. "Albert Einstein," she repeats, her eyelids so heavy it's hard to tell if she's awake or talking in her sleep.

"What about him?" asks Logan, who has more faith in her lucidity than I do.

"He said..." She's quiet for so long that we all gather around her, like she is saying her last peace. "He says, scientists were rated as great heretics by the church, but they were truly religious men because of their faith in the orderliness of the universe."

"What does that mean?" grunts Travis.

I ain't seen half those words in the SAT book.

"It means," explains Logan, "that Christians have always called doctors and scientist anti-Christians because they didn't accept everything on face value, when in fact God is a scientific God to begin with."

Ashley lifts her hand and finds Logan's. For a moment it is just them, like they are all that matter, the two of them in some world alone no one else can enter. And then she drops his hand and begins to shake. It starts small, tremors in the arm that spread quickly until she is seizing full throttle. I scramble to find the call button. Travis is out of the room before I can hit it, yelling like a maniac and raisin' cain until four nurses and a doctor on call descend on us, shoving us aside and out the door to wait and fear.

"You'd let her die?" I'm shaking almost as hard as her. "You believe so much in some righteous stand you'd let your own daughter die?"

Travis begins to cry. I've never seen him cry. You'd think, in all the years we been married I'd have seen him cry, but I haven't. But here in the hospital corridor, he sits on the floor and cries.

"How can I choose between God and my child?"

And I realized why it was never so hard for me as for him. My child always came first.

Chapter Twenty

We call Ashley's pump her Molotov cocktail. Every few days the combination of drugs in it changes. They tried all the kinds of insulin and ruled out everything but aspart, not because Ashley tolerates it well, but because it's the least likely to kill her. They mix the insulin with steroids, something like Benadryl, I think, that's suppose to keep her from blowing up with hives and breathing funny, except they are drugs with longer names I can't pronounce, with lots of o's and p's and y's and n's in them. None have worked well, but every time they try a new one Ashley and I cross our fingers.

The fact that they can't try things faster is frustrating the heck out of me. If she tests at nine in the morning and is given the new cocktail, then tests no different at ten, or at eleven, or at twelve, I ask if we can change and try something else.

"It doesn't work that way, Mrs. Babcock," they say. "It takes a long time for some of this to work, and then we have to let it go through her system and out before we can try something else."

Meanwhile, Ashley's not getting better.

The evening after the seizure, Dr. Benton visits again. I'm afraid he's going to press about the trial. Since the crying incident, Travis and I have a fragile truce that involves not talking about anything important. It's amazing how two people in the midst of a life and death situation can sit around a hospital room and talk about things like the possibility of new linoleum in the kitchen at home or debate the dangers of bumper stickers.

But Dr. Benton don't mention the trial. He sits on the edge of Ashley's bed and pats her leg and says, "What do you think about us getting rid of Max?" Max is the name of her pump. It's what she would have called a dog had we ever let her get one.

"Max doesn't seem to be doing the trick we hoped. And we've about run out of options for what to put in him. Your body is a little resistant here, anyone tell you that before?"

Ashley manages a smile and looks at Logan. "He's the rebellious one." Her voice is still faint, but stronger than before the seizing.

"I'd like to try something else."

"I thought we'd run out of options," I say.

"Not quite. This isn't a long-term solution, but it might help for a while. I'd like to put the insulin directly into your umbilical vein."

"My what?"

"How's that gonna help?"

"When we give you shots, or even with an insulin pump, the insulin goes in and goes through your blood stream," he points to his own stomach and then draws a line with his finger up to his heart, "and then it goes through your heart and back through your blood stream," he drags his finger down his arm and up and down his torso and leg and up back to the start, "and when it finally gets to your liver, it's diluted. I'd like to inject it directly into the vein that will take it to the liver, full strength, faster."

"So she won't be allergic that way?"

"No, the allergy is still there. But at least when we get it to the liver full strength, it has a shot at bring the blood sugar down a bit before the allergy resists it. Like I said, it's not long term, but it may buy us a little time."

"Okay," I say. "Let's do it."

"Wait a cotton pickin' minute," Travis says, going over to Ashley and putting his arm around her. "Y'all are so gung-ho to try new things. What's this going to do to her? I've seen what it does when she gets too much insulin. It nearly kills her. What happens if you give her too much? Won't it kill her that much faster?"

"Shut up, Dad." It's Logan, behind me, who's now standing.

Travis and I are dumbfounded, and Dr. Benton seems embarrassed.

"You all talk like Ashley isn't even in the room. And you," he turns, fire in his eyes, to his dad. "How can you even say the word kill when you're talking about Ash?"

I think he would storm out of the room if he could take Ashley with him.

Ashley, the youngest, the one in the middle of it all, is the one to speak first. "It's okay Logan. I'd rather they talk in front of me than behind my back. I want to know what's going on."

"Ashley is right," Dr. Benton says. "She needs to know what's going on. She needs to have a say in what we do. It's her body, her life. And the rest of you," he looks at Travis and me, "need to come together. Fighting each other isn't going to help Ashley."

I think if this were a movie, it would be the part where he would leave in a dramatic flourish and the scene would fade to black as we all look at each other sheepish-like. But it's not a movie, and so we stand all awkward, looking at each other until Travis finally says flatly, "I'd like to know the risks of putting insulin directly to her liver."

* * * *

It turns out there aren't a lot of risks. Since Ashley's sugar levels are so high, and she isn't reacting to the insulin well, the amount he wants to give her ain't going to plunge her anyway. He wants to start slow, just a little, and so we all decide to do it, Ashley included.

In the morning it's clear Ashley is already better. She's awake and sitting almost straight up when we arrive after breakfast. She's got the computer on her lap and is reading the message boards. It's Sunday, so no one from the church will come today, and Travis and Logan both stayed the night and have the day off today.

"You up for doing something?" I ask.

"I want to know about the clinical trial," Ashley says.

I expect an argument from Travis, but he says nothing. As I hold the folder of information, I hesitate. Opening it is like opening a bag of worms. The fragile peace we have is built on mostly denial and avoidance. But Travis sees me hesitate and he nods, so I open it and we all scoot closer to the bed where we spread out the papers.

For the first time, we sit down as a family and look over Ashley's medical records and the paperwork for the trial, and talk about it together. Ashley asks questions, and I'm surprised that I know the answers to most of them. Logan fills in where I'm blank, and Travis listens, mostly trying not to say something explosive.

About twenty minutes in I realize he is really listening. Not just listening to find something wrong, or to be in the same room and not be accused of fighting, but really listening.

People talk about light-bulb moments—that instant where suddenly everything makes sense. I ain't never had one of those until reading the process papers out loud to Logan, Ashley and Travis.

There's parts of the papers that are all jargony, full of big words and letters Logan calls acronyms. I think it must be the IRS or IRB or FBI or FDA or whatever letters are supposed to be governing it. It sure ain't written for normal folks. But there's a part of it Logan says summarizes the trial, and he wants us to read it. I don't know why he don't tell us what's in it, but he says he ain't sure what it means and he wants to see what we think.

Travis won't read it. It's like he thinks it might send him to hell just by touching it. So I take it, skimming over all the parts with the long words and coming to the section with the heading "METHOD." Logan points to the paragraph.

After withdrawing a blood sample from the patient's bone marrow, stem cells are harvested. The patient receives two weeks of drug treatment to suppress the immune system, along with antibiotics, and is kept in isolation to protect him from infection. The extracted and conditioned stem cells are then injected back into the patient.

"Well? What does it mean?" Ashley asks.

"I think," I say, suddenly understanding the significance of what Logan is trying to get across, "it means the stem cells come from you."

Ashley, who is unaware of all the hullabaloo between her dad and I, just says, "Cool. So I'm healing myself?"

Travis takes the papers out of my hands to look for himself. He flips through a couple and then comes back to the one paragraph I read. "Can they take stem cells from adults? I thought only unborn babies had them."

"No," Logan answers, as though he is some expert, which I imagine after all the hours he is spending on the computer he probably is by now. "Adults have stem cells too. Some researches have found cells in muscle, skin, the brain, eyes. Even baby teeth have them."

I think about the paper I gave Dr. Benton about the baby teeth curing a diabetic. Suddenly, I realize that is what started all of this. This trial is what Dr. Benton meant when he said it could mean something big. I started this, I think. The bad between Travis and me, the good for Ashley's future. I did all this.

"So why bone marrow?" Travis asks. "Why can't they take it from something less invasive?"

"Bone marrow is still the most hopeful because it's been proven it can be used to recreate any type of cell in the body."

"So this has nothing to do with fetal stem cells?" Travis is still hunting through the papers, afraid to find that one sentence that will kill the possibility.

"It's just her," Logan says.

Travis stares out the window for a few seconds, and I know his mind must be swirling with the same questions I have. Why haven't we heard of this before? If adult stem cells work, why are we using fetuses? But now is no time for politics. And it's Ashley who brings us back into the present.

"Dad?"

"Okay," he says. "Let's go through the papers again. Then we can look at the application."

"Cool," Ashley says.

* * * *

Her blood sugar is down to 245 by nightfall. Betsy says we can't bring it down any faster or her body will react like she's having a low, even when she's not, but we're happy for a number in the 200's. Ashley seems to be much better already, not dozing off every few minutes and breathing a bit easier, though that might be my imagination.

It's almost nine by the time Dr. Benton comes to visit again. I notice for the first time how tired he looks. Even when he smiles, the dark places under his eyes show, and he isn't quite as enthusiastic as when we first met him. I realize that all this time he's been keeping up his office back home, and traveling to Austin every morning and night to see us.

"I think we're ready," Travis tells him.

As he pulls up a chair to join us, other things seem to be weighing on his mind. "That's great," he says, but not at all enthusiastically. "I'll call Jack in the morning. I can fax your application over to him and get the process started as soon as possible."

"Fax it? Can't we give it to him when he comes in?"

"Oh, Jack's not at this hospital," Dr. Benton says surprised. "Didn't you know that? He's back at the Johns Hopkins Center for Clinical Trials in Baltimore."

"Maryland?" I asked.

"Yes. I thought you understood that. I'm sure he mentioned that at lunch. It's in the paperwork, I'm sure."

"When will he come back down to do the surgery?"

Dr. Benton looked from Travis to me, obviously a little uncomfortable. "He's not. The trials are in Baltimore. You have to travel there for the treatment."

"I get to go to Baltimore?" Ashley almost squeals. "Cool!"

"We can't take her to Baltimore," Travis counters. "She's not well enough."

"If she wasn't, we'd medevac her there, but I think she'll be fine. She's responding very well to the direct infusion of insulin, and the new corticosteroids. She should be strong enough in a week or so. There's not a starting date on the trial. It's whenever she can join."

"How long is the treatment going to take?"
"Can you take time off?"
"Will we get to ride in an airplane?"
"The insurance—"

The questions are coming fast, the practical side of this taking the upper hand over the grittier aspect of medicine, but it's Dr. Benton who cuts to the heart of it all.

"The cost of the entire treatment is covered by the trial. But you do incur the cost of all the travel. This first trip itself will be at least a month."

"First trip?" Travis says. "I thought the treatment was done all at once."

"It is. But Dr. Van Der Campen will want to do follow up visits with you, tests and such, to make sure it's working well, gauge complications, evaluate what needs to be done better during the next trial phase. Those visits are usually pretty short, but you'll have to check with him about how often you'll need to go back."

"Also, you may want to prepare for the publicity."

"Publicity?" The idea of anyone wanting to know anything about us is crazy to me.

"There's already been a bit of press about this. There always is when stem cell research is involved. It's a great unknown, and there are very opinionated people on both sides. It makes for good ratings, so it gets press time."

"But this isn't the same kind, is it? It's got nothing to do with abortions or anything, does it?" I see Travis's acceptance falling apart.

"Oh no. The stem cells will come from Ashley. But it's a new realm of medicine, and people are always interested in the possibility of new cures, as well as the idea of stem cells. There's strong emotions attached to those words. You'll find some people very enthusiastic about it, people like you who are hopeful it will be the miracle cure, and others who will be in strong opposition to it."

Logan grabs the brush off the desk and tosses it to Ashley. "You may want to use that, first, sis. Hey! I can dye your hair!"

"Not over my dead body," Travis and I both say at the same time, and we all laugh, and it feels like the family we had before the kids grew up, when we was close and liked being together.

Dr. Benton looks at the charts for the day and has Ashley test her blood once more before he goes. "Things seem to be on track here. Unless something changes drastically and the hospital calls me, I probably won't come in tomorrow to see you." Ashley puts on her best pouty face, which makes him laugh as he tousles her hair. "Don't worry. You'll soon be feeling so well that all the guys will be stopping by to see you." He says his goodbyes to us, and when he leaves it feels like something strange has happened, a passing of the torch or something.

I should feel better. The application is done. Ashley's blood sugar is down. My whole family feels like a family for the first time in a long time. But my gut tells me a war is brewing, and we ain't even seen the tip of the iceberg yet.

Chapter Twenty-One

It takes less than three days for the news to hit. Some girl up in New England is the first. She's older than Ashley, almost twenty. It's not on the major channels, but we see the local report on the Internet one night while browsing for more information on the trial. The camera crews catch her leaving a restaurant. She's wearing a red and white striped waitress uniform shirt and carrying a dirty apron. Surprised by the small crew outside, she blinks in the glare of the lights. They fire questions at her, holding out the microphone hoping to see her hang herself. She mumbles and pushes past them and leaves in a beat-up car.

Without a subject to engage, the reporter walks through the small group of people who had gathered because of the camera, and holds out the microphone to whoever wants to get his uninformed opinion on TV.

"I think using people as guinea pigs for some medical experiment is immoral!"

"Did you say stem cell treatment? Isn't that like what they did with that sheep, Dolly?"

"I think it's great they can use aborted babies. At least something good is coming out of that, you know?"

"She doesn't even look sick. I'll be she's getting big bucks to be in that trial. You know—like giving plasma or something. Only this is more dangerous. Didn't you say that? That this is dangerous?"

"I heard that, too—that it's real risky because it's never been done before. I hope she's got a lawyer in case anything goes wrong. Then she can sue the doctor if she dies."

"What idiots," Travis says.

"Do we need lawyers?" I ask.

The second report is in California. This one's on some cable news station, one of many stories all displayed at the same time, with three boxes and two scrolling news lines at the bottom. It's the medical report of the day—a two-minute update on breakthrough stem cell miracles. A boy this time, about Logan's age, being whisked into his house by his dad. The reported stands in front of a handful of protesters on the sidewalk with signs that read, "Who says your life is more important than his?" above a sonogram picture. I keep waiting for one of them reporters to say it's got nothing to do with babies, but they don't. They actually don't give much information at all. They let the crowds do most of the talking.

I don't know how the media is getting the names. The stem cell doctor said they can't give out the names of their patients, and it's clear the patients didn't want to be on TV. I'm hoping it's not a matter of time before we're in the spotlight, too.

The hives are nearly gone now, and Ashley's swelling has gone down enough that it's easy to see how much weight she's lost. They've started her back on real food again, and I worry that when we leave the hospital there will be cameras, and people will look at her and think, "She's not sick enough."

On the calendar there are two dates circled in red. One reads: Ashley goes home. The other, ten days later, reads: Ashley goes to Baltimore; starts beta cell replacement treatment. I've spent the last two days gathering up my things, which have scattered like dandelion fuzzies in a breeze. A coffee mug in the kitchen. A towel hanging in the bathroom. Magazines and books in the common room. Cosmetics in the bathroom in Ashley's hospital room.

Ashley's wearing normal clothes again. She smiles and hums and is sometimes crabby with me when I baby her. I found a new word in a book Logan left the last time he was here: buoyant. I like it. It sounds like we are floating. Which is what it feels like.

When all the days before the red circle are crossed off, I pack my car with the remains of our life here. Bags of books and DVDs, the laptop, a box of cards, and photos Ashley has helped me take down from where the Baptist ladies taped them. We stand in the room looking at the bare white walls, the room stripped of everything that had made it home the last month, and it almost seems sad. Ashley finds a card in the box from one of the kids at church, a sloppy rainbow across the front with the words, *Get Well Soon* in childish writing. Inside, it reads, "*God answers prayers.*" She holds the card to her chest for a minute and then lays it on the white pillow. I thought saying goodbye to this place would be all joy, but turns out it's a bit teary, too.

Travis has gone to drive the truck under the overhang by the front door to wait for Betsy to wheel Ashley out in a wheelchair. Not that she needs it today, but it's hospital tradition, Betsy says, so we agree to it.

Ashley looks around in that saying-goodbye kind of way and walks out to meet Betsy and the wheelchair.

The parents who live with us in the McD house are there to see us off, like I was for others before us. Several kids Ash has made friends with wave from a second story window. I've never seen so many bald children in one place, but our going seems to give them hope. I look at Ashley and think of what we've gone through, of what is ahead, and I think I didn't know hope until this moment.

I watch Ashley and Logan pile into the front seat of Travis's truck, Ashley's feet propped up on dashboard, a grin spreading from ear to ear.

"See you at home?" Travis asks, and I nod. The small crowd waves as they turn out of the parking lot and disappear down the street.

When she's gone, I return to check for anything we might have missed. The sheets are already stripped, and there's a hint of ammonia that replaces the smell of Ashley.

I drive home alone. When I walk in the door it's like the last month never happened, except the house is actually clean and there's no laundry on the sofa. Ashley's in her room, music turned up. Logan's gone. Travis is sitting in his chair in front of the TV, watching NASCAR. I sit on the couch watching with him, not talking, until car racing turns to bull riding and Logan comes home and Travis is hungry, and everything is so old normal I don't know what to do with it.

* * * *

Janise calls a little after ten. "Turn on your TV."

We turn on right as the news anchor cuts to the shot of a reporter standing in front of Children's Hospital. I recognize her as one of those local gals, the platinum blonde, face-tanned reporter whose drawl is just a bit too sugary as she reports stories that aren't sweet at all.

Logan's gone, Ashley's in bed, but Travis and I sit to watch.

"Yesterday we reported on a new treatment for diabetes— called by some a cure—that is being touted as a possible medical miracle. As is usual with many medical breakthroughs, however, there is a controversial side to the procedure. Today, we're learning that many are protesting the fact that this cure comes from one of the leading embryonic stem cell researchers, a Dutch physician named Jack Van Der Campen."

"I thought he's American," Travis says.

"He is."

"It's come to our attention also, through extensive research, that a young Texas girl is the next patient to enter this untried and very

risky treatment."

"Just because it hasn't been done in the U.S. doesn't mean it's untried," Travis growls.

I'm surprised to hear him so defensive when he himself was saying these same things not long ago. I don't get why the news, which always seems on the side of medical research, is now against it.

"Each of the patients in this trial suffer from type 1 diabetes, a disease which has no cure but is easily controlled by a drug called insulin."

"Is this lady an idiot?" Travis says.

"According to the regulations we were given to view, each patient must have some sort of complication that makes the disease difficult to control," she continues. *"It seems that even the doctors running this trial agree it would be hard to justify the type of risks these children are taking."*

"Why does she keep referring to them as children? One is twenty."

"I'd like her to sit up with her kid all night testing her sugar, worried every minute that she might end up passing out." I get up to turn off the TV, but Travis put his hand on my arm so I sit back down again.

"Can you tell us about the procedure and the likely complications?" Bob is saying.

"Certainly, Bob. Firstly, each child will undergo a very painful surgery in which their bone marrow is removed with a long needle."

The camera cuts to a series of pictures of things like needles and blood drops, in case people don't know what they look like, I suppose. Seems to me like they are trying way too hard to make something of nothing.

"While scientists take the marrow and attempt to extract stem cells from it, the child will then have their immune system destroyed by drugs similar to chemotherapy. This is where the majority of the risks are. Besides the usual dangers of surgery, completely killing the immune system leaves each of these children open to many other illnesses and infections."

The camera cuts back to too-tan girl looking very serious, like she really cares about all this. In the background, the sign-wielding morons are jumping up and down and smiling, and I get the feeling they are more interested in being on TV than making a point.

"If stem cells are found, they are cultivated in the lab to reproduce. When the immune system is rendered ineffective, the stem cells are reintroduced and stimulated to create more of the insulin producing

cells in the pancreas. *If successful, this might reverse the disease and the children might be cured. We must emphasize, though, that this has not been proven yet."*

"It has been done successfully," Travis yells at the TV. "Do your research, lady!"

At the bottom of the screen a little graphic of a fetus with one of those DNA strand things through it appears, with the streaming words, *check out our website for more information on embryonic stem cell controversies.* Just the fact that they put this alongside the story about Ashley makes my blood boil. No one will remember what this big-haired lady says. What they will get out of this is that this is about killing babies.

Behind the reporter are protesters standing out in front of the hospital waving posters that show their collective idiocy in matters of stem cell research. On TV, Bob and the blond drone on.

"We've heard a lot about stem cell research, but we rarely hear about the practical aspects of putting this research to use. Are there drawbacks with this type of therapy?"

I hate the way they do this back and forth thing, like they're sitting in a coffee shop having a conversation instead of on TV reporting.

"Most definitely, Bob. Adult stem cells have been known to mutate into the wrong type of cell, which can obviously cause some very dangerous problems, as well as the fact that they have, in the past, had a tendency to increase the risk of cancer."

"Is this true?" Travis clicks the TV off and looks at me. "I don't remember reading about cancer, or about the stem cells turning into something else other than beta cells."

"She don't know what she's talking about." I don't know this; I'm as concerned as Travis, but I am afraid this single blonde bimbo is about to derail our plans to save Ashley, and right now all I know is, cancer or not, this is the only option we have.

"Where'd she get that information?"

"Who cares? It's wrong. You know the media. They just like to blow things up. They exaggerate it to get a reaction."

He considers this and decides I'm right. "We should ask the doctor, though. About the cancer thing."

"Okay," I say. I won't ask, but I don't tell him this. I don't want to know. She dies of diabetes now, or cancer later. I'll take the later and deal with that when it comes.

* * * *

After Travis is in bed I sneak out for my cigarette and think about what the reporter said, and what everyone else is thinking. The protest signs saying we are interfering with God's design. The news that the stem cells could become something other than what the doctors intend. Could they become heart tissue or eye balls? I remember years ago hearing about some lady who had stomach pains and went in for an operation. They found she had teeth growing on her ovaries. Some cells traveled and made their home in the wrong place. Could that happen to Ashley?

I've been so worried about finding some answer, any answer, I wonder if there are some answers that are worse than no answers at all. Is it possible this cure might be worse than the disease?

And then I think of Ashley, barely strong enough to walk, sleeping all the time, not able to eat, wasting away to nothing but a skeleton in sallow skin, and I think anything is better than this life she has now.

"How far will you go?" Travis had asked me that day outside the restaurant, motioning to Dr. Van Der Campen inside munching on chips and salsa.

"As far as I need to," I said.

Right now I hope we aren't going too far. Whatever too far is.

Chapter Twenty-Two

The first time it happens I think it must be some kind of joke. Logan's friends maybe, or a rival baseball team with too much time on their hands with summer break.

I stand in the yard, trying to work it out in my head when Travis comes out to get the newspaper and sees it, too: red paint splashed all over the driveway like blood. We turn and see it spattered on the door and the siding, smears of it forming the words *baby killer,* and it hits us in the gut that this is no prank.

It's a message.

"Keep the kids inside," he says, pushing me toward the house. "I'm calling the cops."

When the two officers arrive they do a quick search and find two paint cans in the bushes near the back of the garage but nothing else. One takes out a notepad and jots down something. I recognize him from our sister Baptist church across town.

"When were you last outside before the paint appeared?"

"It didn't 'appear,'" I seethe. "Someone threw it there."

"Last night," Travis says, laying his hand on my arm. "About 10:00."

"Did you hear anything suspicious after that? During the night, maybe? Anything that woke you up?"

"No," Travis answers, then looks at me. I shake my head.

"Can you get fingerprints from the paint can or something?" Travis asks.

"Probably not, but we'll try. Most likely whoever did this doesn't have a record to have prints on file anyway."

"Why do you say that?"

He shrugs. "Just a hunch. Crimes like this aren't usually done by criminals with records. They're done by people who feel morally obligated."

"You saying this is morally right?" Travis voice is low and growly, the way he gets when he's really angry.

"I'm saying *they* think you are morally wrong. It's not about destroying property. It's about making a point." He flips his notebook closed like he's putting the matter to rest.

"So you're not doing anything?" I say.

Again he shrugs. "Not much we can do."

Travis and Logan spend the morning trying to scrub the paint off. When hose and soap don't work, they pour some toxic chemical on it and go at it with the outdoor broom. Logan don't ask where it comes from or what it means, but I figure he knows. He don't complain, neither, about giving up band practice for cleaning. When I go to the store I buy him a tub of Twizzlers and put them on his bed.

The next day our mailbox is bashed in. The policeman don't even flip open his notebook for this one. "It might not have anything to do with you. Looks like kids just playing pranks after drinking a bit too much."

"But no one else's mailbox is beat up," I point out.

"Well, it's hard to ID the bat that might've done this, so I think you're just gonna have to buy yourself a new mailbox and figure out why you think y'all are targets."

Travis and me look at each other, then back at him. He looks at us like he's waiting for us to say something, admit maybe that we are the baby killers, but Travis clamps his hand over mine and nods tersely. "Maybe you're right, Officer. Maybe it's just kids."

The cop waits a second, and seeing we ain't talking more, gets in his car and drives away.

* * * *

I Google "Jack Van Der Campen" and "embryonic stem cell" and within seconds there are over ten thousand hits. I let my eyes wander over the titles and their descriptions, but I don't click on them. Just the words in their brief summaries are enough to make me sick to my stomach. It don't take many pages to realize he's not just the face on the posters, he's the face of embryonic stem cell research. Aborted fetuses. Invitro embryos. Experiments and research and test tubes and mice. He's neck up in everything bad about stem cells, and I shut down the computer before the third page. *I don't care*, I tell myself. *This is different*. I don't let myself think about how many babies died for him to learn what he needs to make Ashley well. *It's not the same*, I say to myself.

* * * *

Turns out we'd've been better off not fixing the mailbox, 'cause hate mail starts showing up. Not the stamped kind that comes through the post office. It's the kind that's written in cut-out magazine letters and folded without envelopes. No one threatens us. At least not with bodily harm or anything. It's more along the lines of "you will burn in hell." Since it ain't God I'm scared of at this point, I tear up the letters and throw them away.

We don't call the police this time, 'cause we're pretty sure they ain't on our side. For once I wish we lived in some city up north, one of those places way outside the Bible belt with all those liberals and pro-choice democrats.

We don't tell Ashley, and it seems she don't notice. She don't leave the house much. She gabs on the phone with her friends and keeps up on the message boards with her new diabetic friends and in general keeps herself in her room. She's happy thinking life is a little normal again, so Travis and Logan and me all tiptoe around it, trying to make it that way for her.

We don't talk about it with anyone else, either. It's like if we said it happened, we'd be saying we're the ones—putting a big target on our backs or something, and so we don't. We act like it's normal to clean paint off the driveway and replace mailboxes and lightposts and windows, and fill in holes big as a grave dug in the front yard with its graphic paper headstone. We stop reporting it 'cause the police don't do nothing anyway.

There's only a few days left until we leave. Maybe when we're gone it'll all stop. I haven't seen nothing lately on the news about it, so it seems like it's just a local thing now, and I'm thinking it may just be kids, like the police said. A day passes with nothing, and then another one, and I think maybe this all will just go away.

* * * *

"Babs?" It's Janise, and I can tell from the way she says my name it ain't good. "I'm not sure you should go to church tomorrow."

"What?" I wave my hands to get Logan to turn down his video games and press one hand over my ear to hear better. "Yeah, we're going to church."

"I don't think you should," she says, louder so I can hear her plain as frogs on a summer night. I wave at Logan again, and he turns off the games, none too pleased, and sulks out.

"What's wrong?"

"There's a rumor going around. I heard it from some women in my church. I don't believe it, but people are talking."

I can't imagine what people in her church would be saying that would have to do with me and my church. I gather the remotes that are spread out around the room like they got legs and walked away. "So?"

"It's about the news story—the stem cell thing."

I catch my breath before realizing she don't know about Ashley. We haven't talked about the clinical trial and the upcoming procedure to anyone. Other than Donna Jean and Pastor Joel, I didn't think anyone even knows Ashley needs more treatment. As far as everyone else is concerned, we got Ashley's diabetes under control and now she's home.

"People just like to get riled up. You know that. They probably got the news all wrong anyway."

"I don't think so, Babs. That doctor running the trials in D.C.—he's the baby killin' guy all right."

I squeeze my eyes shut and hold a finger to my temple, warding off a sudden migraine. "What does it have to do with them, though? Why do people here care so much?"

She's quiet a second, letting the clock tick tock like a bomb in the room. "They say someone from Collier Springs is doing it."

I freeze, not wanting to hear what comes next. It comes anyway.

"Some are saying it's Ashley."

I sink into the couch and take this in. They can't say it on the news. She's a minor. Dr. Jack has promised us that they can't say anything unless we tell them it's okay. But somehow someone knows.

"Babs?"

"We ain't done nothing wrong, Janise."

"I know that, honey. I do."

"We're just trying to take care of Ashley."

"I know that."

But I don't know that she does. If the folks in town think we're part of some stem cell research for a cure, they're gonna think what they want, which is pretty much what the news tells them to think: that there's something morally wrong with using stem cells. They won't get that this is different. That Ashley ain't using someone's unwanted pregnancy to get better. That she's healing herself. Who's ever heard of that before? Who would believe it if they heard it?

She waits for me, but my jaw is clenched so hard I can't speak.

"There are some groups around town really spun up over this. They're planning some big protest this Sunday. Near your church." She waits but I say nothing. "It's summer. Everyone's bored," she rushes on, as if I need an explanation. "And it's not like it's a big town. There aren't that many sick people here." She waits again. "Babs?"

"Yes?"

When she answers her voice is quiet. "It is Ashley, isn't it? It's y'all that are going to be in this research thing, isn't it?" My silence is the only confirmation she needs. "Oh Babs."

"I should go."

"Don't go. I'm not judging you. You know I don't care so much about that stuff. I'm just surprised is all. You and Travis.... Y'all have been so outspoken about it."

I want to correct her and tell her it's only Travis that's all hung up on this, but I'm smart enough to know this don't make me look better. "It's not like what they're saying."

"Well, of course not. It never is when it's your own child. I expect I'd do the same. You know, see the other side if it would save my kid."

"You mean you'd throw in your morals, too."

"I didn't say that. I'd never say that."

I hang up without saying goodbye. Ashley stands in the hall, watching, as I throw the phone on Travis's chair. "How long you been there?"

"Are we doing something wrong, Mom?"

I reach out and pull her into a tight hug. She's nothing in my arms but elbows and ribs. "Of course not."

She pulls away and I let her.

"Morgan's mom won't let me talk to her. And some of the other girls from school won't answer when I call. Are they afraid they'll catch it?"

How does a mom answer this? There probably are a few, Morgan's mom most of all, but after talking to Janise, my guess is it's much more than fearing they'll catch diabetes. A few suggestive news reports, a few protesters with signs, and we're the enemy. We're the baby killers. And the fact is, if it took that to save Ashley, I would've done it in a heartbeat. So the fact that we're not don't make me innocent.

"Stay here," I say, grabbing my purse.

It takes less than ten minutes to drive to the church, where I park illegally in a handicapped space and march directly to the kitchen. The hospitality committee is exactly where they always are this time each week, their gossiping echoing down the halls off the sanctuary, which might as well be called the sanctimonious. I forget which SAT week that one was.

They stop the gabbing as soon as I fill the doorway.

"The devil has arrived," I say, staring them each down. Yolanda. Gloria. Brenda. Vickie. Dina. Jen. Dot. Erin. Alicia. And two dozen angel food cakes. All their kindness of the past weeks flits through my mind, but I push it out.

"Babs! What are you talking about?"

"Isn't that what y'all are saying? It *is* Ashley. She's the one on the news." Looks pass between them, but no one speaks. "Are y'all part of the protest, too? Are y'all going to be marching down Main Street holding your signs with the rest of the holy-rollers? You going to be praying at the meetings that the government steps in and stops this insanity? You going to show up at Ashley's funeral and tell us how sorry y'all are that God didn't heal her?" I look at each of them, their eyes wide and surprised. "You don't think this *is* the miracle? We prayed, and this is what God sent us. And don't you dare fool yourselves into thinking if this was your son or daughter you wouldn't do the same thing."

I leave and no one follows me. I'm crying by the time I get to the car, and I can hardly see the road on the way home. I sit in the driveway a while, trying to get control before going back inside. When I finally open the door, I see Logan sitting at his drum set in the garage, watching.

"Lord Almighty, can't a woman have a moment alone around this house?" I grab my keys and march past him, thankful he don't say anything.

* * * *

Sunday morning I lay in bed as Travis and the kids get around for church. Logan and Ashley fight for the bathroom, and Travis burns the eggs, and everything seems so normal I almost make myself believe that we could walk into church like every Sunday since Logan was two. But I know it's not, and the thought of facing all those people thinking God-knows-what makes me crawl under the covers.

I can hear the clink of silverware as the kids eat.

Travis comes in. "You getting up today or what?"

"No." I haven't told him about yesterday, about Janise's phone call, about the women at the church and the news reports.

"Come on," he says, dragging the covers off me. "You hate being late."

"Go without me."

"No. This ain't no time to be missing church."

This is exactly the time to miss church, I think, but I sit up anyway. "Go on," I say. "Go eat. I'll be there in a minute."

We're good and late getting out, and by the time we get to church the parking lot is full. A small swarm of activists are milling around in the streets in front of the church. They aren't the reporter types—more like the angry people who show up anywhere there is something to be angry about with hateful signs that say things like, "You'll burn in hell!" I think about telling them if they're so worried about hell perhaps their backsides oughta find a pew in a church somewhere on a Sunday morning rather than raising ruckus outside one.

I wonder if the group will grow when other churches begin letting out, and I don't relish facing that. I begin pulling the kids back to the car. "Let's go. We should get home."

"We can't avoid this forever," Travis says, stopping me with his hand on my shoulder.

"Are they here for us?" asks Logan.

"Cool," says Ashley, feeling more like a celebrity than a target.

Travis leads us through the stragglers, who jostle around us until someone shouts, "That's them!" Suddenly people are crowding around us.

"Are you the girl in the stem cell trial?"

"How are you feeling?"

"You don't look that sick!"

"Why are you doing this?"

"Did you know the doctor doing the treatment learned how to do this by using aborted fetuses?"

"How can you go to church and call yourselves Christians and still do this?"

I notice the lack of reporters. There's no local news crew, no ABC or CBS; I can't even find anyone that looks like a newspaper journalist. Travis pushes the flimsy posters away and makes a path that he shoves the kids through. I follow close, and I'm almost at the top of the stairs when someone yells over the din.

"Are you aware this procedure can kill your daughter?"

Travis whips around, as close to murder as I've ever seen him. "She's dying now, you miscreant."

He pushes us through the front doors and closes them behind us. The narthex is empty. An usher hands us bulletins, and we have to walk up halfway before we find enough seats for all of us.

"Miscreant?" I whisper, laughing.

"You're not the only one reading Logan's SAT book."

A few people turn to look at us, but there seems to be a concerted effort to keep eyes front. Four of Logan's buddies nod at him and he nods back, but he stays with us. Ashley's itching her stomach like crazy but she joins in the chorus, her voice high and sweet next to Logan's low throaty song. Travis puts his arm around Ashley and sings loudly and off-key, which he always says is pleasing to God 'cause if God wanted him to sing praises better he would of given him a better voice. I hold the bulletin in both hands and mouth the words. They're just words.

I go through the motions of the service, stand, sit, sing, pray, shake hands and smile, pass the offering, clap for the soloist, fill out the registration card. I do it because it's what I'm supposed to do, but my mind flits back to why we're here in the first place.

The memory of Donna Jean in the bathroom flits through my mind, and I let my eyes wander across the aisles until I see her, sitting straight as an Indian next to her very expensive and educated-looking husband. She's listening to the sermon. Not pretending, but really listening. It means something to her, something that is just out of reach to me.

Next to me is Travis, who would give up his own daughter for what he thinks God tells us about the value of life.

Last night I snuck the SAT book out of Logan's room to read while I smoked. I got stuck up on the word "elusive." The big black sky, the vastness of space, the stars flung there by a God who is bigger than all of it. A God who wants to love me, if only I'd believe. A daughter whose life hangs on the thread of possibility. One more insulin. One more steroid. One more trial. The answer's there, if only we could find it. Could there be a more heart wrenching word than elusive?

At the end of the service, Ashley begs to go see her friends, so Travis and me watch her scamper down the aisle. Most of them gather around her, but a few avoid eye contact and slip out the back door. Donna Jean comes to say hi as does Pastor Joel and baby Mary Ashley, but most people look away and busy themselves with other things. Pastor Joel presses Mary Ashley into my arms, and I feel the warmth of her tiny body against me. My chest hurts the way it did when I nursed my own, an ache to pour life into her and hold her close and keep her safe. She smells of milk and baby powder, and when I think I can't breathe anymore, I place her back in Pastor Joel's arms and rush out the back door myself.

Travis finds me on the bench in the gardens and sits without saying anything. The sky is so blue it hurts my eyes. I haven't told him about the Google hits on Dr. Van Der Campen, but now I can't keep the secret anymore and it all spills out.

His puts his arm around me, and I finally melt into him. "Are all of them right? Are we doing the wrong thing?"

He puts his lips to my head; I can feel his breath in my hair. "What's done is done, Babs." At first I think he talking about us and the clinical trial, but then I realize as he talks, he's talking about Jack. "We all make mistakes. The best we can do is learn from them and move on. And it seems like Dr. Van Der Campen has done that. He's not testing embryos anymore. And Ashley isn't getting baby cells. She's getting her own."

"Everyone thinks—"

"Everyone thinks wrong. We know. That's all that matters."

We sit in the garden, quiet together, until Donna Jean comes looking for us and tells us the crowd is getting bigger outside, and we should take Logan and Ashley and go.

We don't stay for cookies and punch and socializing. By the looks of everyone not looking at us, there wouldn't be much socializing anyway. We find Logan on the stage looking over the drum set and talking with the praise band members, and Ashley's in the basement with a few friends. We go through the basement walk-up to get to the car and manage to get almost out of the parking lot before anyone sees us.

Chapter Twenty-Three

"There's an article you should read this morning," Travis says, downing his orange juice before heading out to work.

"I ain't got time to read some NASCAR update," I say, punching cereal carbs into a calculator. "You can't have this," I tell Ashley, handing her back the box to put away. Dr. Benton told us no more than fifteen carbs a meal, less if we can do it. The insulin pumped through Max into the umbilical vein is only partly successful, and the last two days I've watched her sugars start to go back up.

"That's okay. I'd rather have bacon."

"We don't got that. Your dad can't eat it."

"How 'bout a hot dog?"

"Fine." I stick a hot dog in the microwave, not caring that it's not exactly a breakfast food. It's protein. It's three carbs. It works.

"It's not NASCAR," Travis says, tossing the paper across the counter. "It's the trial."

"Is it about me?" Ashley grabs at it, eager to see her name in print which, if it's up to us, will be never.

"Eat your breakfast," I say, shoving the hot dog with no bun at her and taking the paper.

"I gotta go." Travis leans over and pecks my cheek, a new habit that's growing on me, and leaves. I sit on the stool at the counter and open the paper. On page two, there's a picture of Dr. Van Der Campen and a short article about the trial, although as I read I figure out it's more about him than anything.

As I read the first paragraph, I worry I'll see all those things from the Internet about him, and I don't want Ashley thinking we could be sleeping with the devil here. As far as she knows, Dr. Benton found him for us, and that alone made him all right in my eyes. But as I skim the article, it's not just about his embryonic research, and I realize how little I know about him as a person and a doctor.

I scan over his credentials. They're a long list of ivy-league sounding names, some of which are overseas, and research grants he's been given. The article explains a little about the trial in the Netherlands, although it fails to tell about how each of the patients is fairing and mostly emphasizes the fact that he did it there 'cause the U.S. wasn't too keen on letting him do it here.

It all seems very unimportant and I'm beginning to wonder why Travis thought I'd be interested when the last paragraph gets me in the gut. I reread it, wondering what significance it might have. Medically, it means nothing. Personally, it changes everything. Despite the way the doctor hardly talks to us and comes off like he's thinking of himself better than us, I suddenly feel kinship with him.

"What is it, Mom?" Ashley is peering over my shoulder, and I consider hiding the article but then decide she might as well know.

She takes the paper and reads the article half out loud, mumbling through parts she finds boring, but getting clearer towards the end as she reads his personal info.

"Van Der Campen was once married with a daughter of his own, when, at age three, his daughter developed type 1 diabetes." She stops and looks at me.

"Go on," I say.

She reads more. "Struck with a complication called hypoglycemic unawareness, his daughter fell into a coma at the age of eleven when her blood sugar plunged, and she died before rescue workers could revive her." Her eyes grow wide. "Oh mom, his little girl died!"

I don't know if she knows what hypoglycemic unawareness is. I remember seeing it on one of the message boards, but I can't pinpoint what it is. Something about high or low blood sugars.

"His wife, also a diabetic, unable to cope with the guilt of passing on the genetic DNA that caused her daughter's diabetes, and ultimately her death, killed herself less than a year later," she continues. "These events spurred Van Der Campen to finding a cure, driving him out of the United States and to another country where he could test his theories, and then back home, in hopes of saving even one family the tragedy that has haunted his own."

Ashley holds the paper a minute, staring at the words before putting it down. I lay my hand on her shoulder, but she brushes it off and leaves the room without another word.

* * * *

The great thing about the hospital was that, when we were there, there's nothing else but Ashley and getting well. Back home, the rest of life waits for us.

After our less-than-inspirational Sunday at church, Monday brings one more thing I'd like to avoid: the county school board.

We missed the end of the month meeting while Ashley was in the hospital, but they've made a special session just for us. The meeting room is small and ugly, too-bright fluorescent lights covering the ceiling and a long, fake wood table that the board members sit behind and try to look important.

I have no idea what to expect, other than a battle, so I'm armed with a folder full of Ashley's school records: her straight-A report card and her student-of-the-month certificates and the bumper stickers we get year after year for her outstanding behavior. I have her medical records from the past few months and the 504 that Travis and I never filled out since she never went back to school.

Turns out I don't need none of them though, 'cause one of the board members holds out a letter from her principal saying she believed the "incident" with Ashley was merely a lack of information on our parts, and that it would be a shame for Ashley to be penalized for something that clearly was not a risk to others. Also, there's the note we sent to the nurse that day, who was out of town and didn't get it in time. She sent in a letter of apology for the mix up.

"Technically," a stodgy-looking man with a bushy mustache says, "we could expel her. Zero tolerance means we don't give exceptions to ignorance." I bite my tongue so I don't say nothing to get us more in trouble and wait for him to finish.

"Clearly, though," a girthy woman with big hair says, "it wouldn't serve either the school or Ashley well to expel her."

I wait.

"Should we vote?" asks the mustache man. "All in favor of dismissing the case against Ashley Babcock, say aye." All five member say aye. "So dismissed," he says. I expect him to bang a gavel or something, but he merely shoves the papers off to the side and opens a new folder.

"Now let's deal with the case against Logan Babcock." The others shuffle their papers, too.

My evidence in favor of Logan is much thinner. He don't have the stellar grades Ashley's got, nor the certificates for behavior. Ashley's case I was mad about. Logan's I'm worried about.

"We have some witnesses, I believe?" girthy woman says, motioning to a woman I hadn't noticed in the back of the room. She nods and opens the door. Three people enter. One is the baseball coach, one is the principal, and the other is a teacher, I think.

The principal begins by explaining the charges against Logan, emphasizing what she calls "the disparity between his grades and his test scores." She's brought his report cards and the standardized test scores and places them on the table in front of the board members like she's some lawyer laying out evidence for her case.

"This is not the first time Mr. Babcock has been in trouble with this school, either," she adds. "He has shown a pattern of disrespect for both the school system and authority and is considered by almost all of the administration and staff as rebellious."

"How so?" I charge.

"Yes," says a tiny lady behind the table. "How so?"

"For one, his clothes and hair. Even though he has received multiple warnings, and I have spoken to Mrs. Babcock here about it several times, he continues to wear his hair in a Mohawk and dye it neon colors. It's extremely distracting to the other students and to the staff members."

The teacher I don't know, who is sitting in the chairs behinds me, clears his throat. "I haven't found it to be at all distracting," he says.

"And it's not against the dress code," I add. "If it were against the dress code, I'd make him change it, but it's not."

"Yes, well..." says mustache man. "If he isn't breaking any rules, we can't exactly take that into consideration in this case."

"But it goes to show his overall attitude towards the school system," Mrs. Gianuzzi says, pulling herself up to her full 5'3" height.

"But this isn't about his attitude towards school or authority," the tiny lady says. "It's about one particular incident, with one particular test. Do you have proof that Logan took this test, and that he used it to cheat?"

The principal starts explaining how she found the test, and how she knows it's Logan's locker, and how she then went to examine his test scores and that the scores shows he clearly cheated in some way. The board members listen with no expression on their faces. My stomach is churning.

"Can I add something," the teacher behind me says, standing up. I've got a sinking feeling like my stomach has dropped into my toes. The mustache man, who I now gather is the head person here, motions him forward.

"It's true that Logan is not the best student. He doesn't always turn in his homework, and he doodles a lot in class instead of taking notes." He looks sideways at me and smiles. "But he is, as a person, an outstanding individual, and smart as they come. He's probably the smartest kid I've ever taught."

I'm sure my jaw is dropping. I clamp my teeth together to make sure I don't look surprised that someone is complimenting my son.

"What do you teach?" asks the girthy lady.

"Science. Chemistry and physics. Logan was in my chemistry class this year. He didn't make A's because he didn't do the homework all the time, but I'll tell you, he never missed one question on a test. Not one. And I can't say that about anyone else in class. He didn't need a cheat sheet to pass that standardized test. He could have done it with his eyes closed."

Mrs. Gianuzzi starts to say something, but the man raises his hand to her and she stops. "Dave, do you have something to add?" He looks past me at the baseball coach, who comes forward as well. I think about the fight Logan got into in the locker room and figure this whole deal is now done. Alternative school, here we come.

But Dave don't say anything about the fight. Instead, he tells about his relationship with Logan over the past three years; how he found him on the middle school baseball team and saw such great talent, and how he feels like Logan is his second son, and how Logan has better sportsmanship than any kid he's taught. "He would never, ever cheat," he finishes. "It goes against everything he is."

There are other things being said, but I miss them for a minute because I'm thinking about Dave's comments. His complete and unswerving faith in Logan and his honesty. Can I even say that about myself? Did I know these things about Logan, his sportsmanship and dedication and ability to ace tests without ever studying for them?

"Mrs. Babcock?" I look up and realize the tiny lady is speaking to me.

"Yes?"

"Do you have anything to add?"

I tell my children to tell the truth, no matter what. But I know Logan hid that test in his locker, and I don't know what they will think if I admit that, even with the fact that Logan didn't use it, even if it wasn't even the test they gave his class. I look from Dave to the chemistry teacher and wonder how strangers can have more faith in my son than me.

"He's a good kid," I say, and I mean it. My entire being fills with admiration and love for this kid I've never quite known what to do with. And suddenly I know. I fight for him.

And I do. And everything the principal throws at me I argue with, and every question the board asks, I answer with passion. I've spent the last few months pouring out my energy on Ashley. Logan is every bit as deserving.

Before they rule, they kick the others out and ask me a few private questions, about Ashley and the time Logan spent away from school and how he's handling this crisis in the house, and I realize he's the glue holding our family together, and I tell them this. They excuse me for a few minutes to talk amongst themselves, and when they bring me back in, they take a vote and unanimously choose to dismiss his case as well.

I don't know if it's a pity vote, but I'm willing to take that over expulsion any day. I thank them and leave before they can change their minds.

* * * *

When Logan gets home from the music store, he stands around the kitchen pretending he's looking for food when I know what he wants is the result.

I hand him a tub of rocky road ice cream and a spoon. "You kicked butt," I say.

"I'm off the hook?"

"Yeah." I turn my back on him to wash off the lunch dishes, and he throws his arms around me.

"Thanks."

I can feel the relief flooding from him and can't believe I didn't notice that he was actually worried about this.

"I didn't do anything," I say, patting his arm and leaving soapy bubbles on him. "You pretty much speak for yourself."

He squeezes me a smidge and leaves the room humming. The feeling in the house is different now, subtle shiftings of the space between us, and I vow that I will never again be the least of his supporters in a room.

* * * *

Wednesday evening I drop Ashley off at youth group and Logan off at band practice. Before I can get out of the parking lot, Brenda comes running down the stairs waving at me. I sigh and roll the window down.

"Can I get in?"

I unlock the doors, and she climbs in the passenger side. "You need a ride?" I ask.

"No. I just want to talk. We ain't talked since you got home. How are things?"

I study her face, trying to figure out why she's here. "You need your casserole dish? I can bring it by tomorrow if you need it."

"I don't need it. I just want to know how you are."

"We're fine."

She fiddles with her purse, latching and unlatching the clasp, and I want to tell her to just get out and go on home. I got my own share of things to do and no time for this.

"I heard about the hate mail."

I raise my eyebrows at her 'cause I ain't told no one.

"Ashley told Savannah and Savannah told Joe and Joe told me."

It's our own church version of telephone. I want to tell her it didn't work this time: the info is wrong. But since it's not, I keep quiet, wondering how Ashley found out.

"I don't know what you think about us, Babs, but you're wrong. We're not against you."

"Did you see us at church Sunday?" I ask. "You'd have thought we had leprosy. Hardly anyone looked at us. Do you really want to get into this?"

She stops playing with the purse and lays her hands in her lap. "I'm not the enemy here."

"I got so many enemies, Brenda, I can't keep them all straight. I got people bashing in our mailbox every other day, and throwing rocks through windows and digging fake graves in the front yard, but the only enemy I care about is the one killin' Ashley."

She looks surprised. "I thought Ashley was doing so much better. I looked up diabetes, and I thought people could live a long time with it. Like arthritis or something."

She takes me a little off guard here. It strikes me as so out of place that she would look it up. I don't know whether to be suspicious or thankful. I size her up and decide I'm either gonna spend my time fighting people's perceptions or fighting for Ashley. I ain't got the energy for both.

"She's not well," I say, and suddenly tears are rushing to my eyes, but I'm not going to cry here in this car with this overbearing lady. I blink them back and grit my teeth while I take in her astonished look. She reaches out for my hand and squeezes it, tears springing to her own eyes suddenly. I stop my jaw clenching and let out a long sigh. "She's really sick, actually."

"She don't look that sick," she says, not letting go of my hand. It's not an accusation but an observation that I admit is pretty true. "I seen her in the hospital, and she looks real good now."

"What do you know about diabetes?" I ask.

"She's not making insulin, and so she has to take shots of it. It's got something to do with eating, right?"

I think of the long days in the hospital, the nurses and the nutritionists and all the medical pamphlets I pored over, and here Brenda pretty much sums it all up in two sentences.

"That's pretty much it. Except, on top of that, she can't take insulin either. She's allergic to it."

I see the information registering on her face, the confusion and then the dawning of what that means. "So she can't eat? 'Cause she can't take the insulin?"

It means so much more than this. At this point, eating is not the biggest of our worries. Whether Ashley eats or not, her blood sugar is going up, but this seems unimportant to explain. It's enough for Brenda that Ashley can't eat. In fact, for Brenda, this is probably the most awful thing that could happen.

"So what are you going to do?"

And there it is. The question everyone wants to know. Are we the stem cell family? Months ago I didn't like Brenda much. She wears too much lipstick, and it always sticks to her front teeth. She has damp patches on her shirt under her armpits, and she smells of too much perfume. She is loud and almost always happy. For some reason this really bugs me.

But here she is, in my car, asking about Ashley. What stands out to me above all these other things is how many times she drove down to Austin to be with us. How many meals she cooked for Travis and Logan, and I wonder how many suppers she missed with her own family 'cause she was ministering to mine. And it all spills out. The days watching Ashley waste away to practically nothing. The hours and hours on websites looking for something that would take the place of the insulin that isn't working. The desperation that there is nothing left, no stone unturned. And then Jack Van Der Campen. And possibility.

"It's not what everyone thinks," I say, maybe a little too defensively. "It don't have anything to do with babies. There aren't any abortions or anything involved. It's a whole other kind of stem cell thing."

She takes in everything I say, real quiet and not talking. Not even asking questions. When I finish, she just nods. "What do you think of Jack Van Der Campen?"

"Well, he ain't the devil like everyone wants to think." She don't say nothing so I keep going. "He's good folk, Brenda. Not what the papers say about him and what the protestors make him out to be. He's like all the rest of us, trying to do the best with what life gives us." I think about the newspaper article and his wife and kid. "If he made some mistakes in the past, he did it with a good heart." I stare at my own hands in my lap. "This is our last chance, Brenda. He's our last hope."

The quiet is so loud I can hear it. I almost stop breathing, waiting to see if I'd gone too far, but when she finally meets my eyes there's only good stuff there. "You think he likes cookies? I make a mean chocolate chip I could send with you when you go."

* * * *

When I get home the house is empty and there ain't no signs of meanness. No paint or shattered glass. No letters in the mailbox.

I don't fool myself in believin' that now the church will be behind us all the way. I figure it's a little like everything else in life: there will be some on both sides of the divide. I count the people for us: Logan and Travis, by far the two most important, and not necessarily the easiest to get; Dr. Benton, whose experience and expertise make his support a hundred times more significant than any cowardly bullies; Pastor Joel and his wife, who gave us not a moment of wavering, even though they mighta felt it at home; Janise, who would stand behind me no matter what; and now Donna Jean and Brenda, two women I barely spoke to before this mess. All in all, it's a pretty good list.

As I start to fix us dinner, I find myself humming.

Chapter Twenty-Four

"Can we go to the beach?" Ashley's been staring out the window for a good minute or more before she drops this bomb at the dinner table.

Everyone's finally home and we're picking over chicken, along with the green beans and tomatoes Janise brought from her garden. Thank goodness salt isn't off the menu yet.

"Why?" Travis asks, reaching for the Tabasco.

"I just want to. It's been a long time since we've gone."

"The youth group went last summer," I say.

"Yeah, but that wasn't the family."

"You want to go with the family?" Logan asks, his mouth full of tomatoes. "Why?" I kick him under the table.

"I just want to." She pushes the food around the plate but don't eat anything.

"You need to eat, Ash. You took insulin already. You'll go low if you don't."

She wrinkles her nose. "I don't see that happening, Mom."

She's probably right. Her sugars are eeking up again, and it's been hard to keep it under a hundred, even without eating.

"How about we plan to go when we get back from Baltimore?" Travis suggests.

"I want to go now. Before we leave."

"Why?" Travis asks again.

"Because," she says stubbornly.

"Because she's afraid she's not coming back," Logan says, tomato juice dripping down his chin.

We all freeze, forks in the air, not believing what Logan just said.

"What? It's true, isn't it?" He looks at Ashley, who scoots out her chair and runs out of the room.

"What?" Logan says, looking at Travis and me. "We all know that's why. We can't say it?"

I give him my best look of disgust and leave him to Travis, who is giving him an earful as I make my way to Ashley's room.

I knock on the door and walk in when she don't answer. "Ash?" She's sprawled out across her bed, her headphones plugging her ears and her eyes closed. I tap her and she don't move. I take the earphones out. "Ashley?" Finally, she looks up. I sit next to her. She rolls over and stares at the ceiling.

"It's true. If that's what you want to know. Logan's right."

"Jeez, Ashley, you think if this thing don't work we're going to leave you there?"

"No. I think if it doesn't work, I'm going to die."

"Don't be melodramatic," I say, sounding much more confident than I feel. It's not that I don't want to admit it's possible. I don't want *her* to admit it's possible. Every motherly instinct is telling me to lie, lie, lie.

"I know what's going on, Mom. I've been sick, not dumb. I don't make insulin. I can't take insulin. It's pretty simple."

I think how casually she tosses out the word insulin, like everyone knows what it is and does, like she's saying *I got a heart and it don't beat.*

"So going to Corpus Christi and watching the oil refineries belch their smoke over the gulf is your dying wish?" Even she can't resist smiling at this.

"Yeah. Camping at the beach. Just like we used to."

I stand to go. "I'll see what I can do."

Travis isn't too thrilled with this idea. "What happens if she gets sicker when we're out there?"

"We bring her home."

"It's so dirty. Maybe we should stay in a hotel."

"She has diabetes. A little dirt isn't going to raise her blood sugar."

"What do we eat?"

"I can cook chicken and green beans just as well over a campfire."

"How will she go swimming with the pump?"

"I don't know. Maybe we don't go swimming. Maybe we just walk on the shore with our feet in the water."

"I don't know where the camping stuff is."

"It's in the garage." This is Logan, who's come into the kitchen to grab a handful of cookies now that Ashley is gone. "So we're going?"

I look at Travis, who looks back at me and shrugs. "I guess we are."

* * * *

We're all actually excited as we pile in the truck the next morning.

I've banned the I-Pods and the cell phones in the spirit of making this a family trip. Ashley's blood sugar continues to rise, and the itching's getting worse, but she's insistent and our plane trip to Baltimore is still a few days off. She could itch at home or on the road, so we throw in the tent and the sleeping bags and the camp stove and take off.

"Can we at least listen to music on the CD player?" asks Ashley, not even fifteen minutes from home.

"And not that country junk you guys like, either," Logan pipes in.

I shuffle through the stack Travis keeps in the glove compartment and pull out the only non-country one he has. It's 50s and 60s music, and the kids groan, but when I turn it off they yell to put it back on, so I do.

It's fun music, and we find ourselves singing along enthusiastically, mostly out of tune, and laughing over the goofy lyrics. When *Wonderful World* comes on we all sing louder, the windows of the truck down and the hot wind blowing away the cares weighing down on us the last weeks. For a few moments, it's as if none of this has happened and we're all back to the way we used to be, years ago, before the hospital and before adolescence, before money troubles and time wore us down.

Travis takes my hand as he sings.

I used to love this song because it felt like my life. It's really just a litany of things I don't know nothing about. Me and Louie Armstrong—neither one of us knew about biology or science or French. But we had love. I liked that all that mattered was love.

I danced around the kitchen singing this song with the kids when they were little. It seemed funny then. A tenth grade education don't seem too bad when your kids can barely speak and they only need to learn colors and shapes and letters, and love is the thing they need the most. But pretty soon it's algebra and dissecting frogs and Spanish and curing major diseases, and love's just not enough.

I let the others' voices carry the song, and I watch the flat ground turn into rolling hills and the clouds gather on the horizon. I ignore the signs that say the next rest stop is 110 miles away and that civilization's behind us, and we are heading further out to where there is nothing if we should have trouble.

* * * *

We set up the tent without making too big of fools of ourselves and decide to go walk along the shore before the sun goes down. Ashley lingers behind us, searching for shells and pretending that she isn't so tired she wants to lay down in the sand and sleep. Logan pretends to be searching for stones to skip, but I see him slipping shells into the bucket Ashley sets down every now and then. We are all pretending this is something it isn't, which is Ashley's version of a "make a wish foundation" request.

At the campsite I cook chicken over the stove, but Ashley picks at it and excuses herself to go to bed. When I go in the tent, she's already half-asleep.

"Did you test?"

"No."

"You gotta test, Ash. You can't just go to bed without knowing what your blood sugar is."

"Why?"

"Why? Why?" I can't bring myself to say why. "Because you have to, that's all."

"It's high, Mom. And more insulin isn't going to help that, so why bother?" She rolls over and closes her eyes.

I hunt through the duffle bag and find the meter. "Give me your hand." She does, begrudgingly. I prick and panic when the number comes up over 550. "Good mother of Moses, Ashley. It's 558."

"Toldja," she says, and tucks her hand back under her.

"Don't go to sleep. Don't you dare go to sleep." I pull her shoulders up so she's slumped upright like a rag doll. "Travis! Travis!" I yell, sure everyone in the campsite can hear us. In a split second he's at the tent flap. One look at Ashley, and he's running to the truck.

"I'm calling Dr. Benton. Logan, put out the camp stove and roll up the sleeping bags and throw everything in the back."

Other campers come over and ask what's wrong and offer to help. In less than ten minutes we have everything in a heap in the bed of the truck and are on our way to the hospital. Dr. Benton tells us to meet him there and to keep Ashley awake and make sure she is drinking water.

This is, I'm sure, the longest three hours of my life. There's no music on the way home. No fun banter, no jokes. I sit in the back with Ashley and try to keep her from falling into a coma.

* * * *

When we arrive at the hospital, a small entourage is waiting. They hook her up to IVs again, and Dr. Benton changes the insulin brand, hoping that'll buy us a little time. He pumps her full of steroids again and we wait.

"How could we be so stupid?" Travis mumbles.

"It would've happened no matter where we were," I justify.

"But if we'd been home, we'd have been three hours closer."

"It doesn't matter now," Dr. Benton says. "She's here. And we need to get her to Baltimore as soon as possible."

Suddenly, Janise is here, hugging me and telling Travis and Logan to go home and finish the packing we started, that she'll stay with me. I don't even ask how she knows we're here; I'm so relieved to see her. It's 2:00 in the morning by the time it quiets down. Janise works the phone and pretty soon has us a new flight out and calls Donna Jean to have her take us to the airport in the morning. Dr. Benton comes in at 5:00 to tell us Dr. Van Der Campen is expecting us and will meet us there.

The new insulin, or steroids, or the IV works, and Ashley is back down in the 200s by the time Donna Jean arrives. Her arms and legs are covered with wheels, the circly, hivy things that come from the allergy, and Travis brings her a light, long sleeved shirt and a long skirt to cover them. It won't be good to have people on the plane worried about her being contagious.

Dr. Benton gives each of us a hug as we leave; the sun is barely up. "Will you be there, too?" I ask.

He shakes his head. "This is Dr. Van Der Campen's baby. I have a job here. But I'll call, okay? You're in great hands."

Janise also hugs us goodbye. "I'll pray for y'all."

"I don't know what I'd do without you," I say.

"Go," she says.

I climb in Donna Jean's Suburban next to Ashley and wave through the window. As she drives away, I think this is not the way I intended on leaving.

Chapter Twenty-Five

None of us has ever been on a plane before. Heck, a trip to San Antonio is as exotic as we ever got. Washington D.C., well, that seems all the way on the other side of the world. We talk about seeing the sights, the monuments and the museums and getting a look at where the President lives. But we all know we ain't gonna see any of that stuff on this trip. If it goes well, we'll be back. We'll be back, and Ashley will be well. We don't think about what it means if we don't go back.

Travis packed what he could find and figured anything else we could buy there, or Travis can bring on one of his back and forths.

Austin's a small airport, and Donna Jean finds a space right near the door. Travis hunts down a cart, and Donna Jean finds a wheel chair. Besides this latest battle with insulin, Ashley's been getting shots every day; something called filgrastin, to make her produce more blood for the bone marrow surgery, and she's complaining that they make her muscles and head hurt. This is in addition to a concoction of drugs called prednisone and azathrioprine, which are suppose to keep her immune system from attacking the few good beta cells she's got left. I'm afraid if someone lights a flame too close to her she might blow up. Surely that amount of drugs can't be good for a person.

We check in without any problems, and when we roll Ashley up to the gate they allow us to board early. We settle her in at a window and check her sugar to make sure it's stabilizing. She drifts off before anyone else even boards the plane.

I sit in the middle seat next to her, Travis and Logan across the aisle, and I feel nervous and anxious and not at all the way I thought I'd feel when I got to this point. This is not how I imagined it would be.

"Is everything okay?" A flight attendant is standing next to me, watching me twist a rubber band furiously around my fingers.

"I forgot something," I say, surprising myself. I can hardly breathe. I feel like I'm suffocating. "Can I get off for a minute?"

She nods and tells me to make sure I bring my boarding pass with me. I'm down the aisle and off the plane, running for the security, through the gates and out the front door into the stifling August heat.

"Donna Jean! Donna Jean!" I'm bent over out of breath by the time I get to her, my chest ready to split in two. "Wait, Donna Jean!"

"Babs, what's wrong?" There is nothing on her face but utter concern. I'm now sobbing, the ugly snotty kind with the gasping, I'm-dying-kind of breathing 'cause I ain't run that fast since I was nine and Bobby Garson hid in the cemetery and made ghost noises at me on Halloween.

"What if..." I'm wheezing. "What if... what if it doesn't work?"

She throws her arms around me, a completely uncomfortable gesture for me, except I find myself hugging her back. I expect her to comfort me. To say what I need to hear: that Ashley will be fine. That in a year we'll look back on this and wonder why we didn't have faith, and marvel at the miracle of medicine and answered prayers. But she don't say any of this.

"Then you have a whole church of people waiting to help you get through it."

It's not the answer I want. It's so much not the answer I want that I pull back like I been slapped.

"I can't tell you it's not possible, Babs." She took my hands. "But I do believe she'll get better. I think this is the answer you all have been looking for. And," she gives me another hug and whispers in my ear, "I hope you personally find the answer you are looking for there, too."

She waves as she drives away, and I realize the plane is going to take off without me. I think about what she said as I'm running back through the airport. What is it I'm looking for? Ashley to get better. That's all. That's all I want.

The last of the passengers are stowing their luggage in the overhead when I squeeze past them and find my seat again next to Ashley. Travis looks over and wrinkles his eyebrows at me. "Where'd you go?"

"I wanted to grab some food." I'm sure my eyes are puffy.

"Where is it?"

"Where is what?"

"The food."

"Oh. I guess I forgot it." Before he can ask, the flight attendants shut the door and the plane starts rolling backwards. I make a big deal of finding the emergency pamphlet and following along with the flight attendant as she shows us how to buckle seat belts and how to put on air masks. I look around for the exit near me and avoid Travis's questioning eyes. I wake Ashley as the plane starts gaining speed and point out the window. She's always wanted to fly, and I don't want her to miss it.

As the plane lifts off the ground, she's all lit up. "There's Town Lake! There's the hospital! Look how small the cars are!" Even Logan, who usually puts up a good show of looking bored, is nose-pressed to the window. When we're high enough that the clouds cover most of the view, they both settle back in their seats. Logan puts on earphones and thumbs through a magazine. Ashley falls silent, but she don't sleep. She continues to stare out the window, across the featureless sky all milky white.

"Are you excited?"

"Hmm." I don't know if this means she's too tired to talk or just don't feel like it. Is it being twelve, or having diabetes?

"Is the plane what you thought it would be like?"

"Sorta. It looks like it does in movies, only maybe with less space. It doesn't feel like we're flying though. It feels the same as driving."

I loosen my seat belt and try to figure how to tilt the seat back. "What did you think it would feel like? Floating?"

She shrugs but blushes a bit. "Maybe."

I find the button to recline the seat but it does nothing. The guy in front of me leans his back so far the seat is less than a foot from my nose and the tray pops out. Ashley giggles, which is the first time I've heard this in a while, and I forgive the man.

"What about the surgery? We haven't talked much about it since we made the decision to do it. You still think this is the right thing?"

"It's a little late to change my mind now. We're on a plane."

I stop fooling with the seat. I take her hands and hold them in mine. "It's not too late. It's not too late until they inject all the drugs into you. If you ever decide you don't want to do it, you say, and we'll go home."

"And do what, Mama?"

"Find something else. We'll find you something else. Some other drug we haven't found. Some other clinical trial that's less risky."

She slips her hands out of mine and tucks them in the blanket over her legs, turning back to the window rather than face me.

"You don't have to do this, Ash. Have you changed your mind?" There's a small part of me that hopes she has. I know that doing nothing is worse than doing something, but to actually choose to do something that could make this nightmare worse...

"I do." She is so quiet I have to lean in to hear her over the noise of the airplane. "I have to do this or I'll die."

Kids are supposed to think they're immortal. That's what the news tells us. That's why they do stupid skateboard tricks off roofs and drag race through town at two in the morning. They think they can't die. And so adults go around trying to pound into them that they're mortal, that they can die. And right now I wonder why. Because all I want at this moment is for Ashley to think she can't die.

* * * *

Our plane flies all the way to the Atlantic and then loops around to land. We come in over the monuments, and Logan moves to our side to point out the Washington Monument and the Capital Building. "Which one is that?" Ashley asks, pointing to a large square building by a long rectangular pool of water.

"The Lincoln, I think," Logan answers and looks at me, but I shrug 'cause I got no clue which is which. "It's the Lincoln or the Jefferson. I can't remember which is the square and which is the round one."

We fly so low over the river I'm afraid we're gonna put down in water, but we land smoothly in Virginia, hardly any bumps at all. We let everyone gather up their stuff and leave before us.

The airline has a wheelchair at the door, and Ashley don't fight it the way she usually does. Dr. Jack meets us at the baggage claim to take us to the hotel near the clinic. The first thing I notice when we leave is that D.C. is just as hot as Texas in August, and the air is so thick I could serve it up with jelly on toast.

Dr. Jack don't talk much about the coming days on the drive. He points out places of interest—the Pentagon, Arlington Cemetery, the Potomac. He asks about our trip, and how we've done with the press. He says he's gotten requests from Good Morning America, The Today Show, and Dateline to do interviews and to follow the stories of a few of the participants.

"I'm trying to get the real information out there about this. It's not as though this kind of stem cell therapy hasn't been used before. We've cured spinal cord injuries, leukemia, even Parkinson's disease. Yet I'm shocked how many people have no idea what it is. Have you ever been to a lacrosse game? We're suppose to have a winning team this year."

I'm worried about the press. I've had enough attention to last me a lifetime. Back home, even if people could understand, they'd never get past him. Him and his past involvement with embryos. I look at him as he talks so casually and wonder if he changed his mind about embryos because he thought it was wrong to test on babies, or because it just wasn't very productive. It's not the stem cell trial that's the lightening rod, I think. It's him.

Up to now I just been seeing him as the doctor, but suddenly I see him as a person like all of us. A mixed-up past full of mistakes and a second chance to make it better. Just because he turned away from those mistakes don't make it wrong to use the lessons he learned.

He don't mention the article about his daughter, or the personal attacks on him. Some parts of our past, I suppose, we got to put a little further behind us than others.

The rest of the trip, Travis and Dr. Jack banter about sports while the rest of us stare out the windows. I can't believe how many trees there are, and how tall they all are. Everything around us is a haze of green. The roads wind up and down over hills, around curves, until I think I might throw up.

At the hotel Dr. Jack helps us haul our luggage in and tells us he'll be back in the morning for Ashley. "The rest of your life starts tomorrow."

Chapter Twenty-Six

After Travis is asleep, I slip out and down to the pool. Logan's there, waiting. I shouldn't be surprised, but there's hardly a thing Logan does that don't surprise me. He's sitting in one of the plastic chairs drinking a Dr. Pepper and bathed in the translucent green light of the pool. He smiles when he sees me and pulls a chair from the table for me.

"I thought you'd be here."

I hold my hands up to him, empty. "I didn't bring cigarettes."

He holds out his hand, one with the Dr. Pepper and one with a small package wrapped in paper. "Neither did I."

I sit down and take the package from him. "What's this?"

"Open it." He takes a swig of his drink and leans back in his chair, head tilted back to the sky.

Inside the wrapping paper is a book. "1000 Most Important Words," by Norman Schur. "What's this?"

"I figured you were about done with my SAT book, and I thought it might be time to move on to something more fun."

Knock me over with a feather duster. "How long you known?"

"Since you stopped looking at me crazy when I used big words on you. I figured you were getting them from somewhere. It just took a while to find out where." He takes the book out of my hands and opens it to a random page. "See? This one's much more interesting. It gives you definitions and contexts, so you know how they're used in everyday language. And it tells you where the word is from—you know, Latin or Greek or whatever—and what the parts of the words mean so it's easier to remember them and figure out new ones." He smiles smug-like and hands it back to me. "You'll blow away every educated person in Texas with a vocabulary from this."

I flip through it, giddy that I actually know some of the words already. When I put it on my lap, Logan's already staring into the starry sky again.

"Why do you pretend so hard you're a rebel?"

"Why do you pretend so hard you're dumb?"

The problem with Logan is that whenever he's being smart-mouthed, he's more smart than mouthy.

"I don't pretend."

"And I'm not a rebel."

I think this would be the perfect time to take a drag, but I've got nothing to smoke. "Jiminy, I wish I'd brought the cigarettes."

"Why didn't you?"

I reach over and take his can and swallow half in one swill. "I don't know. I guess it seemed the right time to quit."

The truth is, how could I possibly keep slowly killing myself by smoking when we're trying so desperately to keep Ashley alive? If there were one thing I could have done in the past to save Ashley, I'd have done it in a heartbeat to keep this from happening. I don't want someone else to be thinking the same thing someday while I'm lying in some hospital bed hooked up to some iron lung, or whatever they do to you when you have lung cancer and can't breathe no more on your own.

"I should get back or your dad will wake up and wonder where I went."

"Mom?"

"Yeah?" Logan looks like he's going to ask something. He stares hard at me for a minute, then his eyes dart away like he just can't get it out.

"Good night."

"Good night." I'm relieved he don't ask, because I feel in my gut it's not a question I want to answer.

* * * *

In the morning Dr. Jack comes to pick us up in a rental car that he says is now ours for the next week, thanks to an anonymous donor. None of us talk much on the drive over. It's not a long way, but there are a million lights and every one of them seems to be red. My stomach feels like it's being tossed around by a wave. From the looks of the rest of the family, they feel it too.

Baltimore's a big city. The buildings are crammed together, and the streets are crowded as we wind our way through them. The building we arrive at, which Dr. Jack says is not technically a hospital but a center for clinical trials, is what the 1000 word book might call imposing. Tall, red brick, white trim, ivy climbing up the sides. He parks the car not too far from the entrance and places a blue card on the dashboard. "If you park here, you need to make sure everyone can see this, or they'll tow you."

Ashley don't want the wheel chair, so we walk very slowly. She leans on Travis as she walks, stopping every couple yards to catch her breath. If I was a passer-by I'd think she was having some asthma attack. It's mostly that she's just tired and weak. Between the high sugars and little food, she's down under eighty pounds, way too thin for her tall frame.

On the sidewalks there is a small group of reporters, craning to see who we are. A few protesters are there, but nothing like in Texas. A few shout angry words as we pass through them, and a few hold political signs for candidates supporting stem cell research. It's such a small and ridiculous group, I nearly laugh at them. Other people are going to and from buildings around us, and no one's giving them a second glance.

He leaves us as we get checked in. I know he's the big wig here, but I'm still put off guard that he isn't going to walk us through this.

Even after the mountains of paperwork we completed in Texas, there's still more here. I hand it over to Travis and Logan, but Logan hands it back to me. "You read it," he says.

Most of it is stuff we've read before. The procedure, release forms, insurance forms, next of kin and emergency numbers. There's a paper that describes some of the resources available to us, including a message board set up just for members of the trial.

"That's a good idea," Travis says, handing it to Ashley. "That way you can make friends with people going through the same thing and keep up with them, even when you're in isolation."

"How long will I be in isolation?"

"A couple weeks, I think. Most of the time we're here," he says, looking to see if there is an answer in the papers, which there isn't.

"Can I still email my friends back home?"

"Of course," I say, although I wonder what they'll talk about. They'll tell her about how school is starting and how horrible the math teacher is and how much they hate having to take showers in gym and how unfair the homework is, and all Ashley will think is that she would give all the flute lessons in the world to be a part of these mundane things.

There's one form that explains the steps of the process and at what points we can change our minds. I suppose it should be of comfort that there are so many times we can back out if we want to, but since there's no other course to take, it isn't so much an option for us. Forge ahead, my daddy would say.

The first test—testing to make sure Ashley still has some remaining functional beta cells—was done at Children's in Austin, but they want us to do it again here since her blood sugars have been so consistently high. Apparently, it's like being a mom of five hundred kids: those little beta cells trying to control all that sugar just burns 'em out. It's a simple blood test, and we wait until a new doctor comes to tell us the results.

He thrusts out his hand and introduces himself. "Hi, I'm Dr. Wong. I'll be the hemotologist working with you during the trial." He's bouncy and young, almost too young, and I consider asking to see his diploma.

"What is it you do?" I'm surprised at how bold Travis has gotten lately. He's never been one to speak his mind, but I can hear in his voice the same questions I have in my head: *Are you some Doogie Howser, 'cause you look thirteen and too young to have any real experience.*

"I'm a blood doctor. I specialize in diseases of the blood. In Ashley's case, I'm the one who removes the bone marrow, and I'll help in isolating the stem cells. I also specialize in autoimmune diseases, which becomes important when we try to keep your body from attacking the new beta cells we hope to give you."

He sits with us and looks at the file they've just begun on Ashley, which I imagine will get thicker and thicker as the weeks go on. For now, it's thin, and probably completely unnecessary for him to look at, since it's all stuff he knew before he came in anyway.

"Speaking of beta cells," he continues, "it looks like you are barely hanging on here, kiddo." He flashes a smile of impossibly white teeth. "You still qualify, but just by a hair. You have the lowest amount of working beta cells allowed. It's a good thing we got you here now. They won't be working too much longer at this rate."

"But the therapy will still work, right?" I say.

"We don't know. There are no guarantees here. Even with a whole batch of beta cells, it could be troublesome. But some are better than none, so let's go with that, okay?" Another flash of teeth.

"What's the next step, then?" Travis asks.

"We move Ashley into a surgery room, and we take some bone marrow out of her pelvic bone."

"Today?"

"Right now. We have a team assembling upstairs."

"They're doing surgery now?" Ashley asks.

"Not surgery, really. More of a procedure. Didn't Dr. Van Der Campen go over this with you?"

"Yes, but it's been a while," says Travis. "We've been a bit overwhelmed with it all and can't remember all the details."

It takes Dr. Wong hardly a minute to explain the process. She'll be under general anesthesia so she won't feel a thing. They'll stick long, hollow needles in her to take out the marrow, and bam! She's done.

"That sounds so easy," I say.

"It is. Getting the marrow isn't the hard part. The hard part will be to isolate the pluripotent stem cells and put them to work." He stands and shakes our hands again. I'll be back as soon as everything is ready."

Once he's gone, Travis turns to me. "What the Sam Hill is a pluripotent stem cell?"

I look to Logan who shrugs. "Don't look at me. I didn't understand half of what he said. I couldn't think, I was so blinded by his teeth."

"They're cells that can become anything." Ashley's voice is tired but knowing. "Like embryonic stem cells. That's why researchers want to study embryonic cells: they can turn into anything in the body." We all look at her with amazement.

"What?" she says. "That last hospital stay was really boring. I had to do something."

"Well, go on then," says Logan, sitting back down.

"Most adult cells are already assigned a job. Skin cells make more skin cells. Brain cells make more brain cells. Blood cells make blood cells. But there are stem cells in the bone marrow, pluripotent cells, that can become anything. At least that's the theory."

We let the word theory hang in the air. It's a reminder of how uncertain this all is.

When they come for Ashley, we let her go with the unanswered questions surrounding us. All the what ifs that are in front of us that start here.

What if they can't get enough stem cells?

What if the stem cells don't work?

What if...

We don't let ourselves get that far. Tomorrow is too big a word for us, and so we take just today. We made it this far. *That's good, isn't it*, I ask myself. And I don't listen when the small voice inside says, *not good enough*.

* * * *

The anesthesia's slow to wear off, and because she's so weak to begin with they want to watch her over night. The room is really too small for all of us. I never thought I'd miss that room at Children's, but I do. It's clean here, and bright, but there's not enough chairs and no sofa, and no desk. Nothing that makes it feel warm. It feels like a hospital.

She wakes groggy and goes back to sleep, and at nine we finally decide to leave and go get something to eat. We find a fast food restaurant that's nearly empty and eat food that has no taste, but we don't care. We only eat because we have to.

I go to bed with Travis, not sneaking out, but curling under the covers listening to his snoring and the sound of the TV behind the wall in Logan's room.

When Brenda's father died a few years back, the church came behind her the way it's come behind us. They fixed meals and prayed for her and mowed her lawn. They sent cards and took her kids out swimming and to the movies. She said she never felt so loved, so completely surrounded by God and friends.

They mow our lawn and fix us dinner and pray for us. They send cards and invite Logan to hang out with their kids. And I've never felt more alone.

The room is so dark I nearly can't stand it. In our home back in Texas, we don't pull the blinds at night and the sky, all wide and sparkly, shines in. When we were young, Travis and I used to lie on the floor in front of the sliding glass door and watch the thunderstorms roll across the wide open spaces towards us, lightening streaking across the sky in great bolts of electricity. It seemed romantic then. Now I worry the electricity will go out or the oak in the backyard will get hit.

Travis rolls over and lays his arm across me, pulling me close. "I thought you were asleep," I say.

"I was." He kisses my hair and tightens his arms around me, pressing me into his chest. It's the safest I've felt for a long time, and I curl into him, breathing him in and feeling the strength of him next to me. "I've missed you." He kisses my forehead, my cheeks, my nose, until he's pressing his lips on mine. It's more need than passion, but in the dark of the room we take what we can get.

I lay, hot and slightly damp, with my head on his shoulder, circling my fingers across his chest. "What if this don't work?" He understands that I'm asking about Ashley and not us, because in the last two months almost all that's left is Ashley. Little of us exists except for this, and this small desperate act to feel connected is related to Ashley, and everything now, even sex, is about keeping her alive, or keeping our will to fight to keep her alive.

"This will work."

"How do you know?"

"Because it has to."

I roll away from him and onto my back, staring into the black ceiling.

"I don't think medicine works that way."

He pulls me back into him, wrapping his free arm around my waist and cradling my head with the other. "Then we find another way." His hands move through my hair, running from my forehead to the base of my neck and back up, this repetitive motion that used to drive me wild.

"I heard about other stem cell research."

His hands stop for the briefest of moments, and then resume. He don't answer and maybe this isn't the best time to bring something else up, but I do anyway.

"They can get stem cells from umbilical cord blood. It's like the embryo cell—pluripotent, or whatever that is—and it can become anything they want it to. She wouldn't even need working beta cells, so it wouldn't matter if she didn't have enough. They engineer them to be the beta cells."

"Can she get umbilical blood cells from anywhere? It seems like there would be some mass market to sell the stuff if it were that valuable."

"No. They usually use it for babies where the parents have already stored it. From when they were born."

"Parents think that far ahead? They're delivering their babies and suddenly think, Gee, I might need this umbilical cord in case my kid gets diabetes in twelve years?"

"Some do."

"And how does this help us? You didn't keep a little jar of it for old-time's sake, did you?"

I try to ignore the sarcasm in his voice. "No. But it's possible to use it from someone else, someone who's compatible, like a transplant."

"And where would we get that?" He's stopped stroking my hair altogether now.

"We could have another baby."

This does it. He rolls me off his arm himself and throws his hands over his head. "Jiminy, Babs. Do you hear yourself?"

"We never said we were done." I sit up and try to make his features out in the dark. "We just kind of stopped after Ashley. But it would be great to have a baby again, don't you think?"

"No. Not for this reason." He swings his legs over the side and gets out of bed. He walks to the bathroom and turns on the light, near blinding me, and shuts the door behind him. I wait. He turns out the light and washes his hands in the dark, taking a long time.

"Not to save Ashley, you wouldn't even think about it?"

He circles the bed and sits on the side, not laying down, putting his head in his hands. "Especially not to save Ashley."

I am so stunned by this I can barely speak. "Why?"

I can see him turn to look at me, but I can't see the expression. "Do you have any idea what that would do to a kid? Knowing their entire reason for being was to provide umbilical blood for their sister? And what, God forbid, if it didn't work out, and Ashley died anyway. What if they felt responsible for that? What if they felt their entire purpose in life was to save their sister, and they failed before they could even eat solid food?"

"We'd never let a child feel that way." I reach over to touch him, but he moves away.

"People feel what they feel, Babs. You can't make them or let them or keep them from feeling just because you want it that way. We are not creating another human life to be the donating stem cells for Ashley."

He fumbles in the dark for the shorts and shirt he flung over the chair and pulls them on.

"Are you going somewhere?"

"Out."

"You can't just leave."

"Watch me." He grabs the key card and lets the door slam behind him.

Behind the wall, the TV in Logan's room drones on. I pound on the wall. "I need a cigarette," I yell.

"Forget it," he yells back.

I flop back onto the bed. Three months ago I'd never have believed I'd be fighting with my husband and asking my son for cigarettes.

Or waiting around for my daughter to die.

Chapter Twenty-Seven

"She'll be here anywhere from 18 to 28 days, depending on how fast the drugs work and how well the beta cells multiply," Dr. Van Der Campen tells us.

We nod and pretend we're listening when the truth is we've gone through this all before. We know the steps ahead; what we want to know is what he can't tell us. How many good stem cells will the bone marrow yield? How sick exactly will Ashley get with the drugs, and how well will they work? Will the transfusion of stem cells help her beta cells grow? In 28 days, will we be going back home?

"We start today with an infusion of drugs that will start to kill her immune system. We're giving her an antibiotic, too, as a backup, but any germ can be dangerous. From this point on, she's going to be in an isolation room. Every time you come and go, you will have to wash your hands in the sink right outside the door. You will need to wear gowns and gloves and masks to keep exposure to infection minimal."

We nod. It's simple enough. Don't kill Ashley by sneezing on her. We buy into this star wars kind of atmosphere. I'm thankful there ain't some huge plastic bubble she'll have to live in. Masks, gloves, scrubs. I can do these.

"The first thing we'll give is the cyclophosphamide, which is the immunosuppressant." He looks squarely at Ashley. "This may make you feel sick to your stomach. We're going to give you something that should help that, but it's still possible you'll experience nausea."

I try counting the syllables in that first sentence, but I can't remember the name of the drug two seconds after he says it.

She already has an IV in, so attaching the water-like medicine to the mix is anti-climactic. He flips the little switch. A small amount of fluid runs through the tube and into her arm. And then it stops.

"That's it?" Ashley asks.

"That's it," Dr. Van Der Campen says. I'll be back in 16 hours to do it again. Do you have any other questions?"

"Are the others already here?" Ashley asks.

"Others?"

"The other kids participating. Do they start today too?" I can see Ashley has in her mind that everyone is lined up through the hall, door after door of science experiments, all doctors synchronizing their watches and flipping the plastic lever at the same time. If she were to run an experiment, it would look like that. But this is life. And life's never that neat.

"Yes, two have already begun treatment. One is five days in, and the other is three days in."

"So I'm not the first?" There's disappointment in her voice, but I feel a rush of gratefulness. If something goes terribly wrong, it won't go wrong to us first.

Dr. Van Der Campen closes the clipboard and checks the drip lines again. "No, but everyone will go at their own pace. It's possible any one of you won't have enough viable stem cells to work with, or that the immunosuppressant drugs won't be as effective as fast. That," he says patting her feet through the blankets, "is why we have staff watching you 24/7."

He's on his way out when Travis says, "So what do we do now?"

"Wait," he answers. "You got a whole lot of waiting to do."

* * * *

Over the next few days there's nothing to do but wait. Not even hope, since there's nothing going on except poison running through her veins. She gets sick like the doctor warned, but since she's not eating, there isn't much to come up. The drug information says she might lose her hair, but the nurses say she probably won't be on it long enough for it to be noticeable.

Boredom sets in. I've stopped Googling answers, because there ain't none left. One point eight million hits, and we've come to the end. Travis is right. This will work because it has to.

We read books and watch TV, but none of it sinks in. They are words, letters, sounds. They mean nothing.

Logan spends a lot of his time downloading new songs on Ashley's ipod and sitting with her as she listens, which is about all she's up to these days. Friends from church and school email songs with notes attached, and Logan faithfully reads them to her, placing the earphones gently over her ears and explaining why each friend picked that particular song. Brian Lee sends an entire mix, and Ashley cries the whole way through the CD but refuses to let us take it away.

Once I overheard Logan on the phone with the band, telling them to find another drummer, that he wouldn't be back for a long time. I asked him if he wanted to go back to Texas for a while.

"Several of your friends' families have offered to let you stay with them. And Dad is going back this week. We can send you back, too. You should be there. It's your senior year. You shouldn't miss that."

"I should be here," is all he'll say, and so that's the end of that.

Yolanda is taking care of the mail this week, and she sends an envelope with some she thinks might be timely. Inside are Logan's SAT scores. I want to open them, but I give them to Logan, and he disappears outside to open them by himself.

When I find him, it's by the hotel pool, leaning back in his chair and staring up at the stars like the first night we arrived.

"Do I get to know what you got?"

He hands the envelope to me, and I move my chair under the dim light. It takes a moment to figure out how the scores are labeled but when I do, I practically stop breathing.

Reading: 790

Mathematics: 770

Writing: 790

"Logan! That's practically perfect!" I try to remember from the SAT prep books he used what the likelihood of this is, and all I can remember is that it's close to none. "How in the world..."

Logan smiles, not an arrogant, I-told-you-so smile but a content one. "Not bad for a hick kid, huh?"

I whack him on the arm with the envelope. "Don't you dare call yourself a hick kid. Look at this! You could get in anywhere you want! I bet you beat out every kid in Texas!"

"It's not a competition, Mom."

"Of course it is!"

"I'm not going, Mom." He can't possibly be saying what I think.

"What do you mean?"

"I'm not going to college. At least not right away."

"Oh yes you are. Do you realize what your Dad and I would do to be able to go back and go to college? Heck, I might just settle for finishing high school. This is the opportunity for you to be something. You can make something of yourself."

"I already am something."

I feel like he's hit me in the chest. "Of course you are. I didn't mean it that way..."

"You did. I know what you think. You think to be someone important you have to go to school and get some degree and know big words and do math most people don't even understand. You think being someone important is moving out of the small town you grow up in and getting some fancy house in a city and having lots of money and a string of letters behind your name."

"That's not it at all." But it is and I know it, and I'm suddenly ashamed at how shallow it sounds. "College is important. Having the degree is important, because people see you differently when they think you're smart. People listen to you. You can do more. Do big things. Lordy, Logan, I have no idea where you got your brains, but they're a gift, and you should use them. Use them to do something really important, like cure diseases, or run the world or something."

"But you don't have a degree and look at you."

"Exactly. Look at me. I ain't nothing but a mom and wife, and everyone in town knows I ain't smart enough to pour spit out of a boot if the instructions was on the heel."

"You're the smartest person I know."

I laugh until I realize he's serious.

"You know more words than me. And you learned them on your own and just because you wanted to, not because you had some teacher hovering over you. And you taught me how to drive a stick shift. And how to dance."

The image of him and I dancing around in the kitchen when he was five floats in front of me. Can he really remember that?

"And you," he stops and swipes at tears, and I realize Logan is near to crying. "You saved Ashley. When no one knew what to do, you found the answers. Not Doctor Benton. You. You are the reason we're here. You never gave up, even when it meant slugging through thousands of pages of medical jargon, you did it."

He takes back the SAT scores and stuffs it in the envelope. "I'm not saying I'll never go. I'm just saying I don't want to think about that right now, because it's not the most important thing in the world. They're just numbers. Everything that's really important is here."

He stands up and stares down at me for a minute. "You shouldn't keep selling yourself short, Mom. Everything this family is, is because of you." He leans over and kisses me on the head, the way I kissed him for years and years before he started pulling away and making faces at me.

I watch him walk away and think, *I can't be all that dumb. I raised some really great kids.*

Chapter Twenty-Eight

Travis leaves for home five days after the poison begins its work. A shuttle takes him away when the sky's still gray, and I stand on the sidewalk until I can't see the van anymore. A small piece of me feels relieved.

Logan stays and we go out for breakfast before visiting Ashley. We haven't talked anymore about college, and I'm surprised to find I'm not worried. The thought of him staying around another year is pleasantly comfortable.

When Dr.Van Der Campen comes to inject more medicine, Ashley cries through the heaving. Her eyelashes are falling out, and dark circles under her eyes give her an alien look.

"How many more days of this?" I ask, squeezing Ashley's hand as she wretches again.

"Another three. By then, we hope to have enough stem cells to transplant back in."

He's efficient. Thorough. Professional. But I miss Dr. Benton and his warmth and the way he winked at Ashley and made us feel like everything would be all right.

When he leaves we start the wait all over again,

By lunchtime Ashley is asleep again, and Logan decides to go grab lunch. I'm not hungry, so I stay. Someone should be here if Ashley wakes up.

A few minutes later someone knocks on the door and opens it just a crack. I look up, and there is Donna Jean.

"What the—"

"I thought you might need some company. Is it okay if I come in?" Already, she's dressed in scrubs and gloves, a mask hanging around her neck. I nod, and she slips the mask up and closes the door gently behind her so as not to wake Ashley, as if a bullhorn could do that.

The relief of seeing her is so huge I want to hug her, but we left things so awkward at the airport the most I can do is motion for her to sit. "How did you get here?"

"I took a plane this morning, rented a car. Travis gave me directions."

"He knew?" I wonder if he set it up, or if she volunteered, but then I realize it doesn't matter. "This must have cost a fortune, Donna Jean."

She shrugs like it ain't no big deal. "Money's just money. There's always more. It was important I come."

"Why?" I don't want to sound ungrateful. I'm not ungrateful, just bewildered.

She sighs, and it comes across as uncomfortable, which is not like Donna Jean at all. "I don't know. I prayed and prayed about it, and it just seemed important."

I don't know what to say to this, so I let it sit in the air until she feels the need to explain further.

"I don't know how to say this. I've been thinking of how to say this for years, and I just couldn't. I wanted to, but I didn't know how so I convinced myself it wasn't important."

She isn't looking at me, and I'm suddenly on edge.

"What's wrong?"

"Nothing's wrong." She laughs, but not a funny ha-ha laugh; one of those cynical laughs, like there's some inside joke I ain't privy to. She glances at Ashley. "How is she?"

"Not good right now. They're giving her drugs to kill the immune system. It makes her real sick. But in three days they start the transplant, where they inject her with her own stem cells. It should get better after that. That's the hope, anyway."

The silence grows again as we both wonder what to say next.

She breaks the silence. "You know the day in high school you walked in on me crying?"

How could I forget? I nod.

She looks everywhere but at me, fidgeting with the buttons on her skirt. "I was ready to kill myself that day."

"What?" I nearly fall off my chair.

"It's true. I'd snuck a bottle of my dad's sleeping pills out of the bathroom. I had them there, in my purse. I just didn't have the nerve. I was sitting in the bathroom praying God would send a sign for me, that there was some reason to live." She laughs again, that same cynical laugh that ends in an almost snort. "Over a stupid boy."

I snag a Kleenex off the nightstand next to Ashley's bed and hand it to her.

"I'm praying for a sign," she says, sniffing, "and then you walk in."

I can't think of a more unlikely sign from God than me.

"Do you remember what you said to me?"

"Don't he know you're Baptist." I say this in almost a whisper, the memory clear as a Texas spring.

She's surprised I remember. "Yes. Exactly."

"It didn't mean what you thought it meant."

She smiles wryly. "I know. I figured that out later. But at the time, what I heard was, 'Doesn't he know that God is more important to you than some silly argument over sex.'"

"That's a lot to get out of "Don't he know you're a Baptist'."

She smiles at me, finally looking me in the eye. "I think sometimes we hear what God wants us to hear. And God wanted me to hear that what he thinks of me is more important than what someone else thinks of me." She reaches out and takes my hand. "You saved my life that day, Babs. I don't know. I may never have gone through with swallowing all those pills. But I do know I wasn't real happy with God at that moment before you appeared. I didn't know who I was anymore. I didn't know why I made choices that ended up breaking my heart. And then you were there, and you basically reminded me that I made those choices because I believed there were rights and wrongs. Because I believed God was more important than what I wanted in a fleeting moment."

"I'm glad I helped." I don't know what else to say. It was so long ago. What could that mean to her now? Why is she here today?

She lets go of my hand and wipes her nose again. "I'm a mess."

"You're beautiful," I say, meaning it. "You've always been beautiful."

She stands and walks over to the window. "It's so lovely out today. It's such a shame that you can't open the window and let the air in."

"Why are you here, Donna Jean?" I don't mean just today, but every day since this started. "For years we been going to the same church, and I barely see you. Ashley gets sick, and you're like some angel. You sit by our side; you bring us stuff that keeps us from going insane with boredom. You give us a laptop, which, frankly, is what's saving Ashley's life. And you show up here, some two thousand miles away, to tell me you remember some conversation in a bathroom near twenty years ago. Why?"

She's still staring out the window, but she answers without hesitating. "When you came running out of the airport you asked, 'What if it doesn't work?' What you really meant, I think, is 'What if God doesn't answer my prayers?'" She turns to look at me, and the intensity of her eyes makes me look away.

"It's the same thing. This working is my prayer."

"Yes." It doesn't seem to be where she was going, but she stops here. "Well, I thought I might fix y'all some dinner tonight. How would that be?"

"Dinner?"

"Yes. You know, that meal you eat when the sky gets dark."

"How are you going to fix dinner?"

"The hotel has functioning kitchens in every room. Weren't you wondering why there was a fridge and oven next to your bed?"

I look over at Ashley, hesitating.

"She'll be fine. I'll fix it, call you, and you can come over and eat, and then come back. I'll clean dishes and everything. Logan can help me."

I try to think of the last meal I ate that wasn't fast food. "Okay."

"Okay." She heads to the door and then looks over her shoulder before leaving. "It's all right that I'm here, isn't it?"

"Yes. It's very all right." I wish I were the hugging type. I want to reach out and show her how much it means, but the distance from me to the door is too much, the contact too intimate. "Thank you. Again. For everything."

She nods and smiles and leaves as quietly as she came.

The conversation rolls around in my head, and I'm struck by how little we truly know of people. How many people in church, sitting next to Donna Jean in high school all fancy and popular and perfectly put together, would imagine the pills tucked inside her purse? Who would see Logan with his multicolored Mohawk and gold hoop earring and imagine he scored almost perfect on his SATs, and sits on his sister's bed and reads her romance stories out of the teen magazines? Who would see me bow my head in church and pray alongside others and guess that I'm speaking into the silence, words as hollow as the hole in my heart?

When I get to the hotel at 6:00, the refrigerator's full and the pantry is busting its seams. Bread and deli meats, eggs, cheese, bagels, cereal, peanut butter, jelly, cream cheese. Lord Almighty she's even managed to find us grits. She's made a list of possible breakfasts and dinners and the ingredients and hung them on the fridge with a Baltimore magnet covered in bright orange crabs.

"This is some primo food," Logan says, licking the spoon as Donna Jean puts a pan of brownie batter in the oven. The smell of garlic and tomatoes flood the room.

"It's just spaghetti," she says, taking a wooden spoon and stirring the pot on the stove. "They don't give you a lot of pots to work with."

"She made enough for leftovers," Logan says, sounding giddy with the thought of so much food.

On the table sits a bowl of salad, with greens and tomatoes and cucumbers and carrots and red bell pepper.

Logan carries a bowl of garlic bread and sets it next to the salad. "We can eat like kings for a week on this." He steals a small piece of the bread and munches on it as he tries to get a taste of the sauce. Donna Jean playfully bats at his hand, and he grins at her. Their interaction stabs at my heart. In all my worry about losing Ashley, I wonder what I've lost with Logan.

He's famished, and while Donna Jean and I banter about the area and the shopping center nearby, Logan inhales ten meals worth of spaghetti and bread.

For weeks and weeks, Travis and I have hardly eaten. I've thought Logan wasn't hungry either. It never occurs to me maybe he needs to.

When he gets up to do the dishes, I notice how tall he is. He's shot up the last couple months and practically towers over us. And he's so skinny. A beanpole. It reminds me of how fast Ashley thinned out. Suddenly I'm wondering how much water he drank at dinner. If he's been drinking a lot lately, whether he's seemed more tired than usual, and if he's disappearing to go to the bathroom more than usual.

"Are you feeling all right?" I ask out of the blue.

"Sure," he says, raising his eyebrows at me. "Why?"

"You're thin."

"I'm fine, Mom." He grabs a brownie off the plate and stuffs it in his mouth to prove it. "Just hungry."

"It's all right," Donna Jean says, laying her hand on my shoulder as if she knows exactly what's going through my head. Not the diabetes part, the bad parent part. The part where I realize I've so neglected my son in the quest to help my daughter that I don't even feed him proper.

"Yeah, mom. It's all right." He grins and takes another brownie. "I met a few kids at the pool yesterday. They were going to play basketball at the court out back tonight. Can I go?"

"I was going back to the hospital," I say.

"Oh." He struggles to keep the disappointment out of his voice.

"No. You go. I just mean, I'm going back for a few hours. But you'll be okay here, right?"

He brightens again, and I think of how much he has sacrificed the last few months. School. Friends. The band. His job. Last week they took senior pictures and he missed that. At the very least he needs a huge meal and an hour of hoops with some strangers.

Donna Jean and I clean up the dishes together, even though she keeps insisting I go back to the clinic. "I made the mess. I promised to clean it. Go be with Ashley."

I take a towel out of a drawer and dry the glasses as she washes them. "It's good, actually, to get a break. I mean, I want to be with her all the time, but it's so tiring. This feels good: eating and talking and doing dishes. Even in a hotel. It feels … normal. I miss that."

"I can't even begin to imagine," she says, handing me a plate with suds still clinging to it.

* * * *

She stays with us for three more days. She fixes breakfast and dinner for us every day, and Logan slaps together sandwiches for us at noon. She washes Ashley's wispy hair and braids it for her so it don't get tangled, and reads books to her while I sneak out and do some laundry. Ashley seems to not be so sick anymore when Dr. Van Der Campen gives her the medicine, but she still sleeps more often than not.

Dr. Wong visits every day as well, taking more blood to test. He announces on the last day of Donna Jean's visit that Ashley must have super-marrow, because he got a very good sample of stem cells which are thriving in the lab and should be good to transplant as soon as Dr. Van Der Campen gives the word. Dr. Van Der Campen, however, is less than eager to move forward as fast as he predicted, although he don't say why. He uses his stethoscope to listen to her lungs several times a day, frowning but saying nothing. I suspect it might have something to do with the other two trial patients and how they're doing, but he don't say. Sometimes it's better not to know, so I don't ask.

It turns out that two of the boys Logan plays basketball with each night are brothers of a girl about Ashley's age going through a trial at Hopkins for cancer. They don't talk about it much, I don't think, but there's comfort in knowing they'll be there every night to hang out with.

We adjust. It amazes me how fast each new hotel becomes our home, how fast the routines become routine. And when Donna Jean says goodbye, the jolt in the new normal is significant.

I'm not afraid to hug her. I am still not sure why she came, but if she says God told her to, that's good enough for me. Having another woman to talk to has been a blessing, and I hold her tight a tad too long before letting her get in the car. I lean over into the open window. "Thank you for everything again. I don't know what we would have done without you."

"Starved," Logan shouts from behind me as he passes to get our car for the drive to Hopkins.

When he's out of hearing distance, I reach in through the window as though I want to touch her, but can't quite do it. "I mean it. I'm not as strong as you think." I think about the bowed head and the mouthing of the songs in church. "I'm not really the person everyone thinks."

She reaches out and takes my hand. "You're not the person you think."

I blink back tears. "When I said that wanting this trial to work was the same thing as wanting God to answer my prayers, you didn't agree."

"I never said that." She lets go of my hand. I feel the cool of the AC on my face even as the sticky heat of the day plasters my hair to my neck.

"I'm asking. What is it you think I want?"

"I can't answer that Babs. Only you know that. If it were me, I'd be praying for God to save her."

"But?"

"But I think you want something else just as much."

"What could I want just as much as saving Ashley?"

She looks at me long, searching my eyes like she's debating whether or not to tell me what it is I want. And then she does.

"I think you want to believe God *can* save her."

Logan pulls in behind her and honks the horn. I'm frozen in place. I want to say the things I know I should say. The easy words. I do believe God *can* save her, I just don't know if he *will* save her. But even as I open my mouth, I know this ain't true. All this time that I've been fooling others, I've been fooling myself too.

"What are you wrestling with, Babs? Whether God is real, or whether he is good?" She reaches out and holds my hand again, the sadness in her eyes too hard to look at. "He doesn't need you to believe to heal her. He wants you to believe so he can heal you."

"I've tried." I am not going to cry. I am not. I am not.

She squeezes my hand. "I know. Maybe stop trying so hard. It'll come."

I want to tell her I've been trying for so long, I don't think it's going to happen for me.

Logan honks the horn and leans out the window. "She's gonna miss her plane, Mom. Just let her go already."

"Why did you come all the way here?"

She lets go of my hand again, like it is too hot to touch. She stares down at her own hands in her lap. "If God lets Ashley die..." Tears suddenly spring to her eyes, and she breathes in deep. "I don't want you to stop wanting to believe."

I want to ask why this is so important to her. Why am I so important to her? Why is it so important to her that I believe? But Logan honks again and the moment is broken. "I'm coming already!"

"I am going to miss my plane," she says, laughing out of nervousness, wiping her eyes. "Everything will be all right, Babs."

As she drives off I hold those words, though I know they're a lie. She don't know. But just hearing them, I feel a little better.

Chapter Twenty-Nine

When we arrive at the hospital, there's a flurry of activity in the hall outside Ashley's room. Doctors and nurses are flying in and out of the room, rolling carts in and out, frantic but controlled.

"What's wrong?" I grab a nurse's arm. "Is it Ashley? What's going on?"

"She's got pneumonia," she says shortly, brushing me off.

Logan and I dress quickly in the gown and gloves and mask. By the time we get in the door, it's just Dr. Van Der Campen and two attendants, and they are transferring her to one of those beds with wheels.

"Where are you taking her?"

"Down to x-ray."

He pushes past me. Ashley's lips are tinged blue and her eyes are dull. I grab her hands in my gloved one. "It's okay, baby. They're going to take you to get some pictures of your lungs. You'll be fine."

"I can't breathe," she says, struggling with every breath. I hold her hand as the attendants roll her out of the room, and then watch as she disappears around the corner.

"She's going to be okay, right?" I ask as Dr. Van Der Campen brushes by.

"This is the one complication we were most worried about," he says, with little feeling. "Even under the best circumstances, pneumonia can be dangerous. With Ashley..."

He don't finish, and I don't need him to. She's got no immune system. She's got no ability to fight off the terrible disease that is squeezing her lungs. Her body's an open invitation.

I'm suddenly sobbing. I sink to the floor, crying so hard I can't breathe. I'm making a fool of myself, but I can't help it. Since that first day in Children's Hospital, that day when the nurse told me Ashley would be fine and live a very normal life, I've known in my gut that this day was coming. Ashley is dying.

And from nowhere there are two hands lifting me up, and I'm in Travis's arms. "It's okay. I'm here." Like I am a child, he picks me up and carries me back into Ashley's room, untying the mask so I can breath and stroking my hair with his fingers. "It's going to be okay."

I cry harder, because I know he don't know this for certain, but I want so hard to believe it. Travis, who has always made everything right, can't control this.

He holds me until I stop crying, and then wipes the tears from my face.

"How did you get here?" I ask, punctuating the question with a hiccup.

"Dr. Van Der Campen called Dr. Benton last night, and Dr. Benton called me. He said he was afraid Ashley might be taking a turn for the worse, and he thought I should be here. I took the red-eye out."

I don't even ask what a red-eye is, I'm just so thankful he's here. Then I realize there were two pairs of hands picking me up, and I look around. "Was that Dr. Benton?"

"He came out too. He thought we might need the support and someone to talk to who understood the medical lingo."

I laugh through the tears, because I can't think of any other doctor who would care whether or not we understood. "Where did he go?"

"I think he went with Ashley," Logan says. "He walked that way, anyway."

I feel completely embarrassed now by my breakdown, but Logan just says, "Sheesh, Mom, you shouldn't bottle stuff up like that. When you explode, you really explode." He grins one of his big, goofy grins, and it makes me laugh.

"Can you go get us some Cokes?" Travis fishes around in his pocket. He finds a couple crumbled bills and hands them to Logan.

When he's gone, Travis sits on the bed next to me. "I'm sorry, Babs. About the baby thing. I didn't want to leave mad, and the whole time I was gone I just wished I could come back and make it right."

"You're right," I say, waving it off and then blowing my nose. "I'm so busy looking at the next step, I stop living in the moment we're in."

"This is gonna work. Dr. Benton says the stem cells are multiplying really well, and they look strong."

"I don't want to replace Ashley with another baby."

"I know that."

"And the baby wouldn't be just a donor. Watching them grow up ... they're almost gone already. In a few months Logan'll be out of the house. Ashley's next. What will I do without babies around?"

He takes my face in his hands, his skin warm against mine. "We'll have each other."

It's such a cornball thing to say I almost laugh again, except Travis don't usually talk like this, and I think he's serious.

Dr. Benton knocks on the door. "Can I come in?"

Travis quickly drops his hands.

"Of course," I say, rubbing at the hollows below my eyes to clear off the mascara I'm sure is smeared.

"They have her in X-ray. She'll be back soon. It looks very mild. Dr. Van Der Campen was very much on top of it. He called a few days ago and was afraid it might be coming on. He upped the antibiotics in the drip."

"Is it clear now?" Logan says, peeking his head in, too.

"Where are the Cokes?"

"Oh." Logan looks surprised. "Did you actually want them? I thought you were just trying to get rid of me."

"I'm going back to x-ray to check on everything. The nurses will be in to disinfect in a minute and you—" he points at Travis, "need to find yourself some isolation clothes. No breathing around Ashley when she comes back."

We go together to find the Coke machine, and Logan runs into one of the boys from the hotel.

"Hey Caleb, what's up?"

"Becca's getting out tomorrow!" His round, pink face is glowing as he rolls his cold can between his palms. "They think she's in remission."

"Sweeeeet!" They bump hands in some macho new ritual, and Caleb takes off down the hall.

"Is she in this trial?" asks Travis.

"No. She has cancer." I think about how the nurse at Children's the first day said that it was better to have diabetes than cancer. One could live a fairly normal life with diabetes, she'd said. I look at us, clothed in scrubs, waiting to hear whether Ashley is going to live or not, and think this is some kind of warped normal.

When they wheel Ashley back in, she's inside a clear plastic tent with tubes up her nose. Her lips aren't blue anymore, but her eyelids are heavier than usual.

"Hey sweetheart," Travis says, holding her hand in his gloved one.

"You all look like aliens," she says, a coughing spasm following.

"You're the one in the plastic bubble," Logan says, poking at her through the blankets.

She reaches out and holds my hands too, so that we are all connected in some way. "I feel like I'm suffocating."

"You've got fluid on your lungs," Travis says, sounding all doctory.

"Are there any other complications I should know about?" Ashley asks. "I seem to get them all." She coughs again and we wait for it to subside. "Just when I think it can't get worse…"

"Oh, it can get worse," Logan says, and we all look at him in horror. He shrugs and pulls a folded paper out of his pocket. "Brian Lee emailed to ask if you'd go to the fall dance with him if you're home by then."

"How's that worse?" Travis demands.

"I don't think her hair will be grown in by then."

* * * *

The pneumonia is a set-back, to say the least. Everything slows down. They cut the drugs they're giving her for the stem cells and her immune system, and they ramp up the antibiotics and a few others drugs I can't name.

We're practically living at the hospital now, afraid to leave. She's lethargic and only half-conscious during those few times she opens her eyes. Every breath is a struggle, and sometimes when I look around at us camped in her room, it seems we're all just waiting around for her to die.

Finally today they come and take the oxygen off, and she eats a tiny bit of chicken broth, and we begin to resume our new normal. When I look around the room at our family, I think no one in their right mind would want to be us, and yet I wouldn't want to be anyone else, anywhere else. It's true that trials make you stronger.

Travis is on the phone with the insurance company, demanding they pay for the Medevac trip to Children's Hospital that first day of our new lives. He's strong and intelligent sounding, and when he looks up at me and winks, I blush. He looks ten years younger, he's dropped so much weight in the last few months. I can't help but think the diagnosis, while terrible for Ashley, hasn't done us much physical harm.

Logan is in the bathroom looking in the mirror and fingering the turquoise that tinges the ends of his Mohawk. I can't tell if he's admiring the recent change or deciding on a new color. He, too, seems more comfortable in his skin. When he glances over and sees me, he grins, and I find myself smiling back at him.

Ashley is asleep, like usual, in her hospital bed, her skin as pale as the sheets around her. Tubing runs out from the IV drip and disappears in her hand. Max the pump lays on top of the blankets and his tubing slithers under the covers and disappears beneath her nightgown. A blood pressure monitor is hooked up to her arm and makes a funny, whirring noise every few minutes as it squeezes her and then releases with a slight whoosh. Underneath all of this, Ashley barely moves. The briefest glimpse and you'd think she was dead.

And yet, here we are.

I remember Pastor Joel saying in a sermon once that spider silk was stronger than steel. I had leaned over and whispered in Travis's ear, "Then I must be Wonder Woman cause I'm brushing them off the porch railings every day."

He snickered, but at lunch Logan said, "That's true. I learned it in science. If you had spider silk and threads of steel the same width, spider silk is five times stronger. It's more elastic and harder to break than plastic."

"That so?" I couldn't tell if Travis was more surprised by the facts or that Logan was actually paying attention in class.

Now, I look at my family and think about that spider web. Alone, we look frail and easy to beat. But we've been steel. Against diabetes. Against the reporters and protesters. Against the school.

I thought for awhile I might lose it all. Ashley and Travis and Logan. But against all odds we're still here.

Chapter Thirty

On the day they transplant the stem cells, we all arrive early. There are no reporters and only two protesters who half-heartedly wave their signs as we pass.

I wash Ashley's hair, what is left of it anyway, and dry it and put it back in a head band. Logan sits at the foot of the bed and paints her toenails, which is about the silliest thing I've seen in a long time and makes us all giggle.

A nurse comes in around eight and ups the saline drip. "The doctor will be in about noon to inject the cells," she says, looking around at our motley little group. "I'm not sure the fumes from the nail polish are good for her," she adds.

"They're toxic, not bacterial," Logan says, using a q-tip dipped in polish remover to clean up the edges. She scowls and leaves.

The plastic bubble is gone, but Ashley still has oxygen tubes in her nose and several IV's and machines hooked up to her, making it difficult for her to move around much. Not that she would, since she don't have energy to do much other than breathe, which we find good enough.

When Dr. Van Der Campen comes in at noon he has a large syringe. "Should we give a drum roll?" I ask. He's amused by this and waits while we all pat our hands furiously on the closest hard substance.

"Ready?"

We nod, and he sticks the needle into part of the tubing and pushes the plunger.

"That's it?"

"That's it. Were you expecting fireworks?"

"It's so—"

"Anti-climactic," Logan fills in for me.

"Climactic isn't all it's cracked up to be," he says, pulling the syringe out and capping it. He attaches two more bags of clear fluid to the IV lines and opens the valves so they can drip into Ashley as well. "These will help the stem cells multiply and do their job on the beta cells. And one will bind the toxins in the stem cell solution."

"There are toxins?" All I can think is more poison. Lord almighty, how much can one person take?

"She'll be fine, Mrs. Babcock. We're almost out of the woods now."

Out of the woods for what I'm not sure, seeing as how she still has diabetes and is still allergic to insulin. As far as I can see, she's in the Black Forest.

So Travis can spend time alone with Ashley, Logan and I have been getting lunch out all week, but today he insists the boys go. It is the first time in several days I've been alone with her, and the excitement of the transplant has her more alert than in several weeks.

"Do you think I'll be home in time for the fall dance?" She unconsciously smoothes her hair.

After all of this I can't believe the dance is the thing on her mind, but I'm glad it is. I'm glad she's looking forward to something other than transplants and sponge baths.

"If we do get home in time, we'll have to go dress shopping. I'll bet you've grown five inches in the last four months."

"Yeah. My other dresses would look like sacks on me now, too. I've lost weight, don't you think? I feel skinnier."

"Quite a bit."

She picks up the brush I left on the nightstand and absentmindedly begins to brush her hair. I watch long strands come out with each stroke, and I put my hand up to stop her. "It's real pretty already."

She reaches out and touches my mask. "Why do you have to wear that all the time?"

"So I don't breathe germs on you."

"Because your germs would make me more sick?" I nod, wondering why this is the first time she's asked this, and wonder if today she's more awake and aware of what is going on around her. She's been so groggy since we got here, living in a fog, accepting everything around her without question because questioning takes too much energy.

She fingers the IV line where it enters her hand. "Do you know anything about the other kids? The ones in the trial?" I shake my head. "I wonder if they got their transplants too. Do you think? Do you think they're well now? If they didn't get pneumonia they should be ahead of me."

"Maybe. We don't know that they didn't get sick, too, though."

"Do you think Dr. Jack would tell us? Could we ask if they are making their own insulin yet?"

"I think that's private." She looks so devastated I add, "I can ask, though. Or, better yet, we can check the message board. We haven't even done that yet."

She brightens a bit. "When I get out, you know what I want?"

"To go to the dance with Brian Lee?"

She blushes. "Besides that. I want a steak. A really big one, with a baked potato on the side with sour cream and butter and bacon, just like they serve at the steakhouse."

"Not a cake?"

She squinches her nose. "No. I don't really feel like anything sweet."

"Okay. Steak it is."

She settles back, and I think for a moment she might be going to sleep, until she talks again. "What if I don't?"

"Get a steak?"

"Get out."

"Oh, Baby, I think you're getting out. They don't want you living here. They got other people they need to put in this bed. And I'm pretty sure they're tired of seeing my mug here." I smile my cheesy smile, but she don't bite.

"What happens if this doesn't work?"

I stop smiling. "You can't think like that. It will work."

"I've had dreams a lot lately."

"Oh yeah? What about?"

"About going to heaven. I drift off on a cloud and Jesus is there, and angels singing the most beautiful music you ever heard. And grandpa is there. And it doesn't hurt anymore. And I'm really, really happy."

"It's just a dream, Baby."

She stares out the window, complete peace on her face. "But I like it. That's the thing. I'm not scared anymore that I might die. Sometimes I dream I'm there, and it's so nice, and then I wake up and I'm here, and I can't breathe, and my head hurts all the time and my mouth feels like sandpaper. And I just wish I could go back to sleep and dream again."

My own mouth is parched suddenly. I don't know what to say. I take her hand in mine. Her skin feels dry and fragile, like onion paper, and I'm afraid I'll hurt her holding it. "It'll get better, Ash. This time next year you'll forget how bad all this was. You'll be back at school, playing in the band, fighting with Logan, eating anything you want, and this whole thing'll be a bad dream."

"But if I'm not..."

"You will be."

She squeezes my hand and lets go. "I'm really tired. I think I'll sleep a little."

"Okay."

I watch her sleep, see the moment when the tightness of her face eases, when her eyelids stop quivering and her body relaxes into itself. I'm selfish to want her here. To want her to keep fighting through all this. Maybe if I were her, I'd just want to let go too.

I slip out and go to the restroom to cry. I wash my face before meeting Travis and Logan, and I don't tell them about the conversation. I pretend to be excited about the transplant and tell them Ashley is curious about the others and that I think she's back to her competitive self because she wants to be the first to have it work. We talk about her name being in medical journals and all the others who will be cured after her. I don't mention her dream. I don't mention death, because today is all about life. I want to hold on to that as long as possible. As Travis and Logan shove down sandwiches and chips, I watch the animation on their faces, their hopes wrapped up in possibility, and I stay quiet.

* * * *

The sun is barely set by nine o'clock, and we say goodnight to Ashley, although she's already asleep again. Logan's invited to go to a celebration dinner with one of his basketball friends, and so Travis and I walk around the Johns Hopkins campus. He holds my hand, and I feel closer to him than I have ever felt. The trees haven't started to change yet, but the air feels like fall already.

I want to ask Travis something, but I can't bring myself to do it. Words have never been easy for me. I open my mouth, and then close it and pretend to find something fascinating about the squirrels running across the path.

Travis, though, feels it.

"All this time, Babs, you were right. This was the right thing to do."

"It hasn't worked out yet," I answer, measuring my words and tempering my hope.

"It will though," he says. "One way or another, it'll be okay."

He squeezes my hand; I squeeze back. "How can you have such faith in God?" There. I've said it. I wait for his avalanche of self-righteousness, but it doesn't come. Travis, it seems, is measuring his words too.

"I think sometimes you mistake me trusting God to answer, for liking what he has to say." He says this slowly, weighing the thought as though maybe this is a new revelation for him, too. "I trust that God will do what is best, because that's what the Bible says. I trust that he hears my prayers, because that is what the Bible says. It also says he always answers, but it doesn't say he answers the way we want him to. Just that the way he chooses will be the best way. In the long run."

He stops walking and stares up into the darkening sky. I wonder if he's looking to see if God is there, or if God will strike him down for thinking what he's thinking. "I believe he can save Ashley's life, but maybe if she dies, something greater will happen. Something good in us, or in someone else." There are tears on his cheeks now, and he turns to look me in the eye. He is more fiery now. "But I don't like that. If he takes Ashley, I may trust that he's going to make something good come out of it, but I'm still going to hate the answer with a passion for awhile."

This is the first time it's seemed possible Travis could be mad at God.

"So how can you trust that he's good, then?" I ask.

"Because the Bible says. Because everything in nature and history shows us that he can make good come of bad. Because," he shrugs. "Because he loves me."

I suddenly have a flashback to a dinner table argument with Logan and Ashley when they were little, about eating broccoli. They wanted nothing to do with the green vegetable. Why couldn't they have candy instead? *I don't like it*, Ashley had whined. *It tastes yucky.*

But it's good for you, I'd said. *You may not like it, but you have to eat it because it will make you healthier.*

Was that like God? Were we just like children who couldn't see for the life of us how something so bad could be good for us?

Travis and I begin to walk again, our fingers still intertwined.

"I don't always feel like God is there," I say.

He nods. "Sometimes it's that way. But he's there."

"How do I know?"

He strokes my palm with his thumb, his fingers running over mine. "Because he promises he will be." It seems like too simple an answer, but then I think of Brenda and Yolanda and Donna Jean and Janise. I think of all the food they made and the laptop that brought us here, to this very place, this very hope. And I suddenly realize God was there, in all of that. He loved me through the people around me.

"I want to believe," I say, stopping again. "I want to trust that God will take care of us, the way you believe it."

He raises his eyebrows at me. "Even if Ashley doesn't get better?"

I suck in my breath. Tears spring to my eyes, but I nod. "I want to trust him even if he don't answer the way I want him too." I hold both his hands in mine and look into his face, wanting desperately the peace he has. "I think, if Ashley doesn't get better, I'm going to need to trust him even more than if she does."

He wraps his arms around me, and I melt into them. He's saying words in my ear, and it takes a minute to realize he is crying and praying. I cling to him under the oaks trees, along some dark and foreign path, and pray with him.

Chapter Thirty-One

One day, suddenly, after nothing for so long, her blood sugar is down. Not all the way, but a good 100 points down, and I stare at the meter. For the first time in two months, the numbers really are going down.

"What's wrong?" Ashley is stronger now, and curious about what's going on with all the doctors and injections and testing. She's sitting straight up today, writing emails to her friends because we got her texting bill last month and took away the phone.

"I need to do it again. I think I made a mistake." She offers her hand out to me without question and goes back to typing, one handed. I wash her fingers off with a washcloth, dry them thoroughly, and prick her again. The meter blinks. 5...4...3...2...1...

281.

Five months ago that would have meant nothing to me. Three months ago that would have been a bad number. Today it is so good it makes me want to cry.

Ashley glances up and sees my face and closes the laptop instantly. "What is it?"

I show her the meter, barely able to keep the smile off my face.

"What was it last night?"

"395."

She searches my eyes, as if asking for permission to believe what this seems to mean.

I nod. "It's working," I say, almost in a whisper because I'm afraid that to say it out loud is to give us unfounded hope.

"Could it be the insulin?" She takes out the pump again and looks at it, as if it will blink the answer in digital code.

"It's the same amounts of insulin you've been getting for weeks."

"So..."

"So it's you." I give her a hug. At first she is limp in my arm, but slowly the realization hits her, and she wraps her arms around me. I feel hot tears hitting my shoulder. Without sound, the tears come faster and faster until her entire body is heaving.

"It's over, isn't it?"

I hold her tight, not wanting to say anything. I don't know if it's over. I don't know what this means, but for the first time I dare to hope.

A knock at the door interrupts us, and we both wipe tears as Dr. Van Der Campen walks in. He stops in the doorway and crosses his arms over his chest. "And I see we have another success."

"Another?"

"It's day five after the first transfusion. The same day both of the other two patients began making their own insulin."

"So it's true?"

"Well, let's see." He asks Ashley to test her blood again. Her hands are shaking so hard she can't get the tiny strip into the meter, and it falls to the floor. I throw it away, take out another, and put it in for her. She pricks her own finger and squeezes the blood out. She hands the meter to Dr. Van Der Campen, who holds it while it beeps five times, counting down.

278.

"I'd say that looks like success."

"I'm cured?"

Dr. Van Der Campen holds out his hands. "Let's not get ahead of everything." He pulls a chair up beside the bed and motions me to sit too. "This process isn't an instant thing. We may not know for a long time what the final outcome of this is. It may take a long time for your pancreas to totally take over regulating your own insulin. And your own immune system might attack it again. We can't know for certain what's going to happen."

"But..." I say, waiting for him to say something positive.

"But, for now, this is very good."

"It's good?" Ashley asks.

"Very, very good." He finally smiles, one of the few I've seen from him.

"So we can celebrate?" I ask.

"I'd say we should all celebrate," he answers. "Where's the rest of the family?"

"They went to throw some hoops in the courtyard. I'll call them." I take out my phone, but Ashley holds her hands out.

"Let me." I hand it to her, and she hits the redial button and waits for the ring. Her face is glowing, the faintest hint of color in her cheeks: something I haven't seen in a long time. I can tell when Travis answers because she smiles even wider. "Daddy? I've got good news." I can hear him whoop through the phone, and she holds it away from her ear, the sound of both Travis and Logan coming through the phone.

"We'll be right there," he yells.

By the time they burst through the door breathless, Dr. Van Der Campen has brought in a round of little plastic tubs of sugar-free jello for each of us to toast. For Ashley this is truly a treat: she's eaten almost nothing since our doomed campout except for some broth. She picks the red jello and peals back the tin foil, digging her spoon deep into it and watching it wobble. The rest of us grab one and open it, even Dr. Van Der Campen joins in, and soon we all have the slimy substance, holding the spoons out towards each other.

"To you, Ashley, and a life free of diabetes!"

We all toast and eat, Logan and Travis huddling around Ashley. The excitement in the room is almost as electric as lightening. I watch Dr. Van Der Campen, and he seems like he might just burst with pride. When he slips out of the room I follow.

"Dr. Van Der Campen?" He stops and turns around.

"Jack. You can call me Jack, Babs."

What do I say? How can I possibly put into words what it means, what he has just done? In this constant shifting sand that is our lives, he gave us something to stand on.

"You're welcome," he says, smiling as if he knows.

"It's working for the others, too?" He nods. "Are there others after Ashley? You said maybe twenty or thirty in this phase of the trial."

"Not yet. The press hasn't exactly been flattering. Sometimes that stops people from flocking to a new trial. But they'll come." He smiles a kind of sad smile. "There will always be people like you—people who need it enough to brave the bad press because there are no other options."

I remember the newspaper articles and the rally posters with the angry red slash across his face. I don't even know the name of his little girl, but I know exactly how desperate he must have felt.

"Like you did?"

"Like I did."

The hall is unusually quiet, no nurses rustling about in their overstarched scrubs, no stretchers or visitors. Hardly a sound except the sound of celebrating from the door behind me. His eyes are a mix of emotions, and I realize what it is. Ashley's life, this miracle today, came at the cost of his own daughter. If she hadn't died, we wouldn't be here.

Suddenly, my heart is so full of gratitude and love and relief it feels too heavy for my chest. I take a step, and then another, and then another until I am within a breath of Jack. And I put my arms around him.

"Thank you," I say.

It takes a moment for him to hug me back, but when he does it's as full of pain as it is with happiness. He lets go and turns quickly, walking away before I can say anything else.

* * * *

We test Ashley's blood every fifteen minutes. She can't wait, hoping to see it plunge, but it's a gradual process. The nurses bring her food, little things mostly, liquid foods to get her stomach used to food again, and she crosses her fingers when she tests afterward. The numbers go up slightly, but they come back down, and in five more days, they are remaining steady around 95.

The difference in Ashley is amazing. She's up and around again, most of the IVs removed, and she insists on taking showers and wearing her own clothes. We take walks around the hospital halls, slow and short at first, her legs weak and her breathing hard until they gradually grow longer. When Dr. Jack approves it, we take short walks outside. Her immune system is slowly building again, and we shed our masks, then the gloves, and finally the scrubs we have come to feel as comfortable in as our own skin.

During the days, Logan and Ashley sit on her bed and work on schoolwork. This is the compromise I've worked with the schools. Before we came out I explained to the principals that we'd be gone for the beginning of the school year, that Ashley was terribly sick and that Logan wanted to be with her. They organized a sort of home-schooling/internet option for him to cover the weeks we'd be gone.

So now that Ashley is stronger, they study together, and Dr. Jack even sometimes comes in and sits for a few minutes to look at the math and science and offer help. He's taken Logan out for lunch several times, and I think they're forming a great relationship that is just as good for Dr. Jack as it is for Logan.

I leave them on the bed studying and head out to the snack machine. A woman is already there, banging her palm against the glass and swearing.

"Can I help?" When she turns around there are tears on her face. She wipes them off, embarrassed. "I can't seem to get it to come out."

I ask which ones and put in more money and push the buttons. The spiral moves and drops two bags of chips. I reach in and pull them out for her.

"Thanks," she says.

"Are you new here?"

She nods. "Son or daughter?"

"Father," she says. "Alzheimer's."

"You're not the first to wrestle with that machine. The one on the first floor works better. But the coffee on the third is better. I think it's their attempt to keep you from getting too flabby from sitting in hospital rooms all day waiting."

She smiles a little, and I'm glad I stopped to help.

"Thanks," she says. "I'll remember that. You been here long?"

I shrug. A lifetime, it seems. Was there life before this? "A couple months."

"Wow. That's a long time. Why are you here?"

"My daughter has diabetes." I say this but then think of her sitting on the bed right now, the last of the IVs taken out this morning, Max the pump packaged back in the box, the blood tests showing normal insulin production. "She had diabetes, I mean."

"But now she doesn't?"

"No. Now she doesn't." I watch these words take effect. I see in her eyes the possibility of her dad regaining his memory of her, of their past together. A few months ago I wouldn't have known what it was I saw in her eyes, but today I know what it is, because I have found it too.

It's hope.

Chapter 32
One Year Later

After an oppressive summer, the air tonight is cool as we sit in the football stands. I lean into Travis, and he puts his arm around me to warm me. A few people stop to chat with us, and then move on as the game begins.

On the track Ashley bounces around with the rest of the cheerleaders, a sight that still makes me laugh.

"For true? A cheerleader?" I asked when she brought the form home and asked to try out.

"It just looks like fun."

I find it hard to say no these days, so I signed the form. She went to tryouts and jumped and yelled and flipped her hair and now is the proud owner of a blue and yellow skirt short enough to give her dad a heart attack.

She waves her pom poms along with the rest of her freshman squad as the football players run onto the field. I look for Brian Lee and find him easily, waving his helmet in her direction and smiling through his black striped face. Ashley is all lit up, her cheeks rosy, her finally thickened blond hair pulled back into a ponytail with blue and gold ribbons and glitter sparkling under the stadium lights. She looks magical.

Logan sees us and climbs the stands and offers us a tray of hot chocolate. Girls walk by and giggle, but he seems not to notice. His hair is short now, and all brown, but he sports a tattoo on his shoulder instead, a small red staff with two snakes circling it. He calls it a caduceus. It's the symbol of doctors. In January he will enter Johns Hopkins University as a pre-med major.

The air smells of fall, that smoky, leafy smell that brings back memories of my own days as a kid. It's the smell of beginnings and endings. It's anticipation.

This weekend I take the GED. I'm not nervous. Logan tutored me for a while, but it turns out I'm not too bad at learning on my own. In the practice exams I've scored nearly a hundred percent. When I showed them to Logan, he just gave it back to me with a smile and said, "See? You were right after all."

"About what?"

"We're two peas in a pod."

Travis thinks I should go to college. Logan suggested UT in Austin, but I may start closer to home in the community college. I'm thinking of being a nurse.

Last year seems a long time ago, and just a minute ago at the same time. We're not the same people, the same family. We can't bring ourselves to say that this whole experience was a good thing. The thought of how close we came to losing Ashley ... it still stops my heart. But we can't say it was bad either.

I lean my head against Travis, and he leans his head on mine. Logan holds his Styrofoam cup out to us in a toast. Ashley beams.

Someone once said faith is standing on a cliff and knowing that if you jump, someone will catch you, or you will be given wings to fly.

I am flying.

About the Author

Heidi Willis graduated from Penn State with degrees in Education and Communications. She taught junior high English in Texas long enough to develop a tolerance for country music but not long enough to speak with an accent. As a type 1 diabetic, she has plenty of experience in poking herself with needles and eating jelly beans and considers herself an expert in carb counting. Heidi is an avid photographer and loves to travel. She currently lives in Virginia with her husband and three children.

Acknowledgments

Many thanks go to Dee Justesen and the people at NorLightsPress for taking a chance on this story and me. I feel so privileged to be among this group: authors, editors, and publishing staff alike. NorLightsPress is a shooting star, and I am honored to be along for the ride! Thanks to my editor, Nadene Carter, for reading with an eagle eye and for always encouraging me when I needed it most.

I owe a large thanks to the extraordinary writing group that is 4Corners. To Jen Blom, Heidi Yantzi, Brit Lary, Erin Halm, Kerri O'Connell and Marcia Keyser, there are no words to express how much you mean to me. Thank you for the many times you've read this, for your critiques, suggestions, and encouragement. But mostly for the friendships. I look forward to many more toasts at the beach house!

Thank you, Tommy Hague, for asking the question that started this whole process. Without you, I might have forgotten the dream.

Thanks to my parents, Rollin and Diana Van Broekhoven, for raising me to believe I could do and be whatever I wanted, and for seeing in me the writer I sometimes lost sight of. You are the best parents a girl could have!

Thank you, Gretchen, for being one of my first readers and for calling me while reading it to say, "That's exactly what it's like!"

Thanks to the scores of parents who opened their hearts to help me understand what it feels like to be the parent of a diabetic child. Your stories of diagnosis, hospitals, comas, worries, and 504s give Babs's experiences authenticity, and I hope I did justice to the struggles you face each day.

Most of all, thank you to my family: to Todd, Ian, Emily and Adalyne. You sacrificed more than I'd care to recall to help me chase my dream. This book is your accomplishment as much as it is mine. I love you all!

Available from NorlightsPress and fine booksellers everywhere

Toll free: 888-558-4354   **Online:** www.norlightspress.com

Shipping Info: Add $2.95 for first item and $1.00 for each additional item

Name _____

Address _____

Daytime Phone _____

E-mail _____

No. Copies	Title	Price (each)	Total Cost
		Subtotal	
		Shipping	
		Total	

Payment by (circle one):

   Check   Visa   Mastercard   Discover   Am Express

Card number_____3 digit code_____

Exp.date_____ Signature_____

Mailing Address:
762 State Road 458
Bedford, IN 47421

Sign up to receive our catalogue at www.norlightspress.com

Made in the USA
Lexington, KY
04 February 2013